Praise for
A QUEER CASE

"With *A Queer Case* by Robert Holtom, crime fans can expect a refreshing treat with all the style and class of a Golden Age whodunit. Slick and clever, it's set in 1920s London, where young gay bank clerk Selby Bigge must navigate a dangerous life of forbidden love while solving a puzzling high society murder. Lively, exciting and delightfully written. Five stars."
Janice Hallett, bestselling author of *The Appeal* and *The Twyford Code*

"Robert Holtom has done something truly special with *A Queer Case*. This is a novel that doesn't just entertain – it thrills. Imagine the sharp wit of classic whodunits infused with the pulse of LGBTQ perspectives, all wrapped in a world of wealth, scandal and secrets. Selby Bigge is an unforgettable protagonist – caught between two worlds, craving more than his stifling existence, yet tumbling headfirst into a mystery that threatens to expose everyone's secrets, including his own. Holtom masterfully blends suspense, social commentary and a deliciously queer lens, creating a novel that is both a love letter to the Golden Age of crime fiction and a bold reimagining of its future possibilities… *A Queer Case* is an instant classic."
Jeffrey Marsh, author of *How to be You* and *Take Your Own Advice*

"A perfectly structured old-school murder mystery with a delightfully decadent twist. It was such a thrill to see the 'degenerates' of Hampstead Heath slink out of the woods of the traditional cosy crime story and take centre stage for once. This is a remarkable debut, full of wit and charm, and with prose as vibrant and sparkling as the gorgeously gay characters who grace its pages."
Russ Thomas, bestselling author of

"Brimming with sparkling dialogue worthy of
this deliciously witty, gloriously queer murder
with all the elegance of Golden Age crime at
Sean Lusk, author of *The Seco*

"Clever, atmospheric and intriguing."

Greg Mosse, bestselling author of the Maisie Cooper Mysteries

"Selby Bigge's yearning for love tugs at the heartstrings, but his irrepressible willingness to settle for sex in the meantime is highly entertaining too. He owes nothing to the cruel world of the 1920s but curiosity, loyalty and goodness combine to turn him into a sleuth, in this clever Golden Age debut, bristling with both clues and charm."

Catriona McPherson, award-winning author of *The Edinburgh Murders*

"Holtom has written an instant contemporary classic. A queer case, where the mystery goes far deeper than murder."

A. J. West, *Sunday Times* bestselling author of *The Betrayal of Thomas True* and *The Spirit Engineer*

"A tremendous start to an intriguing new series, a Golden Age mystery with more than one trick hidden from sight."

Stuart Douglas, author of *Death at the Dress Rehearsal* and *Death at the Playhouses*

"A fantastically fun ride through 1920s London, full of clever plotting and a brilliantly drawn cast of characters, most of all the delightful, acerbically funny Selby. Holtom writes with wit, verve and style."

Eleanor Wasserberg, author of *Foxlowe* and *Light at the End of the Day*

"This vibrant, sexy debut thrums with all the edgy glamour of the Golden Age and the visceral danger of living within the queer underworld of the time. Welcome to 1920s London and the new Poirot!"

Stephanie Scott, author of *What's Left of Me is Yours*

"A marvellously fruity romp through 1920s London. Holtom delivers this alternative take on the Golden Age whodunit with stylistic panache and assured attention to detail. I'm already looking forward to the next Selby Bigge mystery. Fantabulosa!"

Phil Lecomber, author of *Midnight Streets*

A QUEER CASE

ROBERT HOLTOM

TITAN BOOKS

A Queer Case
Print edition ISBN: 9781835413173
E-book edition ISBN: 9781835413180

Published by Titan Books
A division of Titan Publishing Group Ltd
144 Southwark Street, London SE1 0UP
www.titanbooks.com

First edition: June 2025
10 9 8 7 6 5 4 3 2 1

This is a work of fiction. All of the characters, organizations, and events portrayed in this novel are either products of the author's imagination or are used fictitiously. Any resemblance to actual persons, living or dead (except for satirical purposes), is entirely coincidental.

Copyright © 2025 Robert Holtom.

Robert Holtom asserts the moral right to be identified as the author of this work.

No part of this publication may be reproduced, stored in a retrieval system, or transmitted, in any form or by any means without the prior written permission of the publisher, nor be otherwise circulated in any form of binding or cover other than that in which it is published and without a similar condition being imposed on the subsequent purchaser.

A CIP catalogue record for this title is available from the British Library.

Typeset by Richard Mason in Minister Std 10/15.5pt.

EU RP (for authorities only)
eucomply OÜ, Pärnu mnt. 139b-14, 11317 Tallinn, Estonia
hello@eucompliancepartner.com, +3375690241

Printed and bound by CPI Group (UK) Ltd, Croydon CR0 4YY.

A QUEER CASE

The first Selby Bigge mystery

BY ROBERT HOLTOM

For my parents

CHAPTER I

"Truly fortuni," I whispered.

Grey-blue eyes, a fine Roman nose and a generous portion of blond hair oiled back under his trilby. Plump kissable lips I had kissed before and was soon to kiss again. It was the last Sunday of September 1929 as we walked the straight and narrow paths of Hampstead Heath, making our way for the woods. A time of decaying splendour as the oaks turned yellow, the ashes orange and the beeches, my favourite, that vivid, burning amber. For the everyday stroller, the Heath's imminent loss of abundant leaf cover was simply a moment of aesthetically pleasing autumnal display. But for Arthur and I it was the last chance to bare behind the bushes before the bushes themselves were bare.

"Truly fortuni," he echoed.

We'd first met at the Men's Bathing Pond back in the summer. He'd been sunning himself in the changing area in nothing but a piece of string and barely half a handkerchief's worth of cloth that permitted a generous glimpse of what lay underneath. He caught me looking and I'd blushed, but one thing led to another and now here we were, seeking alternative pleasures at a chillier temperature. Up ahead a man appeared, the severe-looking sort in a coal-black suit and bowler. He stomped his way down the path with an ugly little terrier pulling at a leash. Arthur and I wore dark Sunday suits, nothing conspicuous. I had opted for a homburg, grey wool felt and black satin-lined. It was superb quality and kept the chill off my crown, which was getting a fraction chillier these days. With straight backs and broadened shoulders we tried to pass ourselves off as normals. He stomped past us with a harrumph. His dog panted and strained, having caught a whiff of something exciting on the air.

A few minutes later and the woods were looming. Lured by their siren's call we entered. The colours were changing but the leaves were still onside for now. Neither of us had appropriate footwear for the muddy paths but that didn't deter us, led by our urges and keen to satisfy them. Suddenly there was a shout. We stopped dead in our tracks, Arthur almost skidding on the mud.

"That can't be the bloody police, can it?" he muttered. "We're just going for a stroll."

"Old chums who bumped into each other," I replied, trying to sound more confident than I felt. We held our breaths until quiet returned. A few pigeons flapped overhead, their wing beats surprisingly loud, and somewhere another call was issued. "Probably that fellow shouting at his dog."

We resumed our mission. Up ahead lay a fallen oak, as if a Titan's arm had been chopped off mid-battle and now all that remained was the bone. Next to the giant's dismembered limb was a large holly bush with a good covering of berry. It also afforded better cover than any of the nearby trees. We hurried around the oak towards the prickles of the holly. But those sorts of pricks didn't matter as my cold hands went quick to Arthur's warm neck.

We kissed hurriedly and nervously. He tasted of cigarette and mustard and I assumed I tasted of cigarette and bread sauce. I enjoyed the feel of his plump lips as he enjoyed mine. We opened our mouths and our tongues were quick to find one another. My hands slipped from his neck to the back of his head where I could feel the end of his lustrous hair. How I wanted to run my fingers through it but, ever the Englishmen, we kept our hats on. Not one to waste a second, I put my hand to his crotch and gave a squeeze. His person was already starting to stiffen, as was mine. He pulled back from our kiss and we looked a moment at one another. His hands came around my back and patted my buttocks.

"Those will be for dessert," he said with a fruity chuckle.

Something snapped. We froze. The sound had come from further within the woods. We waited, the silence of the air anticipating another sound as a vacuum awaits its filling. We held fast, groins pressed together, our members unsure as whether to continue hardening or to wither. Another snap, then leaves rustling and somewhere much too close a dog yapped. We pulled apart as the ghastly terrier belted into view.

"Bugger," I cursed.

The siren's call proved true. I saw panic on Arthur's face, which he saw mirrored on mine, we had no choice but to run. A subtle departure proved difficult as the leaves beneath our quick retreating feet mocked us with the volume of their crunching and even the branches pointed at us accusingly. The dog's infernal barking was answered with another shout, louder now and much too close for comfort. Our quick step became a run as we escaped that blasted creature and its approaching owner. God only knew what he would do if he caught us. He'd looked the National Vigilance Association sort. We ran and ran, our faces reddening, skirting the oaks and ashes, not stopping to admire the beeches, and then suddenly the trees vanished as we stumbled onto a sturdier path.

We tried to return to a regular pace but were fearful the dog would reappear. My armpits were perspiring and I cursed the stink it would make under my jacket. Arthur was a few paces ahead, his face pink, and I saw his shoes were covered in mud, flecks of which had splashed up onto the hem of his trousers. I looked down at mine and saw the same. Double bugger. We reached a fork in the path and he turned to me, worry in his nice grey-blue eyes.

"Bloody creature," he said.

"Less Hound of the Baskervilles," I replied. "More Terrier of the Heath."

We tried to laugh but our attempts at bravado quite failed.

"Perhaps we could try the South End Green toilets," I suggested.

"I... I'm not sure. I hear the police have been sniffing around there of late."

That familiar look of desire passed between us but the thrill of the moment had died.

"Another Sunday," he said, "we should try the Heath extension."

"We should."

A serious young man appeared from the left fork, strolling purposefully ahead of his companion, a short young woman with a grumpy look about her. He too looked rather bad-tempered and I assumed a lovers' tiff. He was marching in our direction and the last thing I wanted was for his ire to turn on these two uncanny men still trying to regain their breath. I turned on my heel and took the right fork, leaving Arthur to face the couple. We did not say goodbye.

So it was I retreated back across the Heath, heading for Parliament Hill. The sun was lower and the chill intensifying. I pulled my coat tighter around me, regretting my lack of a scarf. My feet were sweating and I could feel them rubbing up against the tight leather of the shoes with only a thin layer of sock in between. The heel of my right foot was beginning to chafe, I'd have a blister sooner or later. Battle scars without victory, just my luck.

Despite these protestations I worked my way to the top of the hill and found my usual bench empty. Its wooden slats provided respite for my unsatisfied buttocks and my fast-beating heart. I admired the view through the trees to that higgledy-piggledy horizon of spires, chimneys and smoke. With a single finger held aloft I vanished whole swathes of the city. St Paul's and Waterloo Station obliterated by the tip of my index finger, St Pancras squashed under a thumb. From here I liked to put London into perspective.

Occasionally I turned my head to observe the Sunday strollers. A handsome young couple with clean skin and rosy cheeks walked arm in arm. They had the look of new love to them, all excitement and adventures to be had. Then came a family of stern father, prim mother and a pair of smaller facsimiles in tow. All wore sensible coats and walked with the lethargy of those mid-digestion, I assumed of a hearty roast lunch. A governess was on hand, the dour and dependable sort, disinclined to marriage. Soon an elderly couple tottered their way across the brow of the hill, unperturbed by their sagging necks and greying hair, the kind to immortalise their long marriage (and approaching mortality) with a plaque on a bench. Like the riddle of the Sphinx, so I witnessed the three stages of normality: from first love to senility by way of family. For those everyday folk, love was something attainable, for the likes of me it was criminal.

"Excuse me, have you got the time?"

I turned to the stranger and almost gasped. Straight nose, slim lips and quiet chin, suddenly I was back amongst those sandstone spires, dressed in black tie and gown, talking animatedly with other men about the pastimes of the Greeks and the latest college scandal. I had only met him a handful of times but even then he'd made an impression. Like a lesser-known Greek god, he had been beautiful, and I saw now that his looks hadn't changed a jot.

"I say, it's Patrick, isn't it? Patrick Duker?"

Shock crossed his handsome face but he was quick to smother it.

"Yes, it is," he replied reluctantly as his eyes narrowed and forehead furrowed. I could almost see the levers and pulleys of his brain clunking away as some distant memory was searched for.

"Oxford," I said. "We were mutually acquainted with Cyril Hughes."

"I'm terribly sorry, I... I don't recall..." But as the words left his lips so his eyes opened wide. "Stuart? It's Stuart."

"Selby. Selby Bigge. Do take a seat."

"I wouldn't want to intrude."

"It would be no intrusion at all."

He sat himself down as I raised my left arm and pulled back the sleeve of my coat to reveal a slender, pale wrist dotted with short, light hairs. The gold face of my watch stared back.

"It's a quarter past three, by the way."

"Thank you." He shuffled around in one of his coat pockets and produced a silver cigarette case. "Fancy one?"

I turned to him, his eyes steadily on mine. What a face to behold and such penetrating hazel eyes. I took one of the proffered cylinders and placed it between my lips. He was quick to produce a box of matches but his fingers were trembling, from cold or excitement I could not tell. The first extinguished the moment it blazed. He tutted quietly as he tossed the used stick into the grass before lighting another. I leant towards his cupped palms and sucked deeply at the quavering flame. I always loved that first rush of smoke as the lungs woke up to the fine taste of tobacco.

"What a funny coincidence," he said after lighting his own. "You were a Balliol chap, weren't you?"

I shook my head, "Fitzalan."

"Never very high up the Norrington Table, if I recall."

"Not very good at rowing either."

"At least you weren't at Pembroke! I was PPE at Corpus. What did you take?"

"Classics," I said. "Always loved the Ancients, especially Ovid and Sappho. Such wonderful poetry."

"Can't stand the stuff myself," he said. "Too flowery by half."

"Not even something contemporary, Walt Whitman perhaps?"

"Not my cup of tea," he replied, quite missing the point of my reference to the famous nature lover and lover of men.

"*I contain multitudes*," I said, quoting one of my favourite lines.

"You contain what?"

"Ignore me, just thinking on Oxford days. I wonder what happened to our chum Cyril."

"He went to prison," replied Patrick quickly.

"Really, whatever for?"

"He... well... he made good on his innuendos and was punished for it."

I knew at once what he meant and, whilst I wanted to ask about the particulars, I could sense his body stiffen. I kept my eyes dead ahead, as did he.

"How unfortunate," I replied feebly. "What brings you to Hampstead on a Sunday afternoon? A stroll on the Heath?"

"I live here," he said rather coldly.

"Oh, I hadn't realised. Bought a house, have you?"

"I live with my father."

His father was one Sir Lionel Duker, a big name in the world of banking. He'd made a killing out of African mines and got a knighthood for funding Great Britain's war efforts.

"That must be nice for you," I ventured, not entirely sure it would be.

"It's big enough for the both of us. He's getting on a bit but he keeps himself occupied."

I felt there was more to be said but he was holding back.

"Jolly good. I couldn't begin to imagine living with my father."

"You don't see eye to eye?"

"If an Englishman's home is his castle then let's say my father has a lot in common with a number of this country's monarchs."

"A tyrant?"

"Aspiring. He only ever achieved a lesser managerial position at a bank in Horsham."

"How rotten. Is Horsham ever so dull?"

"Thoroughly and certainly not a place I can indulge all my vices."

"Bit of a gambler, eh?"

The earnest look he gave me proved a shade confusing. Usually the offer of a cigarette was signal enough up here on the Heath, but he must be playing it safe.

"Something of that sort," I lied. "Still, it's nice you get along with your father."

"Most of the time."

"But not all of it?"

To that he said nothing.

"Families can be murder," I added.

"As a matter of fact, I'm planning one of those."

"What? A family or a murder?"

"The latter."

I blinked, trying hard not to choke on my cigarette.

"The murder of my mother that is."

"Oh dear," I said, waiting for the punchline, "is she ghastly?"

"Much worse, she's my age."

I coughed up a small plume of smoke.

"Stepmother, I should say."

"How dreadful," I managed. "Although I do hear the Oedipal complex is quite the rage these days."

A big grin spread across his face and he started to laugh. His mouth was wide and full of teeth, one or two slightly wonky – the wonkiness a human touch, he couldn't be all demi-god. The laughter persisted for quite some time.

"Dear me," he said. "I haven't had a good laugh in months. You must think me mad?"

"No, no," I lied. "I'm sure many men are plotting the deaths of their stepmothers right this very moment."

"How tactless of me, to tell you all this. We're perfect strangers really, I can't even remember the last time we spoke."

I remembered. It was a Trinity term of my degree and Cyril had invited me to one of his drinks parties at Worcester College. It wasn't often he allowed me to brush shoulders with the upper sets, but he'd needed to make up the numbers. I had always been so nervous at events like that, surrounded by men so much richer and more interesting than I. They never asked after my family or the land we owned. *They can smell the middle class on you*, Cyril had once said. *No one important ever came from Horsham.*

Looking back, I don't know why I'd let him be so mean to me but our acquaintanceship had proved mutually satisfying. With a glass of chilled champagne in hand, I had eyed Patrick across the room, thinking how splendid he looked in his dinner jacket and wishing for him to return my gaze. By my design we left at the same time and I took to talking with him as we neared the duck pond. We were a bit squiffy and I worried we would go over the edge. So we found a bench to sit on to stop our heads from spinning. He'd exuded that youthful beauty so typical of our kind and for a while we talked about nothing or other. It transpired he was in the middle of his finals and I worried I'd never see him again. At one point he placed his palm flat on the bench between us and I had dared to place mine on top of his. We stayed like that for a while until, finally, he kissed me.

"Although when I saw you on the bench I thought you looked the sympathetic sort."

Sympathetic wasn't exactly the word I'd hoped for, but it was a start.

"I had a feeling you'd be easy to talk to and I was right."

"I'm terribly discreet," I assured him. "I'm not prone to gossip."

"To hell with it," he replied, leaning towards me so I could smell the tobacco on his breath. "Her name is Lucinda and I call her the Harpy of the Heath."

"That bad is she?"

"Worse, and my father thinks her an angel."

"A very young angel."

"Exactly. He's too doe-eyed to spot her designs on his bank account and she's too wily to give herself away. I need proof."

"With which to dissuade your father?"

He nodded. "So he'll divorce her forthwith."

I took a long drag of my cigarette and let him wait awhile before I replied. "From my experience if you want someone to reveal who they truly are, all you have to do is let them talk."

"She does plenty of that and it's always so bloody inane."

"But do you ask her the right questions?"

"I try to ask her as little as possible."

"Then therein might lie your problem."

He looked at me, a little bemused, but perhaps just a little impressed.

"I say, Stuart, you're not a private dick are you?"

"No, I'm a clerk at Childs & Co."

"More's the pity, I was just about to invite you to dinner at the Ritz."

"The Ritz!?" I ejaculated, utterly failing to hide the surprise in my voice.

"Father's forced me to accompany him and Lucinda on some God-awful effort at family bonding, not that we ever bonded as a family when mother was alive. Tuberculosis."

"I beg your pardon?"

"My mother died of tuberculosis when I was fifteen years old."

"I'm so dreadfully sorry."

"I was at Harrow at the time. Were you Eton or Winchester?"

"Bledwood."

"That the frightful one on the edge of Cornwall?"

"West Sussex." Even my boarding school had been unexceptional.

"*Stet Fortuna Domus*," said Patrick, with evident pride. "Let the fortune of the house stand."

"*Numquam te videant sanguinem fundentem*," I replied. "Never let them see you bleed."

"It's the Harpy's blood I want. Say, if you were to accompany us to the Ritz, would you be able to get her talking, so to speak?"

"I could give it a try," I said, although at this point I'd try anything to prolong my exposure to Patrick.

"I want you to get her to reveal the truth – that she's a lying gold-digger who my father would be wise to dispatch."

"I'll find the truth," I replied quite shamelessly. "Whether it's one you want to hear or not."

He paused to contemplate my offer, rubbing his chin, and I took as nonchalant a puff on my cigarette as I could manage. Flirting on the Heath tended to be a little more straightforward.

"I like your confidence, old chap, and you're someone who means nothing to the family, so you've the advantage of an outsider's eye." He looked down to check the time on his watch. "I'd best be off but what say you to seven o'clock at the Ritz this Friday, expenses covered?"

"I say, that's very generous of you."

"Anything to unburden me of my second mother."

I'd happily unburden him of a number of things. He rose to his feet and offered me his hand, which I took with swift enthusiasm.

"Selby Bigge, eh? Perhaps I remember you after all."

My breath quickened. Could he really remember our kiss?

"Do say you'll come!"

He spoke with a new enthusiasm, almost boyish, and spread a wonky-toothed grin generously across his face. I had to remind myself to release his hand before it became socially suspect. If our trip to the woods required a detour via dinner with a knight of the realm, then bottoms up.

"I'll come!"

CHAPTER 2

The trials of the week proved unavoidable. Dull conversations with my colleagues at the bank and the endless cross-referencing of balance sheets followed by the prying questions of my landlady, Miss Wickler. I lived in the attic of her house in Pimlico. The damp on the walls and the mice in them were offset by the cost of the rent and the quality of her desserts. On Wednesday evening, I was treated to a tipple at the River Styx in Soho by an older chap with a Mephistophelean beard. The saucy buggeranto asked to squeeze my buttocks and I obliged.

Friday night finally arrived and there I was in black tie standing in the lobby of the Ritz! Plush red carpet beneath my feet and an elegant chandelier above my head, it was the very form of luxury. I'd done my best to look the part in top hat and overcoat, and a dimpled footman had given me the eye before easing my load.

"Selby, hallo!"

Patrick came striding towards me, his hat only just removed and a lock of his wondrous hair hanging down across his forehead. If only I could reach forward and brush it back, but he did that himself once the aforementioned sassy footman had removed his jacket.

"Patrick! Good evening."

"So glad you could come, old chap."

"I could hardly refuse your invitation."

We shook hands and I felt his warm skin against mine, his grip firm and reassuring. How I'd be happy for him to grip any part of my body. He passed a quick glance at the top of my head and my heart sank. I was ever conscious of the march of time prematurely stamping itself across my scalp. I still had a good amount, mind. I wasn't like those unfortunate chaps who were bald by matriculation. With a slick of pomade and some carefully angled combing, it passed muster. Hopefully Patrick would focus on my strong nose and quick wit instead.

"They're already here," he said, pointing me towards the hall beyond the lobby. We traversed more thick carpet, passing between two rows of marble columns with potted plants on top. A profusion of palm fronds and aspidistra heralded our arrival. The hubbub of the restaurant grew louder as did my excitement.

"I appreciate you doing this, Selby, I really do."

"It's my pleasure."

"They met here as a matter of fact."

"Who?" I asked, struggling to keep up.

"Father and the Harpy, some do before Christmas last year.

I should have gone with him but had a dicky tummy, bad oyster. Then the next day he barges into my bedroom and wouldn't stop going on about this beautiful young woman he'd met, called her the angel on top of the Christmas tree, which was enough to give my innards another turn. He invited her to the house a little after New Year's and I could see at once I'd underestimated the severity of his infatuation. They were married by May and she moved in at once."

"Efficient."

"Repellent. I try to lock myself away in the library, but she always finds me and insists on chattering. She asks the most irritating of questions, prying into my secrets."

"Do you have many?"

"None that she'll ever discover, the scheming hussy," he replied defensively and I thought better than to comment on his rather unsavoury descriptions of the fairer sex. "When things get very bad I escape here. Pa is friends with the owner and has access to one of the suites. It has a glorious bathtub."

I pictured him in said glorious bathtub.

"I'm good with secrets," I said. "I'm sure Lucinda has plenty."

"You get me the knife and I'll stick it in."

Quite a violent metaphor but I got his gist. At least my mother had the good sense to still be living and not half as irritating as my father.

"Be careful though," he said, suddenly gripping my upper arm. "She'll try to charm you the way she charmed Father. Be vigilant."

"I'm immune to those sorts of things," I said quite honestly. "I'll get the measure of her, all right."

"That's the ticket." He sneered as we entered the restaurant. "Name's Duker, I'm joining my father, Sir Lionel."

A slick waiter with a pert posterior guided us between the circular tables, each laden with plates of delicious-looking food and ample glasses of wine. I spied lobsters dripping in butter, a trifle covered in a delectable latticework of spun sugar and one of those exciting new tongue dishes. My stomach rumbled. I had eaten a small luncheon on purpose.

Some of the guests watched us as we passed and it gave me a little thrill to be walking alongside Patrick. For all they knew I was one of them and belonged here just as much as they did. Up ahead, at a centrally placed table not far from the great mirrors, a man was rising to his feet. He was a sturdier, taller version of Patrick with a lot more wrinkles.

"There you are, my boy."

Sir Lionel stepped away from the table and squeezed his son's shoulder before turning to look at me. He too had a rather good head of hair, except his was all grey.

"And you're his chum?"

"Yes, sir, the name's Selby Bigge."

He sized me up with a flash of his leonine eyes and I felt the veritable gazelle in the predator's path. I would have to employ all the charm at my disposal.

"Well then, Mr Bigge," he said, gripping my hand. I tried not to wince, it was like a bloody vice. "Allow me to introduce my wife, Lucinda."

Where I had expected to see a winged creature with raven hair, vicious eyes and a hungry mouth, sat someone actually rather beautiful. She was dressed in a gown of pale-blue silk, which left her arms bare. She wore a little make-up and her ash-blonde hair was pulled back in the current style. Not quite the Harpy Patrick had led me to expect.

"A pleasure," she said, reaching her hand across the table.

I took it in mine, not risking bending over to kiss it lest I knock over a glass.

"Be seated, boys," ordered Sir Lionel. "There's champagne and smoked salmon for starters."

With Patrick to my left and Lucinda my right, the gormandising began. We tucked into thickly buttered brown bread with delicious slabs of salmon on top. I added plenty of lemon and pepper to mine, scrumptious! Champagne was poured by the oily waiter and soon Lionel had us all making a toast.

"I didn't think it was possible, at my ripe old age, but it turns out an old man can have a second chance at happiness."

He beamed at his wife and she smiled back. And, if I hadn't been forewarned, I would have said her smile was quite genuine.

"Here's to love."

"To love," we echoed, and I sensed Patrick shudder.

I ordered steak with a creamy, peppercorn sauce and boiled potatoes. Patrick had lobster, Lionel the steak, and Lucinda the confit of duck. The food was pure nectar and my steak perfectly done, which meant very well done. I watched Lucinda out of the corner of my eye as she ate her food. She did so in polite, little bites but whether or not she was planning on stabbing her husband with her fork I could not tell.

As the meal unfolded, so Lionel proved to be his own favourite topic of conversation. With a new audience member to hand he regaled me of his time in the army and the adventures he'd had fighting in a number of wars. All that was required of me was the occasional nod or exclamation. It transpired he'd earned his stripes in the Second Boer War, which resulted in a number of anecdotes concerning the best tactics for massacring the Dutch.

"I've never trusted people who wear wooden shoes," I said in an ill-fated effort at humour. Sir Lionel did not look amused and I returned to my role as audience member.

"It's a shame you and Patrick were too young for the Great War. It's the making of a man." He spoke with a zeal that reminded me of my father. "And after victory comes the next best thing: the spoils."

At this he reached across the table and took his wife's hand in his. He slowly and delicately, given his strength, raised her arm so I could see the bracelet on her wrist.

"Each one half-carat," she said. "Aren't they beautiful."

"Truly."

A thin band of gold interspersed with diamond after diamond. It was as if the restaurant went quiet and maybe the rest of London too as the glittering band twinkled in the low, electric light. Her naked wrist was slender and pale, the perfect setting for this piece of jewelled splendour. Perhaps now I was looking at her motive for marriage.

"That's what I fought for," said Lionel, and suddenly the room was all clattering cutlery and chatter again. "Gold and diamonds. It's a better life owning mines than living in a trench, that I can assure you."

He bent his head forward, almost in supplication, and kissed his wife's hand. But whether he was bowing to her or the bracelet I could not tell. Then followed a lengthy autobiographical account of how he'd made his fortune in the mines of South Africa. After ousting the Dutch, he'd struck immeasurable riches and was quick to climb the ladder of power. He even supplied gold to the Bank of England.

"You can't build an empire with guns and ships alone. You need the money to buy them first!"

"You're quite right," I said. "We're on the gold standard, after all, and that requires full vaults."

Unsurprisingly, Sir Lionel cared little for my experience of working at a bank, much preferring the sound of his own voice. I didn't even get the chance to impress him with my degree from Oxford, not that I ever shared the specifics of my finals result.

I kept Lucinda in my periphery. She must have heard these stories numerous times before but she managed to keep a polite smile on her face. I wanted to see the mask slip to reveal the calculating conspirator beneath but either she was an actress worthy of a West End role or just an attractive young woman who'd struck gold.

"Another bottle, sir?" asked the slick waiter.

"Oh dear," boomed Lionel. "I'll be done for."

"Don't be silly," chided Lucinda. "It's a special occasion."

"You know I'm just an old man who can't take his drink."

"Nonsense, you're not old to me."

"And you are much too good a liar."

"Hush."

He reached out and traced the back of his index finger along her cheek, an act I was worried would induce Patrick to return his lobster to its shell.

"If a serpent bit your ankle," said Lionel, still gazing at his wife, "I would bribe the ferryman of Styx with gold and bury Cerberus in a pile of diamonds."

I always appreciated a classical allusion and while the story of Orpheus and Eurydice was quite an obvious choice, it seemed to be doing the trick. Lucinda looked on enraptured.

"I would follow you into the very depths of Hades and guide your spectre all the way back home."

"But you mustn't look back," she said, almost worried. "You mustn't."

"No," he said plainly. "From the moment I met you I have never looked back."

They stared deeply into one another's eyes and I couldn't help it, I was touched. How lovely to be able to look at someone like that in a crowded room of strangers without the least hint of self-consciousness or worry. To be able to touch someone else's hand, maybe even kiss them on the cheek, and not fear any recriminations. For the possibility of police involvement to seem so palpably absurd it wouldn't even be given a thought. I could quite understand Patrick's bitterness, denied even this most basic of human needs, but it was clouding his vision. With patience and tact I might be able to incline him to a sunnier disposition.

"My God."

"What is it, darling?" asked Lucinda.

"It's... it's him."

Sir Lionel looked utterly furious. She followed his gaze between Patrick and I, her smile quickly becoming a grimace.

"Do not worry," she whispered. "They won't let him in. He can't afford here."

"I won't have my evening spoiled."

"Darling, please don't make a scene."

I shifted in my seat to get a better view and looked across the tables of conversing guests. It was hard to know of whom they spoke, but on the far side of the room a new arrival was arguing with the maître d' – a youngish chap in an immaculate suit with the air of the dandy about him. From the waiter's gesticulations it was clear the man didn't have an invitation. As he argued, his eyes roamed the room until they stopped at our table. He gave a sly little wave and Lionel choked.

"If that man takes one more step, I'll kill him."

"Darling, please."

Lucinda's voice was one of pleading as she placed her hand delicately on top of her husband's. He was gripping the side of the table, scrunching the tablecloth beneath his fingers. Her marvellous bracelet glittered in the low light.

"I'll run my steak knife through his heart…"

"Ignore him, he'll go."

"… and feed it to the foxes on the Heath."

"You will do no such thing, darling."

"There's no place for sodomites here," spat Lionel.

The word hit me with its violent mix of sibilants and plosives but I hid my discomfort, an act I was so skilled in that it had long become a habit. Like boxing at school, I had learned to take the blows.

"Sorry, Selby," said Patrick quietly. "This is a most unfortunate situation."

"Who is he?"

He leaned towards me and I smelt the citrus scent of his eau de toilette masking the musky tang of his sweat.

"Morrow Davenport."

"Does he have a grudge against your father?"

"You could say that."

Patrick looked back across the room, his lips slightly parting to reveal the wet of his mouth within. There was moisture at his temples. We were all perspiring in this place, filled as we were with alcohol and food, and wrapped in so many layers.

"Dammit," he whispered.

The unwelcome guest had wheedled his way into the room and was making his way between the tables. The maître d' hovered at his side, buzzing in protest but unable to stop him. The dandy paused to observe the waiter then reached forward as if to caress his cheek. The maître d' staggered back. He looked utterly terrified, as if his skin might burn.

"Pay him no heed, darling," said Lucinda, trying to calm Sir Lionel's fury. But its object was swift approaching and all we could do was sit politely in our seats. An electric hum of excitement filled the room as some tables fell to silence and others whirred with speculation, forkfuls of food paused halfway between plates and open mouths. Then he was upon us.

"Good evening," he said, evidently relishing this moment. "What a pleasant surprise to find you all here."

He gave us a wicked, white-toothed smile as he took us in one by one. I cannot lie, he was very handsome, with a trim moustache and bright, green eyes. His hair was chestnut brown and voluminous, cascading down to beneath his ears in a wavy, Wildean manner. His eyes eventually met mine and his eyebrows rose in involuntary surprise.

"There is nothing pleasant about it," said Patrick, speaking before his father could.

"I beg to differ." His words were slightly slurred, the joker was half-cut!

"Go back the way you came, Davenport."

"Leave us alone," begged Lucinda.

"*Leave us alone*," he mimicked.

"You're a beast!"

"And you're just the latest in a long line of women." He swayed on his feet. "Women with spacious morals."

"Not another word," warned Patrick.

"But London needs to know that my column isn't mere gossip, it's the truth. Isn't that right, Lionel?"

It was at this point that the artillery fuse triggered the shell as Sir Lionel slammed his palms against the table and rose to his feet in an explosion of anger. Cutlery rattled, a wine glass toppled and his chair crashed to the carpet as he confronted the interloper.

"Get out," he roared, "you vile..."

He employed a slur I knew all too well, as shocking as it was offensive. His explosive outburst spread as shockwaves throughout the room, slamming into the ears of the silent onlookers and crashing against the gilded mirrors. But the man in question remained unfazed and he simply laughed, the machine gunner's rattling response to the artillery.

"Be quiet!"

Sir Lionel stepped away from the table, ready to kill, and Davenport's laughter was quick to die as he staggered back in surprise. The millionaire raised his hand, the fingers clenched into a fist. Patrick leapt to his feet and took hold of his father's arm. He was smaller and possibly weaker than his father, but his action did the trick, stopping the man in his tracks. It was at this point I heard her gasp.

The others missed it but I turned at once to Lucinda, her hand held out in front of her, blood trickling from her palm. Beneath her hand, the wine glass's stem remained standing on its base but the bowl had vanished.

"Quick," I said, taking her hand gently in mine and turning it to reveal her palm. A nasty shard of glass stuck out from her skin as the blood pooled around it. "This will hurt but it's for the best."

I placed my index finger and thumb on either side of the fragment and pulled it quickly from the flesh. Tears rolled down her cheeks. I picked up her glass of water and poured some across the wound. Some of the blood drained away onto the tablecloth but more was quick to come. I saw another smaller piece of glass poking into her skin, which I also removed. Hoping that was it, I wrapped her napkin tightly around her hand.

"Hold it high," I said. "It will lessen the bleeding."

"I... I can't," she gasped, audibly in pain.

"You must, there will be help soon."

A flurry of waiters was fast approaching the table, like the reserve troops who had missed the battle. I lifted her hand up and held it there.

"Thank you," she whispered, her face deathly pale. "I hate blood."

"So do I," I said in sympathy, and I wasn't lying, it was horrible stuff.

"I'll have you in prison, Davenport," shouted Sir Lionel. "I will see justice done."

"I'll have you ruined, Duker," he retorted, as two waiters escorted him away. "I know all your secrets."

Lionel righted his fallen chair and it was only at this point did he see that his wife was in agony. His face changed from fury to panic in the blink of an eye.

"My God, you're hurt."

"It's… it's… nothing," she lied. "Just a scratch."

"A doctor has been summoned," said the maître d', suddenly deciding to make himself useful. "Perhaps Lady Duker would care to reside somewhere a little more private."

"Take me away, please."

The gathering waiters helped her to her feet, offering their arms for support, and slowly Lucinda was guided from the table. She looked as fragile as the glass she had just broken.

In my life, dissemblance was key. I lied on a daily basis simply to protect myself and over the years I had got rather good at it. I also had to be good at detecting the lies of others, be they a chap of similar persuasions or a policeman in disguise. Lying, or perhaps the concealment of truth, was my stock in trade. But watching Lucinda retreat, I didn't see a dissembler or harpy, I saw a young woman in distress. After a few paces, she turned her head on its elegant neck to look back at me.

"Thank you," she said breathlessly. "You're my hero."

CHAPTER 3

"It's a shorter story than it should be and I don't know the half of it."

Patrick and I were seated on two very low yet expansive armchairs in a corner of one of the bars. A circular, marble table was between us and on it two tumblers of amber whisky. Scottish malt was one of his favourites, and he'd been kind enough to buy it, but the stuff burnt like a bumblebee's behind. The drama of the dining room was not long past but at least it was over. Lucinda had been taken to Lionel's usual suite to have her wounds tended to, while Lionel fumed at the manager, demanding to know how *that painted cockatoo* had got himself into the Ritz.

"He writes a gossip column, of all things," explained Patrick. "Like that pretentious drivel people used to write in the *Cherwell*, remember?"

I did. Oxford's aspiring journalists liked nothing more than swiping at their fellow students by way of scathing articles in the University newspaper. The members of the Union often got cut the deepest, but then what's worse than an aspiring journalist but an aspiring politician? The Union, *petri dish of the mediocre but affluent*, as one particularly bitter hack had called it.

"It gets published in that God-awful magazine, *Whispers Allowed*."

"This doesn't sound good."

"It's not. Earlier this year his vile little column claimed to know a *twelve-carat truth* about *the Knight on the Heath*. Doesn't take a genius to deduce to whom he was referring."

Clearly I was no genius as I racked my brains trying to put the pieces together. Then it clicked – a knight of the realm living on Hampstead Heath, Sir Lionel.

"What was the so-called truth?"

Patrick struggled forwards in the large armchair, which looked as if it were about to swallow him up, something I happily would have assisted with.

"That my father had engaged the services of…" He looked hurriedly around the room for eavesdroppers and lowered his voice. "… a prostitute."

"Oh dear," I said, trying to keep my sympathy at a discreet volume.

"Utter rubbish. Father was livid."

"I bet."

"He didn't waste a minute, bought a number of copies of the magazine and gave one to a friend of his at the Yard and another to a barrister chum. He wanted Davenport in prison before the end of summer."

He swigged down the last of his whisky as I took a polite sip of mine, trying not to wince.

"Unfortunately it hasn't proven so simple because for something to constitute libel it has to be plainly written."

"What do you mean?"

"Well, if Davenport had written that my father engaged… well, you know. If he'd written it all down in black and white, then there would be something tangible to point at and call libel. But he minced his words and put it all down in flowery metaphor and insinuation: *the lonely knight atop the heath* with his *precious gems*, rubbish like that."

"So he could have been writing about someone else?"

"Of course not," he shot back, speaking with a vehemence reminiscent of his father's. I couldn't help but feel stung. I was only trying to help.

"Sorry, old chap," he said, relenting. "Didn't mean to bite your head off. This damned business is making monsters of the lot of us."

"I understand," I replied diplomatically. "Especially with Davenport still at large."

"But not for much longer."

"Oh yes?"

"Father's not one for losing. He got more lawyers on the case and one has come up with the goods – an historic case of a similar sort, namely, defamation by florid prose. The perpetrator was jailed and that's all that matters. Father can get Davenport behind bars and take the magazine down with him for publishing such slanderous filth."

"And, in the meantime, Davenport stumbles around London

making a fool of himself. Does he have a death wish?"

"He thinks he's got away with it but he doesn't know we've got the ace. He's in for a nasty shock."

"Why was he foolish enough to take on your father?"

"This is where the story gets interesting but I can't get hold of all the chapters," he said with an unexpected flourish of metaphor. "This isn't Davenport's first attack."

"He's come at your father before?"

"Not my father but Lucinda."

I could taste the bitterness with which he said her name, or perhaps that was just the whisky.

"It all came out in one of her many bouts of histrionics. Shortly after the *Whispers Allowed* column was published, she came crying into the drawing room with tears artfully painted on her face. It turns out that Davenport had got his claws into her first husband and torn their marriage apart. Father took her into the study at this point so I heard no more but it would seem Davenport has a grudge against the Harpy."

"Do you have any idea of what he had on her first marriage?"

"All I know is that the ex-husband was called Pethybridge, West Country money I think, and now he lives abroad. Whatever Davenport had it was big enough to break the couple in two and send him packing."

My head was spinning and it wasn't just the alcohol. There was I, naively anticipating a three-course meal at the Ritz with an extra helping of family tension, only to find myself served a much more sinister affair. I needed my wits about me.

"If I could just get the dirt on Lucinda I'd be able to warn Father before he writes me out the will and leaves it all to her."

"You really think he'd disinherit you?"

"Lovestruck old fools do all sorts and her Harpy's claws are in deep. She'll drain him of every penny he's got, wearing Mother's diamonds while she's at it."

I decided not to remind him that said *Harpy* was currently having her bloodied palm attended to. His resentment was understandable but not all of us were born to riches. God knows a big house and a nice man were just the sort of thing I'd settle for.

"Perhaps I could help."

The words jumped from my mouth. I think I was as surprised as he was.

"Dig the dirt, you mean?"

I nodded slowly, aware that my heartbeat had quadrupled in an instant. "I have a little experience of these things." This was sufficiently vague to not be an outright lie. "I'll find out what Davenport's got on her."

"Really?"

"I'm not one of the family, so he needn't feel threatened by me, and nor does the sight of him make my blood boil, yet."

"You'd be discreet, wouldn't you?"

"Discretion is my modus operandi." This was mostly true.

"What do you charge?"

"Oh, nothing for an old friend."

"That's very generous of you." He sounded a little sceptical but I could tell the idea had taken hold. "You'd really do that for me?"

"Absolutely," I said, holding back on all the other things I'd do for him. "But first there is something I must ask and you might not like it."

"Fire away."

"Davenport's libellous comments about your father, are you sure it's all smoke without fire?"

I prepared myself for a hostile comeback, but instead he looked into his tumbler, then at his feet and finally to the ceiling before returning my gaze.

"My father loved my mother very much," he said. "He used to call her the best of diamonds. When she died it tore him apart, right at the seams. I saw him cry on at least three occasions, not the sort of thing a fifteen-year-old boy should ever have to witness. For quite some time he was depressed, worried he would be alone forever, and how he moped. But, as the years went by, the gloom alleviated and we finally resumed a more normal relationship. We frequented Ascot and took the occasional trip to the Continent. It was not an unpleasant life. That was until last autumn."

"This was before Lucinda?"

"Yes, he invited a woman to dinner. I'd never met her before in my life. We ate sole and calf's liver, I think, and none of us had much to talk about. After dessert, Father asked her to leave."

"And you think she might have been…?"

"He never said as much, but he did confess to me that he was lonely and his loneliness had made him weak. He saw sense though and dismissed her before anything unfortunate could happen. Then came Christmas and bloody Lucinda materialises."

"Loneliness can get to the best of men," I said quite truthfully. "But don't worry, I'll get to the bottom of this."

"Thank you, Selby, you're a true gent." He smiled and the grumpy son of a knight vanished, once again revealing the handsome youth I'd admired at university. "I don't know how I'll ever repay you."

"I'm sure we can think of something."

"I know," said Patrick. His enthusiasm was still high and, for a moment, I thought he was going to invite me to the suite with the glorious bathtub. "You should come up to the house."

"On the Heath?"

"Just the one."

"That would be lovely."

"Yes, yes, this is all coming together very well. Next Saturday is Father's seventieth. You should come as my chum."

He winked at me and I tried not to blush. Things were moving quickly and in a rather favourable direction.

"I would be delighted."

"That gives you plenty of time to talk to Davenport and get the goods on Lucinda. He'll be in prison and she'll be divorced before the year is out." He spoke with an alarmingly menacing enthusiasm but I put it down to the drink. He raised his tumbler. "The cockatoo and the Harpy – here's to killing two birds with one stone!"

CHAPTER 4

It was the Wednesday following the affair at the Ritz and the evening was cold. October had begun. The day's feeble sun was long gone and a grim mizzle slicked the paving slabs. I was dressed in my usual pinstripe with homburg. The bowler always tempted me with its air of officialdom, but I worried that if I purchased one I would be giving myself up to the City once and for all, chained to my desk until they put me in my coffin, bowler glued to my crown. I arrived outside a tall block of London flats in Bethnal Green; a solidly built red-brick affair that was quick going to seed.

I'd started my search to find this place by ringing up the office of *Whispers Allowed* and having a lovely chat with a Cockney receptionist. After a number of compliments and mistruths, I soon had Morrow Davenport's personal telephone number, which I tried on the Monday and again on the Tuesday, finally getting through to him. I'd referenced the Ritz and a shared dislike of one Lucinda Duker and he said he'd get back to me, which he did, with a time and address. This amateur sleuthing business was really rather simple, I didn't know why Sherlock Holmes made such a fuss about things.

I mounted the steps to the large front door, old dark wood covered in dents and scratches. A single doorbell was close at hand but I noticed the door was ajar so I gave it a prod and let myself into a dusty hallway, poorly lit by flickering bulbs. It was colder inside than out and there was no porter there to greet me. I shivered. It was just the sort of spot for a haunting. Further into the gloom I spotted a cage lift, which looked like some sort of medieval torture contraption, so I took the stairs. I spiralled my way up, wondering when I was going to bump into one of the occupants, but the doors on each floor were closed and no light came out from underneath. Davenport lived on the top.

It didn't take long to get out of breath. I'm not an unfit sort of chap; I love a good stroll and sometimes manage some swimming, but stairs really are the devil. The sound of a gramophone became audible as I climbed higher and higher – something simple with violins. My knees clicked as I ascended and my footsteps echoed in the gloom. The music called me on, it was positively eerie. I finally reached the top landing and paused to recover. There was only one door up here, a little way off to my right. A soft orange glow came from the edges as did the music. I approached the door, ready to knock, when...

"Oh, good evening!"

The voice came from the other side, animated and loud. It was Davenport's all right. Except the door was still closed and I hadn't knocked. He must have another guest.

"Welcome to my humble abode."

How exceptionally awkward. I noticed more stairs to my right, not the spiralling kind but a steep staircase ascending into deeper darkness, probably to the roof. I climbed a few of them and waited.

"How are you?"

I was hiding, how bloody foolish of me! But I felt self-conscious, not wanting to be seen by the mystery guest, although how I'd explain myself if either of them saw me, I did not know.

"You look divine!"

The walls must be paper-thin. I could hear everything, even the shuffling of his feet.

"How *are* you?" he repeated. "How are *you*!"

No one answered him and it dawned on me that he was speaking to himself – rehearsing for my arrival! I almost laughed, thinking on the times I had done such a thing. He must be more nervous than I was. I took a deep breath, descended the steps and knocked loudly on the door. I had good practice in faking confidence.

"Mr Bigge!" exclaimed Davenport as he flung the door open, "How are you?"

"I… I'm well."

I didn't know where to start. First of all, he wasn't wearing many clothes. A silk dressing gown with a peacock-feather pattern was loosely tied around an otherwise naked torso, save for a fair smattering of chest hair, and further down was a pair of silk pyjama bottoms and some comfortable-looking slippers. He held the door open and ushered me through. I took my coat and hat off, quick to realign any misplaced hairs.

"Welcome to my humble abode."

It was a large, rather barren room, sparse in furniture. The walls held little artwork save for two staid pastorals depicting trees, sheep and fully clothed shepherds. The violin music tinkled away from a gramophone placed dejectedly on the floor but even that was only Brahms. I have to say I was disappointed, having expected the flat to match the artistic temperaments of its resident.

"It can get chilly up here," he said, closing the door. "Care for a drink? I would say a gin and tonic, but let's go for brandy, you look frightfully cold."

"Do I?"

He stared at me, those brilliant green eyes again, and was quick to look to my crown. He instinctively ran a hand through his generous locks and I couldn't help but grit my teeth. It was all well and good for men like him to have plenty of wonderful hair but they didn't have to make those of us who were less endowed feel all the worse for it. He turned his back on me and sauntered over to a drinks cabinet in front of one of the windows. It looked out into the dark, punctuated by the orange lights of similar abodes. The weak rain pattered against the glass, an accompaniment to the strings.

"Take a seat," he said, casually waving at the settee on the other side of the room, next to which a fire burned merrily in a small grate.

I did as commanded and appreciated the warmth. An old trunk acted as drinks table and there were a number of copies of *Whispers Allowed* on top. Can't say I'd ever read the thing. A door on the other side of the room presumably led into a kitchen or bedroom. There was something quite lonely about the place and I felt a little sad for the chap.

"Drinkies," he said, bringing them over, one in a mug and the other in a water glass. "I hope you're warm enough."

"Quite cosy, thank you," I said.

He plonked himself on the other side of the settee, ensuring a respectable distance between us, all the better for him to size me up.

"You live alone?" he asked.

"I rent a room in a house. The attic room, as it happens."

"Creaky floorboards and a leaky ceiling?"

"And a nosy landlady."

"Here's to locks on the door."

We clinked drinking receptacles and took a swig. He swilled the brandy around his mouth before gulping it down very loudly. It is the birthright of men of the Greek persuasion that we can detect our fellow Grecians with ease – the cut of the jib, the step of the walk or look of the eye – but, while some chaps are so Greek as to be almost Aristotle, Davenport proved harder to read.

"So, Mr Bigge, you wished to speak to me of a mutual acquaintance?"

"I… I do, yes," I replied, momentarily distracted by his good looks. Pull yourself together, Selby! I took a bigger gulp of brandy. "One Lady Lucinda Duker."

"The Harpy of the Heath," he replied with clear disdain.

"Is that what you call her?"

"I have a few other names, but they're not quite so polite. How do you know her?"

"I don't as a matter of fact. That night at the Ritz was the first time I'd met her."

"Oh yes?" He raised a single eyebrow in an effort at dramatic intrigue.

"Patrick facilitated the introduction, he's an old chum of mine."

"An old chum, *really*?"

"From university," I said, trying to keep my tone as even as possible. "We were up at Oxford at the same time."

"Oxford, very impressive."

"Different colleges, mind. He was Corpus and I was Fitzalan."

"Corpus and Fitzalan, what funny names! Still, I like yours, Mr Bigge."

"You can call me Selby."

"I can, though you don't have to call me Murchadh."

"I beg your pardon?"

He laughed, a deep and brassy sound, more a trombone than a trumpet. "Murchadh. My mother was a proud Scot. It's got something to do with the sea, not that I've ever enjoyed swimming, leaves my hair all crusty." He ran his hand through said hair, curling a lock around his index finger, and I wondered if he was flirting or teasing. Probably both. "Father's family were a Cheshire lot, hence the Davenport, and I grew up on the outskirts of Manchester. Not that you'd tell." Indeed I couldn't, his voice was just a shade less clipped than mine. "Call me Morrow. It slips off the tongue a little more pleasurably."

"Quite." I gulped.

"What about yourself?"

"Shropshire on my mother's side and Sussex on my father's."

"And you grew up in either a tiresome village or an emerging suburb where everyone was very dull and quite unlike yourself?"

"Something like that," I said.

"I think the suburb a vile creation of modernity. The name says it all, *under-city*. Grim! All those identical houses filled with identical families, no wonder the Germans wanted to annihilate us."

"I'm sure they have suburbs too."

"Moving to London was the best thing I ever did. So many parties to attend, so many interesting *people* to meet."

He winked at me and I couldn't help but smile, noting the lack of specified sex of said people.

"You keep yourself busy, then?" I asked.

"I try. Anywhere you recommend?"

One is never wise to reveal personal details to a stranger, however handsome; trust must be established first. But my job wasn't to bed the chap, it was to get him to answer my questions. So I offered him something without giving away too much.

"The Cantering Horse attracts a nice crowd. Although rumour has it a policeman was there the other week, pretending to be a punter."

"Oh dear."

"They always stand out like a sore thumb. You ever have any trouble?"

"Me?" He seemed surprised at what I thought was a perfectly natural question. "Oh no, I'm a good boy."

"Nothing with the Lilly Law?" I asked.

"I'm much too well-behaved, but she does sound rather fun."

"Just one of the orderly daughters."

"Oh!" he said, his smile slipping, "Man in a dress type?"

I didn't reply. I just held his gaze and sipped.

"Can't say I've ever seen the attraction. I like my men to be… manly."

He clinked his glass against mine.

"More!"

He was quick to his feet and quicker still to the bottle, bringing it back as he glugged the amber liquid into his glass. He was a tricky one, all right, and not brushed up on his Polari either. As he leant down to top me up, his dressing gown came undone, revealing the rest of his rather nice chest.

"Oops," he said, not bothering to tie it back up. "Now, do you want to talk about Lucinda Duker? Or maybe you have other things in mind?"

"I do," I replied, willing my member to stay down. "I got the impression that you like neither her nor Sir Lionel."

"Whatever gave you that idea?"

"Insults, shouting and a near-fistfight might have given me a few clues."

"You are observant."

"Who do you like the least, the husband or the wife?"

He took his time to reply. There was no quick batting back of badinage, instead his forehead creased and something approximating unhappiness dimmed his face. "It's Lucinda," he said, his words slower than before. "We have a history."

I thought saying nothing would be better than trying to prompt him to say more, so I settled for another sip.

"She stole something I cherished."

"I'm sorry to hear that."

"Oh, Selby, I'll be straight with you." The words gushed out, perhaps he'd been drinking before I'd arrived. "The something was a someone and the cherishment was love. Proper love. The type Shakespeare wrote sonnets for, the type I write doggerel for. Do you know what I'm talking of?"

"I do." And I wasn't lying this time. "A little, at least."

"Then you know how rare it is to find another..." His green eyes reflected the firelight. "To find another man, damn it, in this cruel world we live in."

"I know."

"I was at a party in Marylebone, hosted by some chap who worked for *The Times*, horrid little fellow, very fat, with a few too many chins."

The way he phrased this description reminded me of the bullies at my school, ever ready to shame someone for their physical appearance. I said nothing but silently marked a point against Mr Davenport.

"It was a boring party with tepid champagne and soggy blinis, but that didn't matter because I was there with my... friend. He was all I saw, he was my everything. Until *she* arrived, in a sparkling green dress and pearls. And those dark, smoky eyes. I'll never forget the way she looked at me, then him." His own eyes drifted to the ceiling as he got lost in his memories. Then he snapped back to me and his tone sharpened. "As it transpired, she was just a tart in a frock who soon set her sights on *my* chum. I shan't relive all the details but let's just say she stole from me the best thing I ever had."

"Pethybridge?" I asked, quoting the name Patrick had said.

"Yes! How did you know?"

"Scandal spreads."

"Dear Rupert, how I loved him. But that Lucy took him from me." His top lip raised into a snarl. "I don't know if you've ever hated someone, Selby, truly hated them, but, let me tell you, once you accustom yourself to the burning sensation, it keeps you warm. After she stole him there was only one thing I wanted."

"What was that?"

"Revenge."

He savoured each syllable, like slipping a sharpened knife into soft flesh.

"Did you get it?"

"I did! I dipped my pen in poison and made ruin."

Hell hath no fury like a vengeful poof, as the normals are wont to call us.

"But if you had your revenge, why are you back for more?"

"Because ruining her life gives purpose to mine. God knows my literary ambitions were greater than *Whispers Allowed*, but here I am with more gossip columns to my name than poems. I can't even fill a chapbook. What are you?"

"A clerk at a bank."

"Are you living the life of your dreams, then, the life they promised you?"

"Not yet."

"Then you know what it's like to be not far from thirty and forced to watch the rest of them revel in their happiness as they fill the suburbs with their ugly houses and even uglier brats. She's unremarkable by background, purely middle class, but now she has everything. It's not fair."

God, the man was bitter.

"It's awful, Selby, being this lonely."

I wanted to wince but wouldn't let myself. He spoke his pain so vividly and it was like he'd cut open my skull and taken a look at the thoughts inside. I did hate so much being so lonely. My life wasn't all bad, though. I did have fun, yes, I had lots of fun in London's underground but that didn't warm the sheets for long. Fun was not love.

"Don't you have chums?"

"I have brandy," he slurred. He leant forward and retrieved the bottle from the floor before taking a big swig.

I was a little perturbed by his behaviour, given I'd only just met him, but he was being very candid. At this rate I'd have plenty to report back to Patrick.

"Haven't you taken it too far, this time?"

By way of an answer he reached out towards the magazines and plucked one from the pile. He rifled through a number of pages and then began to read:

"Once upon a time there was a lonely knight atop the heath who had lost his damsel long ago. How he pined for love, offering all the precious gems he could to any lass who might ease his grief, as deep as any mine. Then she appeared, the lady of the knight, with her firm hillocks and golden hair, offering the lonely chap his very own happy ending. And now for the twelve-carat truth, dear reader, the old goat accepted her offer!"

"Firm hillocks?" I said, "It's hardly subtle."

"It's *Whispered Allowed*, it's not meant to be."

"I can see why Sir Lionel is angry."

"Good!" he almost shouted. "That was the point. Duker can accuse me of libel all he wants but it won't stick."

"Are you sure?"

"I have no intention of letting that man put me in prison. You know what it's like for our kind. I'm going to teach him and his detestable wife a lesson."

He enjoyed his hyperbole; he was clearly a writer.

"What lesson would that be?"

"One that involves the barrel of my revolver."

"You have a gun?" I couldn't hide the panic from my voice as my eyes scanned the room for said weapon.

"My father gave it to me after the war. I hadn't fought. It was his way of telling me to make something of myself or die trying."

"He can't have meant that!"

"Oh, please. I bet your father wouldn't care if you wound up at the bottom of the Thames."

"We... we don't see eye to eye," I stuttered. "But he doesn't want me dead."

But nor did he know the truth of who I was, or my mother and sister for that matter. They could never know the truth. It would spell excommunication.

"They all want the likes of us dead," he said, shuffling closer to me. "But I'm going out with a bang."

"You mustn't do anything rash," I said, rising from the settee.

"And I'm taking the Dukers with me."

"Mr Davenport, I'm sorry Lucinda stole your lover, but you really must pull yourself together."

I sounded like my father! Morrow just laughed.

"Or you could pull me together," he said.

One minute he was raving then he was flirting, I was quite fed up with him.

"Thank you for the drink." I made a beeline for the hat stand and heard him coming after me.

"What about something stronger?"

"I should be getting back."

"Where is it you live?"

"Near Waterloo."

"Very nice, whereabouts exactly?"

I reached the door and opened it, letting in a nasty gust of chill.

"Stay awhile," he implored. "Keep me warm."

I turned around as I placed my damp hat back on my head. Yet where I expected to see the pleading eyes of a desperate man and maybe even a quivering lip, I saw only a hard but handsome face.

"You really want me to stay?" I asked.

"I… I do."

"You don't sound so sure."

"I'm sure," he said, this time without a stammer. "I've never kissed a Fitzalan fellow before."

What I did next, I did very quickly (I'd had some practice, after all). I placed my hand at the back of his neck, pulled his head closer to mine and kissed him hard on the lips. He gasped and pushed back, forcing our bodies apart. He tasted of brandy.

"Not to your liking?"

"I… Maybe I've drunk too much."

All bark and no bite; all puff and no poof.

"Maybe you have," I said, putting my overcoat back on. "You must leave them alone, I'm warning you. You've already had one revenge. Why bother with another?"

"Because my appetite is insatiable."

"I'm not so sure about that. Good evening, Mr Davenport."

I turned on my heel and marched back into the gloom. The door slammed shut behind me, the bang echoing down the stairwell as I quickened my step. This was the second man I'd met who loathed Lucinda Duker. But while Patrick's hate was restrained, Morrow's was verging on lunacy. And to think somewhere in his rooms was a revolver. I'd come here to find Lucinda's secrets, only to discover that this madman wanted her dead. I had to warn her.

CHAPTER 5

Situated not far from Spaniards Road, Sir Lionel's house was an impressive if crass piece of architecture. Built entirely of red brick, it was like an overgrown toy castle. On the right was a narrow turret with a pointed roof and giant, stone spheres sitting atop each crenellation. On the left was a great bay window that ran from the ground to the first floor, jutting out like a rugby player's jaw. It was approaching five o'clock; I had been instructed to arrive after tea but before canapés. The morning's grey clouds had dispersed to ensure an afternoon of blue skies. I passed through a wrought-iron gate and crunched my way over the gravel of the drive. Funny to think that on the occasions I'd enjoyed the Heath's alternative pleasures, Patrick had been but a stone's throw away. For all I knew, I'd fellated him in the dark. I climbed the steps to the front door, flanked by four red pillars, and tugged the bell pull. Chimes echoed from within and soon the door was opened by a suitably imperious-looking butler.

"Hullo," I said.

"Good afternoon, sir."

"Selby Bigge, I'm here for the party."

"Right you are, sir."

I stepped into the hall, which was just as showy as the rest of the place with black-and-white marble flooring and a big staircase that split in two directions halfway up. What fun for a game of cat and mouse!

"And you might be?"

"The name's Pinks, sir."

"Worked here long?"

"I arrived a year after Sir Lionel."

That didn't quite answer my question but he appeared the loyal sort. A tall chap with a bald pate save for a few delicately combed strands. His suit was impeccably pressed and even the lines on his forehead were straight.

"Allow me, sir."

He took my hat and coat, and I followed him into the room at the base of the turret, a very grand cloakroom indeed. It was pentagonal in shape with a number of windows looking out over the gravel. In the middle was a circular table with a telephone on it and over in one of the many corners was a busy coat stand. The heavy oak door closed itself behind me and I suddenly found myself shut inside with the butler.

"Dear me," I said, groping for the knob. "I didn't know it did that."

The look he gave me was most peculiar.

"The guests are gathered in the drawing room, sir."

"Good-o."

We crossed the hallway to the right of the stairs and entered a large dining room. The table was covered in a white cloth laden with silver and glass, and I counted seven places. Only a select number of guests, then, and to think I was one of them! The chaps at the bank would turn green with envy when I told them whose birthday party I'd attended. Pinks opened a door opposite the one we'd come through.

"Mr Selby Bigge," he announced.

Three pairs of eyes found me as I entered the drawing room and I was disappointed that none of them belonged to Patrick.

"Colonel William Price."

That was the stern-looking older chap with a giant, white moustache stuck in the middle of a very circular head. He looked every bit the retired military man (with far too many war stories to hand).

"Mrs Octavia Stubbs."

Golly, the famous crime writer. Well, famous-ish. She wore round spectacles, had lots of grey hair and was dressed up in some purple contraption, which created the impression of a discoloured meringue. What a treat!

"Miss Theodora Smythe."

The final guest was most striking. She wore a long, silver dress and had dark hair cut alarmingly short. A similar age to myself, there was something decidedly mannish about her, which confused my attractions no end.

"Good afternoon," I said, affecting my most charming smile, which appeared to do little for any of them.

"Do take a seat, sir. Drinks will be served later."

"Marvellous."

The drawing room was expectedly magnificent with lots of sash windows overlooking the garden and a large pair of French windows. A profusion of furniture fanned in a semi-circle around the fireplace. The Colonel was in an armchair nearest the fire and Mrs Stubbs and Miss Smythe on the adjacent settee. I sat on one opposite, a splendid Persian rug between us.

"Salby what?" asked Mrs Stubbs in an imperious sort of tone.

"Selby Bigge."

"Selby? But that's a town, in Berkshire."

"Yorkshire, as it happens."

"Bigge. There are Bigges in Cornwall, I believe."

"Quite possibly, yes."

"You must be related to Hortense and Arthur?"

"I don't think so."

I'd often contemplated inventing a more illustrious background for myself but a few probing questions and soon the whole pack of cards would come tumbling down. All roads led to Horsham, after all, and that would be the end of it.

"Are you a friend of Sir Lionel's?" I asked.

"Yes."

"Marvellous." I longed for a glass of something to hide behind. "It really is an honour to meet you, Mrs Stubbs, your books are most admired."

"They are."

"I do like your detective, such a clever chap."

"Which one?"

Bugger, I'd forgotten she had more than one sleuth. Scarcely a minute in and I was already tripping over my own feet. The last of her novels I'd read had been set on a barge and the twist something to do with a dog and a hosepipe. Amusing, but she was no John Rhode (but I thought I'd keep that observation to myself). The detective had been some run-of-the-mill policeman called...

"Inspector Glover!" I said, relieved to have remembered.

"Aunt Oscar has such a way with words," said the younger woman.

Octavia Stubbs wrote all her novels under the name Oscar Trolloppe, hence her niece's pet name. That the two were related I couldn't believe, the family resemblance was entirely non-existent, although they both seemed to share a passion for the withering glare.

"Which is your favourite of Glover's mysteries?" asked Miss Smythe.

The fiend!

"The Isle of Savages," I said quickly, picturing the memorable front cover: a tribal headdress resting on a skull, the feathers covered in blood. Lots of people trapped on an island getting killed off by a madman and there was a ghost if I remembered correctly.

"That's not a Glover," shot the young woman. "No one survives."

"You're quite right," I replied, stalling for time, "My top Glover would have to be... *Who Killed Cock Robin?* I was so impressed by how the nursery rhyme was tied into the solution of the crime."

"That was impressive of me," the crime writer agreed.

Ha, one point to me, Miss Smythe!

"And the soldier in the insane asylum was a twist I didn't see coming," I added, on the verge of overdoing it.

"A soldier, you say," barked the Colonel, suddenly coming to life. "You're a soldier?"

"No, I work at a bank as it happens."

"Fought in the trenches, eh?"

"I was a bit young for that."

"How young?"

"Too young."

He glowered at me, the purple of his nose contrasting with the white of his moustache. All that time in the trenches must have made him fond of the drink.

"I led troops at Verdun."

"Oh yes?"

"And Passchendaele."

"We owe you so much, Colonel," said Miss Smythe, with just the faintest hint of sarcasm.

"Great Britain was truly great, once."

"I quite agree," chimed Mrs Stubbs. "Nowadays all the young care about is sex and tittle tattle. God must be turning in his grave."

"God isn't dead, Mrs Stubbs," said the Colonel.

"Quite so," she replied with an impish little grin. There was a sense of humour there yet. We were saved any further discomfiture by the opening of a door on the far side of the fireplace. In walked Patrick, looking just as handsome as ever.

"Hello, Selby!" he said, visibly pleased to see me. "I trust you're making friends with everyone."

"Absolutely," I lied.

"Mr Bigge was going to tell us his *second* favourite Inspector Glover mystery," said Miss Smythe.

"Come, Theodora, no teasing."

The woman batted her eyelids and, oh, if I could hold up my index finger and vanish her.

"It will be champagne and canapés soon," explained Patrick. "Dinner will be served before seven. Pa doesn't like being too late to bed."

"Quite so," I said, "Where is he?"

"Taking a nap."

"And Lucinda?" I ventured.

"Powdering her nose."

As long as the pair weren't being shot at by a venomous gossip columnist then all was well.

"First things first, I want to show you the garden."

"The garden?" I replied, but I'd barely sat down.

"Yes Selby, the garden."

He emphasised the request and I realised he wanted to get me alone for a moment. How exciting! Miss Smythe turned her deep, brown eyes on me and appraised me with a look that was oddly reminiscent of some of the men I passed on the Dilly. I looked away, my gaze falling on the carriage clock on the mantelpiece, an ornate, golden affair that must have cost lots of money. There was also a pair of silver candleholders and one of those old-fashioned spill jars in the shape of a fish with a great, gaping mouth.

"Come on, some fresh air will do you a world of good."

"Right ho."

I jumped to my feet and followed him over to the French

windows. Three pairs of eyes watched me go, doubtless willing I didn't return. The air proved much too fresh for my liking as my breath misted in the afternoon chill. The setting sun illuminated the garden's splendour and I spied a well-tended lawn bordered by flowerbeds and a number of apple trees still laden with fruit. At the far end was a high brick wall with an ornate metal gate built into it. Beyond were plenty of tall trees.

"Is that the Heath?"

"The extension."

"Gosh, what a splendid location. It must have been such fun to grow up here."

"You see the old gate," he said, pointing. "I used to climb through the gaps as a child. I got lost in the woods a number of times."

"Do you still spend a lot of time on the Heath?" I said, trying to sound casual.

"Absolutely, got to get away from the Harpy. She's been insufferable this last week, playing Lady of the Manor. Reduced poor Agnes to tears a number of times and even lost her rag with Mrs Fairbanks."

"Agnes and Mrs Fairbanks?"

"Our maid and housekeeper. We've never had trouble with them before, but Lucinda is kicking up a fuss because she wants new staff. She's even got Pa on side. After them, I'll be booted and then she'll finally have everything she wants. Queen of the ruddy castle."

He took me up the garden path to a walled herb garden. It was enclosed on all sides, meaning no one in the house could see us. There was a rosemary bush doing very well for itself, some thyme, a bay and various other things that the cook must make good use of. Just the sort of place young lovers might abscond to.

"Tell me then," he said, sitting himself down on a bench. "What have you found out?"

I sat next to him, the wood cold against my buttocks, hoping this would be the location of our next bench-based kiss. I recounted my trip to Morrow's, although I did omit the nice tufts of hair around his nipples and the bit about my kissing him.

"So that's the crux of the matter," said Patrick. "Davenport hates Lucy because she stole his…"

"Chum," I chipped in as we caught eyes, our cheeks turning bright pink. "And that's when he found his purpose in life."

"Whi… which is?" managed Patrick, his pink becoming scarlet.

"Revenge. He can't bear the thought of her being happy, so he's come back to ruin her second marriage."

A few pigeons flapped over the walled garden and our gazes were taken upwards to the darkening sky. God, it was cold.

"I suppose if we can get proof it will add weight to the case against him," said Patrick. "A drunk *and* degenerate libelist versus a knight of the realm. The judge will pass a harsher sentence."

"I assume he will have burned any proof of that," I said, suddenly feeling a little guilty for having ratted on a fellow Mary Ann. "If he's got any sense."

"We know he doesn't have any of that because he was foolish enough to get my father caught up in his petty revenge. He'll probably enjoy prison, though, given the company he'll be keeping."

The lady protesting too much was a common play in a game where one's true desires had to be kept close to one's chest. Although Patrick played it with a little too much relish.

"But she's the one I want rid of. Father's too spellbound to care she's a divorcee and whether or not her first husband was a pervert is immaterial. I just know she's up to something; she's been scheming all week. It's a shame your investigations have proven so fruitless."

"I... I am sorry to have disappointed you, Patrick," I said, my heart sinking. "But I really don't think we should underestimate Davenport, he's deeply unhinged. He even spoke of wanting to kill Lucinda."

"Don't we all."

"He wasn't joking. He said he owned a revolver."

"What of it? I have one, don't you?"

"I don't as a matter of fact," I replied defensively. "He hates your father too."

"A high-pitched, prancing pervert is no threat to my father."

As it happened, Morrow had quite a low timbre of voice and I'd certainly never seen him prance, nor even flounce for that matter.

"Although if he did shoot Mother it would prove most convenient."

I stared at him, unable to hide my shock, but he simply laughed.

"Don't be silly, Selby," he said, getting up from the bench. "I'm teasing, no one's going to get hurt tonight."

And then, quite without warning, he reached out and touched my cheek twice, something between a pat and a slap.

Was it manly affection or something more? I rose to my feet, much to my numb posterior's relief, and for a moment our faces were mere inches apart. How I yearned to reacquaint myself with those full lips.

"Do you remember that soiree at Cyril's?" I asked, thinking back to our first kiss.

"Cyril had so many bloody soirees," he replied breezily. "Come on, time for some canapés, and I want you to spend some more time with Theodora."

"Really, is she a good friend of yours?"

"Oh, didn't I say?" he said over his shoulder. "She's my fiancée."

CHAPTER 6

"Don't get me started on the degenerates!" said the Colonel.
"Indeed!" chimed Mrs Stubbs.

Patrick and I had returned to the drawing room to find Colonel Price and Octavia Stubbs holding forth on the decline of Western civilisation. Inter-breeding in foreign lands, the poor manners of the working classes and the Irish had all been suitably blamed, now it was my turn.

"Infecting our men with their vice and decadence."

Sounded like good fun to me!

"I remember Verdun, we caught two of them at it, an officer and his batman. Utterly disgraceful."

"Utterly."

"Had them shot for cowardice to save the officer's family a worse scandal."

"A kindness, really."

I inwardly screamed, willing the carriage clock's minute hand to hurry up. Perhaps the fish-shaped spill jar could also swallow me whole.

"Young men aren't what they used to be," trilled the crime writer. "There's a degenerate in my twenty-third novel, *Last Train To Death*. He's quite horrible, with a womanly sort of voice and elaborate clothes. After the first murder, he's the prime suspect but he's actually a red herring. Ends up taking his own life on the train tracks."

"Oh, Auntie! You do love killing people, don't you," said Miss Smythe, her voice rich and throaty.

"It's my favourite pastime."

"It must be fun having a famous writer in the family," I said, forcing myself to be nice to the stealer of Patrick's heart.

"It is. She always told my siblings and I the most gruesome of bedtime stories."

"Character building," said Mrs Stubbs.

"Do you have many siblings?" I asked.

"Two brothers and a sister, which puts me far from the title."

"Oh, a title?" I squeaked.

"My father is the seventh Baronet Smythe of Etherley."

Bang went the next nail in the coffin of any possible romance with Patrick. He'd never elope with an untitled Horshamite.

"Although I think I'm perfectly capable of holding the fort."

"You are capable of many things," said Mrs Stubbs. "Including knowing your place."

"I could run the estate just as well as you can write your novels."

"Indeed," I said. "But I, for one, am glad Agatha Christie never took to land management."

"Agatha Christie!" said Mrs Stubbs, almost spitting the

words. "That woman is a stain on the name of literature."

I had made my remark in jest but might as well have stabbed the butler.

"She churns out novels like the Americans churn out sausages and that's exactly how I'd describe her books. They appeal to the basest sort of reader who gobbles them up with no regard for taste."

"She'll go out of fashion soon enough, Auntie," said Theodora. "No one can top your canon."

Canon was quite a generous term with which to describe her collection but I thought it best to keep that to myself.

"Quite right. I know a murder mystery isn't just an elaborate crossword puzzle, it's a work of art! Readers don't want a parlour game, they want the very human heart dissected to reveal what wickedness there resides. And ghosts, readers want lots and lots of ghosts. Christie can do a good twist, I'll give her that, but where are all the ghosts?"

"Do you really think the human heart is such a wicked place?" asked Patrick, his cheeks rosy from the fire's heat. And what kissable cheeks they were.

"Humans are capable of all sorts of evil."

"But we're good at heart," I said. "Surely?"

"Nonsense, humans are wicked creatures, any crime writer worth her salt knows that. Even Christie. One need only read the papers to see how good we are at killing one another. Although nine times out of ten, murder is a tawdry, matrimonial affair – a put-upon wife poisoning her husband or a cuckolded husband butchering his wife. But who wants to read of such classless occurrences?"

She glared around the room, her eyes wide and penetrating, and I thought better than to answer a clearly rhetorical question.

"I'm a killer."

It was the Colonel who spoke, causing us all to turn our heads in surprise.

"I killed for King and Country. I killed for God. And I refuse to be tarred with the same brush as some cheap little wench who can't keep her marital vows."

"You killed for God?" asked Theodora.

"Yes," he replied gruffly, forced to reply to a woman. "There are killings He permits and those He does not."

"How do we know which is which?"

"Because He tells us."

"By telegram?" she muttered under her breath.

"Come, Theodora," chided Mrs Stubbs. "You owe your life to the Colonel."

"I still think killing is wrong, in wartime as well as peacetime."

"That's easy to say from the comfort of a drawing room," said her aunt. "But you haven't been pushed to the edge."

"We do all have our limits," said Patrick. "Don't we, Selby?"

"I... I would like to think I'd never kill anyone."

On that note, the door beyond the fireplace burst open and there stood Sir Lionel and Lady Duker.

"No one shall kill anyone tonight," announced Lucinda. "Not while there's still champagne to drink!"

We laughed politely as the couple took centre stage. He stood tall and smart with a maroon bowtie and matching cummerbund. There was no denying his magnetic presence. If Patrick grew into that, he'd be doing well for himself. Lucinda looked divine in a gold crepe de Chine number embellished with golden beads. She positively shone.

"Sir Lionel and Lady Duker," I said, rising to my feet. "How good to see you both again."

"You the banker chap?" he asked.

"I am indeed."

He harrumphed by way of recognition before seating himself down in his armchair throne by the fireplace.

"Selby, what a pleasure," she gushed. "You must call me Lucy."

I took her hand and kissed it. Her skin was soft and she smelt of roses, a breath of fresh air in this fusty old room. She motioned for me to sit back down and plopped herself next to me on the sofa.

"It's healing nicely," she said, showing me her left palm. She'd covered the wound with one of those fancy new sticking plasters.

"I'm glad to hear it."

"Selby saved me from a rather nasty scrap last week," she explained to the others. "He's my hero."

She made light of Morrow's histrionics, clearly unaware of what a danger he truly was. I'd have to get her alone to explain things, I couldn't just blurt it out in front of everyone, it would be improper.

"I do like your necklace, Lucinda," commented Mrs Stubbs, indifferent to my heroics.

"It was a present from Lionel."

Lucy ran her fingers down an elegant, golden chain at the end of which was a vivid blue gem mounted on yet more gold.

"Lapis lazuli?"

Lucy nodded, "It took me forever to decide which pieces to wear. I have so many!"

"Lucky you," said Octavia. "Anything special?"

"They're all special if they're from my beloved."

The Colonel choked and it wasn't clear if he was signalling his dislike of women's jewellery or the beginnings of a heart attack.

"There's a lovely diamond bracelet that Selby saw last week."

"I want to see it too," said Mrs Stubbs, a little too enthusiastically. "It's quite wrong that pretty little creatures like you get to hoard all the finery."

"Now, now, Auntie, your jewellery is more than splendid enough." Theodora spoke with a lightness of tone but I detected an edge. "And you have so much of it."

"It's always nice to have more."

The familial double act was interrupted by the arrival of the canapés – smoked salmon, devilled eggs and olives. These were brought in by an older woman with hair so tightly scraped back it was almost a scalping. Mrs Fairbanks the housekeeper, presumably.

"You're late," complained Lucy.

"Sorry, ma'am, things are taking a little longer what with Mrs Stonehouse away and all."

"Excuses, excuses. Pass them around. Mrs Stonehouse is the cook," explained Lucy, placing a hand on my arm. "She had to head north, death of a nephew or cousin, scarlet fever. Thoroughly bad timing what with Lionel's birthday. Still, I never thought devilling an egg could take so long."

Then came a maid in the usual servant's black with a white apron and one of those silly little hats, the purpose of which

I never understood. This must be Agnes. She carried a tray of champagne glasses, fluted rather than bowled, which clinked ominously against one another. Finally came Pinks with the champagne, and he popped the cork to a quiet round of applause.

After the glasses had been filled, Agnes began walking from guest to guest with the tray. Things were going well at first, no drops or spillages, and nearly everyone had a glass in hand save for me. I saw the look of relief on the maid's face just before she snagged her foot on the edge of the rug. The final glass leapt for freedom, as did its contents. Champagne spilled as the flute fell to the floor below. It was death by decapitation as the head left the neck, but otherwise it was a clean break.

"You stupid girl," said Lucy. "What have I told you?"

"I'm so sorry, your ladyship, I really am..."

"Enough with your apologies, get out."

Agnes hovered above the breakage, her knees half bent.

"I said, get out!"

Tears welled in the young girl's eyes as she scurried away. I didn't envy servants one jot. After my botched finals at Oxford, I'd been forced to work under my father at the bank in Horsham for a while. That had been quite bad enough.

"Mrs Fairbanks," said Lucy, shifting her line of fire. "This is unacceptable."

"I do apologise, madam, I really do."

"Apologies won't fix that glass, or the teacup from last week, and the vase the week before. I told you to give her extra training, do you remember?"

"Yes, madam."

"A task you have evidently failed at."

While there's nothing worse than bad service, Lucy did seem to be relishing in the ritual humiliation of her staff a little too much. Sir Lionel displayed no signs of discomfort. If anything he looked approving of his wife's behaviour. The couple were clearly of the same mind.

"Now pick up that glass at once."

"Yes, madam."

We all watched Mrs Fairbanks as she entered the ring of seats and bent down to retrieve the breakage. Broken glasses were proving something of a theme with the Dukers. The housekeeper showed no signs of having been emotionally distressed by Lucy's words, unlike Agnes who was probably filling the kitchen sink with her tears. With the head in one hand and the stem in the other, she departed. One had to hand it to her, she may have lost the battle but she wasn't going to let us see her bleed.

"One just can't find the right staff these days," said Lucy. "How do you cope, Mrs Stubbs?"

"With a high turnover rate."

"Exactly. They're too busy becoming secretaries."

"Or marrying rich men," said the Colonel pointedly.

Lucy's grip tightened on her glass and I worried she'd end up with shards in her right palm as well.

"Happy birthday, Pa," said Patrick, leading the toast as everyone, except for me, raised their glasses and echoed the sentiment.

"Happy birthday, darling," gushed Lucy. "It's going to be such a memorable evening."

CHAPTER 7

Dinner was served in the grand dining hall with its wood-panelled walls and deep, crimson carpet. Expensive paintings were in abundance, including a foreboding portrait of Sir Lionel, which squared his jaw and darkened his grey. A true aristocrat's house would have portraits of ancestors dating back to the invention of paint, but the Dukers weren't true aristocrats, they were a family that had struck gold and diamonds. I'd have settled for either. We ate six courses and by number three I was struggling. I had the misfortune of being seated next to Mrs Stubbs, who still hadn't forgiven me for mentioning Agatha Christie. Fortunately, she absconded for much of the fourth course. By dessert, the Colonel was long past half-cut and, just when I thought it was all over, Mrs Fairbanks wheeled in a giant birthday cake and Lucy led us through a tuneless rendition of "Happy Birthday".

After cake, my priority was to relieve myself. I must have

drunk at least a bottle's worth of liquid. I slipped quietly into the hall, shutting myself off from the hubbub. The dinner had been satisfying but, while everyone had chattered and smiled accordingly, I couldn't help but sense an underlying tension. I knew of the hidden strains within the room and while an Englishman, or woman for that matter, can hide anything behind a blank face, it's only a matter of time before something gives.

I crossed the black-and-white floor around the staircase to a door on the other side of the hall. A gloom lurked within the house, amassing in the corners as shadows, rendering it the perfect place for a gothic melodrama or one of Mrs Stubbs' interminable ghost stories. I shivered at the thought. Surely our earlier conversation about killing had been purely hypothetical? I entered a darkened corridor at the end of which was another door that led back into the drawing room. Possibly. The house was worse than the labyrinth of Knossos. Halfway down were two doors opposite one another. Patrick had said the WC was on the left, hadn't he?

Turned out he hadn't as I entered a very lavish billiard room. A single, orange lamp lit the scene: a huge billiard table covered in pristine, green felt and walls lined with bookshelves full of ancient tomes that looked expensive but unread. On the other side was a set of French windows, the curtains pulled back to reveal the darkness beyond. A breath of fresh air, yes, that was a good idea. I tiptoed across the room and found the key in the lock, good-o. Less fresh, more freezing, but it did me good to shiver a moment on the patio.

A waxing gibbous moon hung among the stars and I wondered who might be out and about on the Heath tonight.

Perhaps blue-eyed Arthur? A fresh wave of goosebumps prickled my skin. I'm not one for hunting but, for a moment, I had the distinct impression that someone was watching me. I imagined that lunatic Morrow hiding amongst the shrubbery. He would be a fool to turn up tonight but people with nothing to lose did all manner of foolish things. I slipped back inside and locked the door. There were voices coming from the corridor, hushed and purposeful.

"What have I told you, silly girl?"

"I'm sorry, Mrs Fairbanks, but I don't know where it is."

"If you're not breaking things, you're losing them."

"But why would I take the cloakroom key?"

"You tell me!"

Poor Agnes sounded truly panicked. She really was the lowest in the pecking order.

"Lady Duker will have your guts for garters, and then she'll have mine."

"I promise I don't know where it is."

"She wants us out and you know it. We can't give her any ammunition."

"I promise..."

"Stop your whinging, Agnes, and find that key."

It suddenly occurred to me I was hiding, as if I were the one who'd misplaced the cloakroom key. I strode forth and announced myself with a cough, even if it sounded more like a hiccup.

"Good evening, sir," said Mrs Fairbanks without so much as a trace of surprise while Agnes looked like she'd seen a vampire. "Can I be of assistance?"

"The water closet?"

"This one, sir." She pointed at the other door.

"Aha, thank you."

"My pleasure, sir."

She gave me a curt nod and was on her way.

"Why can't anyone find the lav?" asked Agnes, as she hurried after the housekeeper. "That writer lady was up in one of the bedrooms looking for it."

"Be quiet," scolded Mrs Fairbanks.

Finally! I locked myself inside and fussed with my trousers and union suit a while before eventually releasing my pecker. I heaved a sigh of relief as I emptied myself into the bowl. One of the Soho queans once told me she'd been with a gent who'd requested she urinate upon him. I'd said I didn't see the appeal and she'd said she charged him extra. How we cackled over our sherries! I flicked off the drips and tucked myself back in before pulling on the chain. Nothing happened, so I gave another tug, still nothing. The chain hung from the cistern above, well out of reach. I pulled again, to no avail.

"Victorian plumbing," I grumbled. At this rate I was going to have to climb onto the seat and start rootling around the bloody cistern. Fortunately my fourth pull proved successful as the water came rushing down, threatening to bring the whole of the plumbing system with it. It was a pokey little room given the immensity of the rest of the house and there weren't any windows. It wasn't English to acknowledge one's more animal practices, that was for the Americans. I washed my hands in the basin, rearranged my hair in the mirror and turned right down the corridor for what I hoped would be the drawing room.

Charades was the preferred method of torture for the evening as we ambled and flustered our way through a number of Greek tragedies, Dickens novels and religious scenes. I was rather shocked to witness Octavia Stubbs hanging herself while her niece stabbed her own eyes out, but then I realised it was *Oedipus*. The price of getting it right was being next on stage, but Patrick came to my rescue as I repeatedly stabbed him in the back for *Julius Caesar*. We were applauded at the end of our rendition and Patrick gave my shoulder a quick squeeze. I dared to look him in the eye but he was looking at his fiancée. Lucy guessed it to more applause and, for a moment, the group was united in a game of mild humiliation.

"Looks like you could do with a rest," she said as I plonked myself next to her on the settee.

"I think we all could," said Lionel from his armchair.

"Have you done much acting before?"

"I dabbled very briefly in the OUDS," I told her, "I think I mentioned I was at Oxford."

"Have another glass, darling," she said, offering hers to her husband.

"I couldn't," said Lionel. "I've had too much already."

"Spoilsport," she replied.

"You go on without me."

"Oxford, did you say?" she said, taking the smallest of sips.

"I did. Classics."

"How fascinating! You must tell me *all* about it."

"Where to begin…"

"I love all those old paintings of gladiators and gods," she interrupted. "So terribly dramatic. I was admiring them at the

National Gallery just the other day."

"How marvellous," I replied, trying to keep up. "Am I right in thinking they've got *The Siren*?"

"Which one's that?" asked Lucy, her eyes wide and unknowing.

"It's a Waterhouse, his best work, I think. A drowning sailor clutching at the feet of a young siren."

"Oh yes, I think I did see that one!"

"She's playing the lyre and doesn't seem to mind he's not going to make it."

"Awfully rude of her!" She paused a moment and her smile slipped. "Although, if I'm perfectly honest, I didn't much enjoy my trip to the gallery."

"Why ever not, darling?" asked Sir Lionel.

"I think I had a shadow."

"A what?" he blurted.

"I think someone was following me."

"You never told me this. Was it that horrible queer?"

Sir Lionel and I looked equally taken aback. His thinking was the same as mine, even if I would have expressed it a shade differently.

"I… I don't know, I didn't see him."

"He should be strung up," said Sir Lionel.

"Let's forget him," said Lucy. "This evening is for you."

"I'll come with you next time," he said, reaching out to stroke his fingers along her arm. I had to admit to feeling a little relieved, knowing he was at her side. "Where's your bracelet?"

"I couldn't find it."

"Where did you look?"

"Everywhere, even under the bed."

"Where did you last have it?"

"I thought I left it on the dressing table. I'm always misplacing things." She laughed, trying to make light of the situation. "I'd lose my own brain if it wasn't sewn into my hat."

"I want you to look again."

"I will, darling. I'll look later."

"Good, I like to know where my possessions are."

"I'm right here, darling."

"Did you say a missing bracelet?" asked Miss Smythe.

"I did," said Lucy coldly.

"That's a shame."

"Why aren't you wearing your engagement ring tonight, Theodora?"

For once the other woman looked taken aback as she stared at her empty ring finger.

"For refitting," said Patrick, but I wasn't half-convinced.

"When will you two lovebirds finally end this interminable engagement?"

"When the time is right," replied Miss Smythe.

"A girl mustn't be single for too long," chided Lucy. "People will say all sorts."

"I don't care for what people say."

"Clearly not."

"Besides, a good marriage cannot be rushed," said Miss Smythe. "One would hate to find themselves attached to the wrong sort."

As if there had been any doubt, it was now quite clear that, of those gathered, the only one who actually liked Lucinda was her husband. What with a scheming son-in-law, disapproving guests and disgruntled staff, Morrow might not be the only one loading his revolver. If this were one of Oscar Trolloppe's novels, it wouldn't be long before Inspector Glover appeared, sniffing for clues.

"Oh dear, almost eleven o'clock," announced Miss Smythe, interrupting my macabre thoughts. "I think it's time I headed home."

Finally!

"Must you, Theodora?" asked Patrick.

No, don't encourage her!

"I need my beauty sleep."

"That you do," shot Lucy.

I suppressed a giggle.

"Did you drive?" asked Patrick.

"I did. Lovely new motor, runs a dream."

"In that dress?" asked Lucy.

"I wore trousers."

"You changed in the car?"

Theodora just nodded.

"My, my, you are a funny fish. I much prefer to be driven."

"Come on, Aunt Oscar," she said, ignoring Lucy's jibe. "I'll drive you home."

"Don't worry about that, I'll get a taxi."

"I'm much faster."

"And cheaper," said Lucy.

"But it's so delightfully warm in here."

"And, if you're not careful, you'll go the way of the Colonel."

As if on cue he snored and Mrs Stubbs paused to weigh up her options. It was clear she wanted to stay, to doubtlessly drink more champagne and bemoan the state of the mystery novel. But there was an undercurrent of insistence to her niece's words, even if the words chosen were harmless enough.

"If you say so," said Octavia, rising unsteadily to her feet.

"I'll have you home in no time."

The men, save the slumbering Colonel, stood to mark their leaving, but Octavia was quick to order us back down.

"We'll show ourselves out," she said.

"Are you sure?" asked Lucy, more out of courtesy than anything else.

"Quite sure. Pinks must be around somewhere."

"Yes, where are they all?" asked Lionel.

"I told them not to disturb us," said Lucy, "and to see to the dining room instead."

He nodded his approval.

"Such a wonderful evening," said Miss Smythe, overdoing the enthusiasm. "So lovely to see you all and to meet you, Mr Bigge."

"Lovely to meet you," I said, and I bet she knew I was lying.

Exeunt stage right Octavia Stubbs and Theodora Smythe. The latter offered an arm to the former and slowly they made their way across the room. They were a funny double act and I still couldn't believe they were related. Their departure was almost rehearsed, as if they'd been through this rigmarole many times before. Come to think of it, there was something decidedly theatrical about the whole evening, as if something more sinister was being staged. But who were the players and who the audience I was yet to discern.

"Shall we play more charades?" asked Lucy. "Or pass the fruit?"

"What's that one?" I asked.

"It's terribly fun. There's lots of fondling plums."

"Darling, it's much too late for that."

To prove his point, Sir Lionel stretched his arms and let out a yawn much resembling a grumpy lion.

"You're not tired are you, birthday boy?"

"I'm seventy. I'm allowed to be whatever I want."

"You must be thirsty too. More champagne?"

She reached for the nearest bottle but he put his hand on top of hers.

"I've had enough," he said.

Colonel Price let out another loud snore of agreement.

"We should put old Bill to bed," said Sir Lionel. "Patrick, help me get him upstairs."

"Yes, Pa."

"Come on, old chap," said Sir Lionel, crossing to the Colonel's chair. "Stand to attention."

So it was father and son struggled to get the Colonel to his feet. He was unsteady to say the least, staggering one way then the other. At one point it looked as if he might take a dive for the fireplace if Patrick hadn't blocked his forward trajectory.

"Selby, do help," whispered Lucy, and I was up in a jolt, taking one of the Colonel's arms as Patrick took the other.

"Father, you open the doors."

Not quite the blind leading the blind but certainly the half-cut leading the half-cut. I wasn't doing too badly, the drumming in my head had lessened to a patter, and I could remember how to walk, which was more than could be said for the old brute. We manhandled him down the murky corridor past the billiard room and water closet, and back out into the hallway.

Lucy followed in our wake, issuing useless if well-intentioned instructions. The first set of stairs, before it forked, seemed like the ascent of a small mountain.

"Do be careful," cried Lucy.

"Do be quiet," whispered Patrick under his breath.

"What, what? A riot?" blurted the Colonel, suddenly deciding to recover the faculty of speech.

"No, Bill, just getting you to bed," said Sir Lionel, a few steps behind, much steadier on his feet than his wartime chum. "Almost there."

While Hercules did have to hold the weight of the world on his shoulders for Atlas' sake, he'd certainly never had to get a drunk man upstairs. We paused for a moment on the first landing, as the stairs forked to our left and right. An austere portrait of the first Lady Duker watched us. She looked most unimpressed.

"This is where we part," announced the man of the house. "I'll take myself to bed."

"Darling, are you sure you don't want a nightcap?"

"Not for me. I'll be asleep as soon as my head touches the pillow." He yawned again. "But you can, my dearest. Have another glass for me."

"I will."

The young wife leant forward to kiss her older husband briefly on the lips. It was a happy moment to witness – two lovers in defiance of a hostile world. She loved him, that much was clear, and cared dearly that he'd had a good evening. One day I'd have someone like that in my life. At this point, the Colonel recovered a modicum of his former strength and stepped back from

Patrick and I. We rushed to stand behind him, lest he fall down the stairs and we had to repeat our Sisyphean task.

"Aha, Pinks," said Lionel. "Where have you been hiding away?"

"Overseeing the clearing of the dining room, sir."

He materialised from the shadows of the hallway as if his job were to frighten us half to death rather than attend to our every whim.

"Mrs Fairbanks should be able to do that by herself," said Lucy, not missing an opportunity to criticise the staff.

"Quite right, madam."

His tone was neutral. Who knew what he thought of the housekeeper or his mistress for that matter? Or me!? A butler's inscrutability was not to be underestimated.

"Are the guests retiring to bed, sir?"

"I am, and old Bill."

"I shall help with your dress, sir."

"That's all right, Pinks, I'll put myself to bed. You help Bill. You can retire once that's done."

"Thank you, sir."

"Good night one and all."

On that, Sir Lionel smiled and ascended the stairs to whichever wing of the house he lived in. I always liked that about the houses of the rich, they had wings, as if one day they might take flight for warmer climes. Pinks climbed the stairs to join us.

"We're off to the Blue Room," instructed Patrick.

"Quite right, sir."

"Selby, you head back to the drawing room with Lucinda."

"I can put myself to bed!" blurted the Colonel as he ambled

across the landing, barging into Lucy. She stifled a cry as Pinks and Patrick leapt forward to pull him back. But I'd seen it, the slightest of movements and quick as a flash, as the Colonel had put his hand out and squeezed her left buttock. Her face remained impassive but I could tell she was gritting her teeth because her cheek muscles were clenched. He'd been rude to her all evening and now at the end of it he'd groped her, the swine.

"Shall we?" I asked, offering my arm as the quickest means of escape.

"What a gentleman."

We beat a quick retreat as Patrick and Pinks struggled with the recalcitrant Colonel, still adamant he wasn't drunk. I overheard him trip on one of the steps, but whether he fell forwards or backwards wasn't my most pressing concern. Now the other players had left the stage, I finally had Lucy to myself.

CHAPTER 8

We returned to the pleasant warmth of the drawing room, not quite so stifling now the fire was low. Agnes was there, painstakingly collecting the champagne glasses, some empty, some full. She looked thoroughly guilty, as if we all knew she was about to drop one.

"You can stop that," ordered Lucy. "I shan't have you breaking anything else tonight. Is the dining room cleared?"

"Yes, your ladyship."

"Then that's enough for the evening. You and Mrs Fairbanks can sort this out tomorrow. Have an early night, Agnes, you've earned it."

"Thank you, your ladyship."

Off she went, performing a cumbersome half-curtsy in the doorway. She was pretty, in a youthful, friendly sort of way. Perhaps that was another reason Lucy didn't like her, although

Sir Lionel didn't appear the sort to let his eye stray. That was the Colonel's job.

"Honestly," said Lucy, collapsing into one of the armchairs. "That girl doesn't tidy up, she rearranges mess."

I laughed as I took the armchair opposite, the one Lionel had been in.

"Have you enjoyed your evening, Selby?"

"I've had a lovely time, thank you."

"We're not too mad for you?"

"Not a patch on my family."

She laughed. It was a pleasant sound and the right sort of accompaniment to my humour. She was laughing with me, not at me, unlike so many before.

"I can see why Patrick likes you."

My heart skipped a beat.

"Yes, he's a good friend," I said, trying to keep my tone neutral.

"You Oxford boys are always thick as thieves. I can picture you both, heads bent over those dusty, old books. The dreaming spires, what a world!"

"It was."

"Is Fitzalan near Corpus?"

"It's a short walk but…"

She suddenly shut her eyes, as if in pain.

"… I don't believe I told you which college I went to."

This was true, like everyone else, she hadn't asked.

She paused a moment, perhaps recovering.

"I'm so silly, I shouldn't have said anything."

"Whyever not?"

"I've given it away, haven't I? Patrick will be most upset."

I try not to be dense but Lucy's sudden reluctance rather confused me. I inclined my head a little, hoping she would explain.

"I've let slip he's been talking about you."

"Has he?" I asked, affecting nothing approaching indifference whatsoever.

"He has." She smiled, seeing straight through me. "Nothing scandalous but enough for me to realise you're significant to him."

If my heart had already skipped a beat, it now came dangerously close to stopping altogether.

"I am?"

"Selby, my husband's son and I rarely talk, but when he does deign to acknowledge my existence I know that whatever he mentions carries weight. And he's mentioned you more than once."

So he did think about me when I wasn't in the room. I couldn't believe it! I wasn't the only one tossing and turning in my bed picturing all sorts of possible scenarios.

"What about Miss Theodora Smythe?"

"Don't get me started on her!" she said, tracing a finger along the arm of the chair. "Driving in trousers, whatever next? As for that haircut, quite risible. I think she has some bizarre notion that if she looks like a man people will take her more seriously. The opposite is true, of course."

"I didn't warm to her much."

"I wonder why?" she asked, with that little grin back on her face.

"Well… um… she was impolite."

"Oh dear, you must be careful with your heart on your sleeve like that, it could get snagged on something."

Perhaps it was the effects of the champagne or the conspiratorial hush that resided in the room now the others had gone, but I felt Lucy was a woman I could be honest with. We were kindred spirits, almost, both attracted to Duker men. Although her attractions were evidently reciprocated.

"I do love Lionel," she suddenly said. "I really do."

"Of course."

"I shan't pretend having money isn't nice. I like my life in this castle on the hill, but the ones who judge me get to take their wealth for granted. Whereas someone middle class like me is just a nasty little gold-digger."

The more she spoke, the guiltier I felt, given the reason I was here was to prove how much of a gold-digger she really was. She looked to the crackling embers and I admired her profile. There was something regal to it, as if she had just as much right to be here as anyone else.

"You know something of love, don't you, Selby?"

"I... I... Yes, I do," I stammered, caught off guard by the question and thrown back to my Oxford days and a chap I'd known much better than Patrick. But with the recollection came the familiar memories of heartbreak.

"Then you know what it's like to be wrapped in another's arms and for that to be enough. For your heart to thump at the sound of his foot on the stair. For his voice to make you smile regardless of the words he says."

She looked me in the eye on that penultimate word, the specificity of its sex quite purposeful. I gulped and managed a small nod, still unable to commit myself to the truth out loud.

"I did love my first husband, whatever those wretched newspapers said, but I was young and caught up in his looks. As it transpired, he was much less caught up in mine. In fact, the looks of women never really interested him."

"Oh."

"We did try to love one another, we really did, but then that awful man had his revenge."

"Morrow Davenport?"

"He hates me more than Patrick, more than Agnes even, more than any of them. He thinks I stole Rupert from him, but it was Rupert who proposed to me. All we wanted was a happy life but Davenport wouldn't let us. The newspapers called the divorce a scandal but Rupert did it for me; he didn't want me to get caught up in an even bigger one. In the end he retreated to Germany – they're a bit friendlier to his sort over there, or so I've been told."

She was right as far as I knew. I'd heard all sorts of stories from Berlin; they called themselves urnings and enjoyed many more freedoms than us English. It was true of the Russians as well, the Bolshies had even decriminalised sex between men (perhaps Communism wasn't all bad?).

"I know what it's like to have people judge me. To be hated simply for loving. But I refuse to let them win. I will fight for my love."

"Of course," I said emphatically. "You must follow your heart, it's the best thing."

"It is." She seemed genuinely grateful to have someone on her side. "There's nothing I wouldn't do for him."

She spoke with true conviction, the fire dancing in her eyes, and how alive she looked. I pitied anyone who stepped between her and her love. She rose to her feet, her gold dress catching the low light, and crossed the room to the French windows. She pulled back one of the curtains and, for a moment, I thought she was going to go outside. She'd bloody freeze wearing only that. Instead, she stared at the panes of black glass. The world beyond was invisible, it was only her reflection she could see. And in that moment I saw how truly exposed she was, surrounded on all sides by people who wished her harm.

"You must be careful, Lucy."

"Whatever for?" she asked, looking back over her shoulder.

"You're in danger."

"Me? In danger?"

"Yes," I said. "There are people who want to hurt you."

"But I'm so lovely," she said with a big smile, as if to dismiss my worries.

"Not everyone would agree, especially not Davenport. He's not right in the head."

"Oh, Selby, this isn't one of Mrs Stubbs' awful novels. No one's going to hurt me."

"But don't you think some of the guests tonight, not to mention the staff, have been acting most strangely?"

"No more strangely than usual."

"What about your downstairs water closet? It feels positively haunted."

"I have nothing to fear from ghosts."

"And the cloakroom key's gone missing."

"What?" she asked, genuinely surprised.

"And a certain author was seen sneaking around upstairs."

"My, my, you are an observant one."

"I can't shake the feeling that something bad is going to happen tonight."

"Nonsense! You'll have to do better than a missing key and a haunted toilet!"

She eyed me for a moment and I wondered what was going through her mind. "Although…" she began, leaving her thought tantalisingly unfinished.

"What?"

"Of all of them, I see Agnes as the sort to slip something into my tea."

"Really?" I replied, aghast. "You think Agnes is planning to poison you?"

"I've seen the way she looks at my jewellery."

She spoke with a flippancy that implied she was having me on, but I couldn't be sure.

"You must tell your husband," I said.

"Perhaps."

She turned back to the window and raised her right hand towards the glass. From the darkness beyond, a hand reached out to touch hers as her fingertips brushed the glass. It was an arresting image, Lucy and her reflection, and it painted her in a most vulnerable light. She came across as confident and gay but, like her reflection, she was an outsider looking in, begrudged by those with more than her – and those with less.

It was at this point that Patrick reappeared, coming through the door that led onto the corridor with the WC and billiard room. I caught an echo of the ancient plumbing system rattling and gurgling. He must have just passed water.

"All well with the Colonel?" I asked.

"He was horizontal and still breathing when I left him."

"Where's Pinks?" asked Lucy as she drew the curtain.

"I dismissed him after we'd undressed Bill. Not a pleasant task."

"I can imagine," I said.

"How about a nightcap, Selby?"

"Yes please!" I replied, far too eagerly.

"I shall retire to bed, then," said Lucy.

"Don't let us stop you," replied Patrick.

The conspiratorial warmth that Lucy and I had briefly enjoyed now cooled in the presence of Patrick's icy disregard for his stepmother.

"At least walk me to the stairs. I don't like the dark."

"Yes you do," muttered Patrick. "It's your natural habitat."

"Perhaps Selby will walk me."

"Absolutely," I said, standing to attention.

"What a gentleman. There aren't enough of those in this house."

"Oh, I'll come," added Patrick. "To ensure Selby remains a gentleman."

We escorted her down the gloomy corridor and out into the hallway. It was pretty chilly. I imagined Sir Lionel the sort to spend a fortune on dinner but to scrimp on burning coke. The rich could be funny like that.

"Goodnight then, boys," she said at the foot of the stairs, looking every bit the lady of the house. "Don't make any mischief I wouldn't."

I couldn't tell if I should be laughing at her joke or embarrassed at her innuendo. Patrick clearly didn't find it funny.

"It was lovely to see you again, Lady Duker," I said.

"You must call me..."

But her voice trailed off, interrupted by a quiet tapping sound. We all froze. It came again as our heads turned to face the front door.

"What on earth?" whispered Patrick, even he was spooked.

The hairs stood up on the back of my neck as, once again, there came a quiet rapping at the door.

CHAPTER 9

"Who the devil?" said Patrick as he made his way across the black-and-white tiles. "At this hour."

Lucy came to stand next to me. She wrung her hands and I worried for her wound. Even I felt a little on edge, although it was probably just Mrs Stubbs come back to collect a misplaced stole. We watched as Patrick unlocked the door and twisted the knob. He slowly pulled it back.

"You!" he hissed.

"Happy Birthday," slurred the arrival, none other than Morrow Davenport! "I've come to join the party."

"You're not welcome here," said Patrick with a newfound authority. It was quite attractive. He went to close the door but Morrow blocked it with his foot.

"I am welcome," he said, his words garbled and difficult to hear. "To wish the old bastard all the bloody best."

"I'm going to call the police."

"No, Patrick," said Lucy, leaving my side and rushing to the door. "We can't make a scene, Lionel's had such a lovely evening, let's keep it that way. Mr Davenport just needs to go back the way he's come, doesn't he?"

"Don't you tell me what to do, bitch."

She gasped, lost for words, as was Patrick, even if he might have agreed with the sentiment.

"You've ruined my life," he hissed, pushing at the door, but Patrick held him at bay.

"You've ruined your own life and now you're ruining it further," said Lucy.

"You're a thief, always taking what isn't yours."

"Leave me alone."

"It's too late for that. I won't let your horrible husband put me in prison."

"It's where you belong."

"I'll shoot the bloody pair of you."

On that, he shoved against the door with his shoulder and Patrick staggered backwards. In strode Morrow – his grand entrance – and, while he was as handsome as the last time I'd seen him, there were great shadows under his eyes and stubble on his chin. I worried he'd be brandishing a revolver but fortunately his hands were empty. He saw me lurking in the background.

"Come to feed at the trough, eh?"

"I… I was invited."

"Greedy little pig, oink, oink."

"Ignore him, Selby," said Lucy, turning away from the intruder to offer me an imploring look. "I'll fetch Pinks and we can deal with this discreetly."

"No you fucking won't."

He lurched forward and grabbed Lucy by the left wrist, his big hand enveloping hers. I expected her to scream but she was more collected than that, issuing only a gasp.

"You'll pay for what you've done."

Patrick and I watched on in horror as the two held hands. She tried to pull free but he gripped harder. She squirmed but still he held on. She gave one final tug and managed to escape the drunkard's grip. Tears welled in her eyes as she held her left hand aloft – there was blood on the palm. The devil had reopened the wound from the Ritz.

"She bleeds," he sneered.

Without a moment's hesitation she slapped Morrow across the face. I felt it myself as the sound echoed through the hall. He stumbled back, putting a hand to his cheek.

"Oh dear," she said, looking at the blood. "I... I feel faint."

"Lucy, let me help." I rushed forward to offer my assistance again.

"No, I need a sink, I'll get blood everywhere." She took a deep breath. "Patrick, I think the police a good idea after all. Mr Bigge, keep an eye on our unwelcome guest, don't let him out of your sight, not even for a moment."

"You won't get away with this," Morrow jeered, but Lucy turned her back on him and made her way for the corridor.

"You've gone too far, Davenport," I said, trying to sound braver than I felt.

"And you haven't gone far enough."

He slithered for the front door, about to make his escape.

"Oh no you don't!"

I rushed forward but he was too quick as he slinked back into the night. I turned to Patrick for help, but he looked like a rabbit caught in the crosshairs of a farmer's gun. A very attractive rabbit, mind.

"Selby, don't let him get away," pleaded Lucy, as she struggled to open the door to the corridor. "Patrick, you must telephone for the police."

I tried for a look of masculine confidence, though God knows what I achieved, and dived into the night in pursuit of that desperate man. The air was even colder than before, but I was wearing an extra layer of alcohol this time. I scanned the driveway, worried Morrow had already got to the road, though he couldn't be that fast. The dim hallway light didn't offer much help, providing only a rectangle of illumination around me, but the moon was bright. I zipped down the steps, my feet skidding on the gravel, and, in response, I heard more stones crunching. I looked to my left and thought I saw a shadow slinking around the side of the house but then I looked to my right and thought I saw another shadow. Left or right, it felt like a most significant decision. I opted for the latter.

I rounded the edge of the house but couldn't spot him; the slippery fish must have slipped the hook. There was a length of lawn to my left filled with flowerbeds and shadows, and beyond that was the high stone wall that bordered the garden. He could hardly have scrabbled up that. I carried on, trying to keep my footfalls quiet, but the heels of my shoes kept making an awful clicking sound. I passed a pair of French windows and realised I must be alongside the billiard room. The dim lamp was still aglow and I saw the large billiard table and the closed door beyond. Onwards I went, reaching the next corner and coming out into the garden proper. Shadows huddled in the distance but I assumed them to be the trees of the orchard. My eyes were adjusting and I saw the walls of the herb garden not too far away. He better not bloody be in there; I didn't want to get a flowerpot full of sage bashed on my head. I waited for a while, rubbing my hands together and blowing onto my palms.

"Where the hell are you?" I whispered.

In response, feet came clattering down the patio behind me.

"There you are," he gasped.

"Bloody hell," I yelped, almost jumping out my skin.

"You need to bugger off," he snarled.

"You're making a fool of yourself, Morrow."

"I don't care."

"You hate her that much?"

"She took the only thing worth having."

"You can find someone else."

"Ha! You know that's not true. You know love for men like us is rarer than any gem."

"Patrick's calling the police."

"Bastard."

He stepped off the patio onto the grass and started off across the lawn. I almost felt sorry for him, he was a broken man with nothing to live for. But how could I face Patrick if I let him get away?

"You're not going anywhere, Davenport."

My feet trampled the soft grass as I gave pursuit. He picked up his pace, so did I, and we ran through the moonlit scene, like two billiard balls bashed across the felt. He crossed the lawn in no time and I struggled behind, following him up a precarious flight of stone steps into the orchard, my heart racing, lungs pumping, mouth gulping as I dashed after his shadow through the trees. Then I leapt, his figure before me, only to find myself wrapping my arms around a tree trunk.

"Bugger."

An angry grating sound greeted my exclamation and I tried my best to find its source. My toes pushed up against the end of my leather shoes – more blisters to look forward to – then I was at the garden wall, all brick and ivy, save for a large, rectangular gap. The gate! He'd pushed it open and fled for the trees of the Heath extension. I couldn't see anything in the pitch dark beyond and didn't fancy my chances. So much for my would-be heroics.

Tail between my legs and fingers like ice, I returned to the house. I climbed the steps to the front door and stepped back inside. I had a number of excuses and apologies ready but there was no one there to greet me. Lucy must still be tending to her wound at the sink and Patrick must be talking with the police. I'd spotted a telephone in the turret room when Pinks had put my coat there. I went for the door and turned the knob. It didn't budge. I tried again.

"Who's that?" came a voice from within.

"Patrick, is that you?"

"Get me out of here."

"What?"

"The bloody door's locked."

A trapped prince in a tower and I his saviour! Fortunately, the key was still in the lock and, once I'd turned it, he flung the door open.

"What the hell happened?" he asked, his face red and angry.

"I… I don't know. Morrow… I mean, Davenport, got away. He ran through the garden, found the gate in the wall."

"Then who locked me in here?"

My mouth gaped but I had no answer. An uneasy silence lingered between us as he eyed me suspiciously.

"It wasn't me, Patrick. What an absurd thing to do."

"Where's Lucinda?"

"I'm not sure. I imagine she's still…"

But he didn't care for my answer as he barged past me and made for the corridor. I followed him as he wrenched the door open and marched to the water closet. He tapped the door.

"Lucinda?"

There was no answer. He knocked again before trying the handle. The door opened and he switched on the light.

"What the devil?"

I came up behind him and peered over his shoulder. The tap was still running and there was blood on the edge of the sink. Not much, but enough to indicate this was where she'd been. A bloodied bandage lay unravelled on the floor and there was blood on the side of the toilet as well. He turned the tap off and pointed for me to leave.

"Where is she then?"

"I don't know, Patrick."

"Is everything all right, sir?"

"Bloody hell!"

We had another fright as Pinks appeared in the corridor, his ghostly demeanour somewhat undermined by his long dressing gown and slippers.

"Pinks, what are you doing skulking around?"

"I heard voices in the garden, sir. I thought it best to check up."

"Voices? Was that you and Davenport then?"

"Yes," I blurted. "I tried to reason with him but he wouldn't have any of it."

"That man can't be reasoned with. You should have hit him with a brick."

"There wasn't one to hand," I replied drily.

"Have you seen the mistress of the house, Pinks?"

"No, sir. Perhaps she has retired to her bedroom."

"Good point, I'm sure there's nothing to worry about. There's been a commotion, you see. That nasty hack turned up out of the blue and tried to ruin our fun. The police are on the way but we should find Lucinda before they get here."

He sounded genuinely concerned, which might have been the first time he'd felt such a thing for his stepmother.

"Whatever you do, don't wake Father," he said. "The police will be worry enough without bothering him over Lucinda's whereabouts. She's probably powdering her nose. Selby, you go pour out some stiff drinks in the drawing room. Pinks and I will search the house."

I did as I was commanded and retreated to the drawing room. It was the least fun of the jobs but, as I had just chased Morrow through the garden, I thought I deserved something alcoholic. I retrieved a bottle of brandy and some glasses from one of the corner cupboards and poured myself a hefty slug. With all the drama my heart didn't know whether to speed up or simply to stop. I dropped myself onto one of the settees with a sigh of relief and allowed myself a moment to close my eyes. An image of Lucy's pained face flashed before my mind as the beast had dug into her wound. Soon Mrs Fairbanks and Agnes were bustling into the room, also in dressing gowns, and a Victorian-looking nightcap for the older woman.

"Sorry to disturb you, sir," she said. "But we've been alerted to her ladyship's absence."

"Quite so. Patrick's gone to check upstairs."

"Very good," said Mrs Fairbanks. "I'll take the attic."

"The attic, do you really think that's necessary?"

"It's worth checking everywhere, just to be sure."

"Shall I do the coal cellar?" asked Agnes.

"You stay here. Get the fire going again and check the milk. We can offer them cocoa."

"Yes, Mrs Fairbanks."

Before I could offer any assistance, the housekeeper was back out of the room and Agnes was prodding at the coal dust with a poker. She bent down to blow and a hint of orange appeared. Then she took some kindling sticks and arranged them in a neat pile and put some scrunched-up newspaper inside as well. She turned and caught me looking. I wasn't sure she appreciated me watching her every move.

"I'll... well... I'll nip off and help with the search," I said.

"Yes, sir."

I didn't really know what I was planning when I went back into the corridor. It was hardly as if Lucy had fallen into the loo. Although in our haste none of us had thought to check the billiard room. Who knows, maybe she'd slipped inside for a quick nap or to read some Shakespeare. As it transpired, someone's line of thinking was ahead of mine. The door was ajar. An orange glow lined the gap and, in a moment, Pinks emerged, closing the door quietly behind him.

"Is everything all right, sir?"

"Quite all right. I thought maybe Lady Duker might be in there."

"You won't find anything in there, I'm afraid."

"That's a shame."

"Would sir like assistance with anything else?"

More a subtle dismissal than an actual question. He was good!

"I'll be all right, Pinks. You keep looking."

"Right you are, sir."

I returned to the drawing room, nearly hitting Agnes with the door upon my re-entry. She leapt back in fright, clearly having been listening at the keyhole.

"Run out of matches, sir," she said, quick to make an excuse.

"Bad luck. You should probably fetch some."

She bowed her head and slipped past me. Before I could even concoct a witticism for how strangely everyone was acting, Patrick appeared from the dining room. The evening had more entrances and exits than a French farce.

"Any luck?"

"None whatsoever. I even peeked into Father's room but he was alone in bed, snoring like a donkey."

"And the Colonel?"

"What?"

"Is he all right?"

"I assume so. I'm hardly going to go barging into his room. What are you suggesting?"

"Nothing at all, quite the opposite I'm sure."

He looked too frustrated to pay my words much heed.

"I need a drink."

He ignored the brandy and took a whisky bottle instead.

"It's so typical of her," he said. "She always has to be the centre of attention."

"You really hate her, don't you?"

My bluntness surprised me but everything about this evening had turned topsy-turvy. I knew Patrick had invited me here to find out her secrets, but the poor woman had just been attacked.

"Of course I hate her. Ever since she arrived, things have gone downhill. My father distracted, the staff miserable, our guests disgruntled, and that odious man trying to slander my father with *her* secrets. We've all been dragged into her mess. I hate her with every fibre of my being."

It was at this point someone emitted a high-pitched scream.

"Bloody hell!" I screeched, my heart almost ejecting itself from my chest by way of my gullet.

"Christ," Patrick blasphemed. "Now what?"

He stormed past me, slamming open the door with a bang, and then came another scream, louder now. I rushed after him and almost ran into his back as he stopped abruptly by the billiard room door.

"Agnes, what is it?"

She was standing on the other side of the billiard table, staring at her feet in wide-eyed terror. Whatever she was staring at, I couldn't see, but her face had turned deathly white.

"She... she... she's..."

Agnes's words were garbled as she collapsed onto all fours and retched. Patrick rounded the billiard table and I watched his face as his eyebrows rose and his mouth opened in a look of pure shock, maybe even terror.

"Oh dear God," he cried. "She's dead."

CHAPTER 10

The first thing I saw was her eye. The right one was closed, but the left was open and where there should have been white was red. It was as if she were winking – a most shocking, bloody wink. Her lips were swollen and her mouth open to reveal a thickened tongue. I wanted to vomit but left that task to Agnes. The site of greatest violence was concentrated at her neck. Red, puce, blue and a colour that could almost be black circled its circumference. Even from where I stood, I could see some of the individual marks left by the murderer's fingers. Her body was in front of the French windows, and she lay on top of her right arm but her left was stretched out, as if to grip the carpet. There was a bandage wrapped around it but the blood had seeped through.

"Agnes, Selby, back outside," ordered Patrick, chivvying the maid back onto her feet. "This room is for the police now."

He slammed the door shut behind us just as Pinks and Mrs Fairbanks arrived.

"I heard a scream," said the housekeeper, her usual poise replaced by genuine panic. "What happened?"

"It's Lucinda. She's dead."

Even in death, he could not call her Lucy.

"Dear heavens." A hand shot to Mrs Fairbanks' mouth and for once Pinks looked taken aback.

"Dead?" he asked.

"Murdered. Strangled."

I let out a gurgled cry, my stomach churning.

"Pull yourself together, man," barked Patrick. "Everyone to the drawing room."

Like sheep that had just witnessed the butchering of one of their flock, we were herded away from the horror. Pinks took to pouring everyone a stiff drink: whisky for the men and sherry for the women. Patrick allowed the staff to sit on the comfortable seats as he paced up and down the room. Mrs Fairbanks took the box of matches that Agnes still clung to and quickly set to relighting the fire. I couldn't believe it. Only moments ago I'd been enjoying the pleasure of her conversation. She'd been so alive, so in love, and now she was dead.

"What to do about Father?"

"Shall I wake him, sir?" asked the butler.

"I... I don't know. This will kill him."

"Perhaps best to inform him before the police arrive."

"You're right but I... I can't. He'll hate me for it."

Of all concerns the moment called for, that one struck me as decidedly odd. Would Sir Lionel resent hearing the news from Patrick because all along this is what his son had wanted? I dismissed the thought the moment it entered my head. What a horrible thing to think. Plenty of people fantasised about the death of those they hated, but that didn't mean they relished the moment when they actually died.

"I will tell him, sir."

"You will?"

Pinks nodded solemnly.

"Thank you. You've always been good to my father, always loyal."

The butler bowed his head and left to do his awful duty. It was at this moment the doorbell rang. Patrick cursed quietly to himself and he too departed. I offered an awkward smile to the women, but Agnes was too far gone to even notice. Her eyes were glazed, as if she were staring into the depths of Hades itself, or back into the billiard room. Mrs Fairbanks sat next to her on the sofa and placed an arm around her shoulders. It was a kind gesture, a human one, and it stood out in stark contrast to all that had gone before.

Things progressed equal parts slow to quick. Every minute in that room felt like ten, yet the affairs of the night rushed forward quite beyond my control. Out of a cosy night of drinking and dining, I had stepped into the scene of a crime. My wit and charm were useless now and all I could do was obey the orders given me. A young constable appeared, his uniform dark blue and immaculately pressed, holding one of those big helmets at his side. He told us his name but I forgot it at once, then he proceeded to take our particulars. Noises came from the billiard room as the necessary procedures were undertaken. What exactly they were I didn't know; my knowledge of crime scenes originated entirely from mystery novels. The reality was decidedly lacking in fun as Lucy's bloodied eye still winked at me. Patrick briefly returned with another man. He was older, with a big, bushy moustache and a flatter hat than the constable's. He was much more intimidating as he gave us the once-over, his eyes resting on mine for a spell, before moving on to Agnes. She was called away.

At some point Mrs Fairbanks was granted permission to leave the room to make us cocoa. Her face was still drawn but she retained her dignity. Mine was all in pieces as I tried not to let out another cry. If only I'd left when Theodora and Octavia had, I'd be tucked up in bed by now and none the wiser. But I'd wanted some time alone with Lucy, to warn her, and she'd simply laughed my concerns aside. I should have insisted, I should have acted as her bodyguard, I shouldn't have left her side for even a moment…

"Mr Bigge?"

I started, realising my name had been spoken a number of times.

"Yes," I said.

"Chief Inspector Lisle will see you now."

"Right, good, yes."

I stayed sitting, staring at the young constable.

"This way."

"Of course."

For the umpteenth time that night, I was forced along that horrid corridor. It was swift becoming the stuff of nightmares and it didn't make much difference that the doors to the WC and billiard room were closed. I heard the murmur of voices from within as I assumed the police dusted for fingerprints and checked for cigarette stubs, or whatever it was they did.

One of the doors in the hall led into a study – a grand panelled room with emerald-green wallpaper and similarly coloured carpet. It smelt of stale cigar smoke. Occupying centre stage was a huge wooden desk, topped with dark-green leather. Copies of the *Spectator* and *Punch* lay next to one another, alongside a pot of ink and a silver fountain pen. Sitting behind the desk was the man with the bushy moustache, while the young constable who'd escorted me stood guard at the door.

"Please take a seat, Mr Bigge."

"Yes, thank you. Chief Inspector Lisle, is it?"

He inclined his head.

"Terrible affair, quite terrible."

"Most distressing," he agreed. "For all those gathered."

Now it was my turn to incline my head.

"May I ask your connection to the family, Mr Bigge?"

"You may," I replied. "I am a friend of Patrick's. We were at university together."

"Would that be the University of Oxford?"

"It would."

"Very good."

I was glad my academic credentials counted for something.

"Was it Mr Duker who invited you to the birthday supper?"

"Yes, it was very kind of him. I was flattered."

The chief inspector raised a bushy eyebrow. Perhaps flattered hadn't been the best word.

"You're close friends with him?"

"Not too close. I hadn't seen him for years, but I bumped into him the other week, in Hampstead."

"That was a fortunate coincidence."

"Quite fortunate."

So far his tone was sufficiently respectful. I was the guest of an aristocrat after all and that association afforded me deference. Class mattered when it came to murder.

"In your own words, Mr Bigge, would you tell me what happened this evening?"

As best I could, I led him from my arrival through canapés to dinner. I skipped the part about my trip to the herb garden with Patrick because I didn't think it important. I mentioned talking with Lucy and then Morrow Davenport's drunken arrival.

"You heard him knocking at the door?"

"We all did. We had gathered in the hall."

He scribbled something in a small notepad and nodded for me to go on. I explained how Patrick went to call the police and I went after Morrow.

"Where was he when you stepped outside?"

"He'd run off around the side of the house, so I pursued."

"Did you find him?"

"No."

"More's the pity," he said with a little too much emphasis. "Which side of the house were you on?"

"That's a good question. The east-facing one I believe."

"They found a footprint in one of the flowerbeds on the west side."

Oh God, if only Morrow hadn't eluded me so quickly, I might have stopped him.

"I assume it's his footprint?"

"I'm afraid I cannot divulge that information," replied the

chief inspector. "If you were on the east side, then I believe that puts you on the side with the billiard room."

"Yes, I believe you're right."

"Describe the scene to me, as you walked around the house."

"Yes, well, I suppose there was the patio and the lawn, and trees. It was rather dark."

Unlike one of Octavia's fictional witnesses, I lacked an uncannily perfect memory of events.

"Then?"

"I reached the far side of the house and that's when he snuck up on me."

"He came from behind?"

I nodded.

"Along the patio or from the lawn?"

"The patio."

"Are you quite sure?"

"Yes, I think."

"Then I believe you spoke to him?"

How could he have known that? Pinks must have told him!

"He spoke to me first," I said, silently cursing the lately loquacious butler. "And I told him he was behaving like a fool."

The ensuing silence implied the chief inspector might think me the fool.

"How long was it between your leaving the house and meeting Mr Davenport again?"

"Gosh, I… um… it would have been a few minutes, I think."

"Could you be more specific?"

"Maybe two or three, I really couldn't say."

"More's the pity."

It was like being ticked off by a very polite schoolmaster. I tried to look the chief inspector in the eye, so as to appear confident and not at all suspicious, but I lowered my gaze to his nose. While he had a generous array of hairs growing above his upper lip, there were also a number poking out from his nostrils. I plucked mine; dastardly painful.

"I am sure I need not remind you that while you were wandering through the garden Mr Davenport had re-entered the house in order to strangle Lady Duker."

"I was hardly wandering!"

My protest was futile; every moment Patrick and I had prevaricated gave Morrow the precious minutes he'd needed.

"Oh dear," I muttered, the little resolve I had left disintegrating. "I... I... couldn't have a cigarette could I?"

"After we're finished."

It's hard to describe exactly where the feeling of guilt begins, whether it's somewhere in the heart or the gut, but it is quick to spread. From my fingertips to my toes, all my nerves twanged with the recognition of my utter failure.

"Oh dear," I whispered, willing myself not to cry.

"You are aware you were seen exiting the billiard room earlier in the evening."

"What?"

"You heard me, Mr Bigge."

"I did go in, yes. I thought it was the WC."

"But it wasn't. What did you do in there?"

"Well, I... I went outside as a matter of fact, to get some fresh air."

"Through the glass door?"

I refrained from telling him it was called a French window and just nodded my head.

"It was unlocked?"

"No. I unlocked it, the key was in the door."

"How long were you outside for?"

"A matter of moments."

"Any chance of a little more specificity?"

"I really..."

"... couldn't say?"

He might as well have pulled my trousers down and started caning me on the backside. My association with aristocracy didn't count for much when my behaviour was painting me as the prime suspect.

"What happened after those moments?"

"I came back inside and locked the door."

"Are you sure?"

"Quite positive. Yes, absolutely. Most definitely."

With every affirmation I sounded less sure, but I distinctly remembered turning the key in the lock and hearing it click. Yes, I definitely did that. Didn't I?

"That's strange, because we found the door unlocked."

"I... I don't know anything about that."

The chief inspector's face proved infuriatingly neutral.

"Were the curtains open or closed when you left the room?"

"Open."

"And the lights on or off?"

"One of the lamps on the tables was on when I came in. I left it that way."

"So, if someone were outside the house and they happened

to look in, they would see a partially lit billiard room?"

"Yes! That's exactly what I saw."

"I beg your pardon?"

Now I'd bloody gone and done it.

"When I was walking along the patio," I explained, "I did look into the billiard room and it was empty."

"You saw nothing?"

"No."

"You didn't, say, see Davenport strangling Lady Duker?"

"I... I didn't, no."

"More's the pity."

Our conversation was proving a veritable goldmine for pity.

"Do you have a wife, Mr Bigge?"

I didn't respond at first, as I was rather taken aback by the question, which was doubtless the point of it.

"No, I don't."

"A fiancée?"

"Not yet."

"You're how old?"

"Twenty-five."

"Not good to be a bachelor for too long. Isn't that right, Constable Stovell?"

"Yes, sir."

I turned to eye the constable. He was one of those frustratingly handsome young men with blunt features and smooth skin. I bet he was married to his childhood sweetheart with a blue-eyed son and another baby on the way.

"Were you familiar with this Morrow Davenport?"

"Not particularly."

"But marginally?"

"I'd encountered him, yes."

"At the Ritz, I believe."

Why did this man insist on asking questions he already knew the answer to?

"Mr Duker told me about that evening he showed up. A nasty piece of work."

Had Patrick also told him about the task he'd set me? What if they found out I'd gone and visited Morrow's apartment? My imagination raced ahead of my reason as I saw all manner of grisly consequences, most involving a prison cell and some the hangman's noose.

"His kind are impossible to trust, isn't that right, Constable?"

"That's why we lock them up, sir."

My buttocks squeaked against the leather of the chair.

"Before they can do anything worse."

"Quite right," I said, through gritted teeth. "A dangerous lot."

"But we were a bit slow this time."

I could feel the constable's eyes drilling into the back of my head as the chief inspector's drilled into the front, the worst possible sort of drilling. Surely they didn't know. They couldn't know. I was just a normal chap like any other.

"It's been brought to my attention that one of Lady Duker's bracelets has gone missing."

"Yes, it was mentioned after dinner."

"A gold one with diamonds."

"The very same."

"Any thoughts as to where it might have ended up?"

"None whatsoever."

I wondered if long silences were part of police training, taught between classes on eyebrow-raising and pencil-chewing.

"Thank you for your time, Mr Bigge. You'll need to provide your fingerprints before you leave."

"Anything I can do to be of assistance."

"Constable Stovell will take you."

"Right ho." I rose to my feet. "I do hope you catch Davenport soon."

"As do I."

That was my dismissal. With great restraint, I managed not to run from the room but walked in as straight a line as possible. Too much sway of the hips might raise suspicion. Back in the hall, I saw the Colonel traipsing down the stairs. His eyes were bloodshot and the skin beneath puffy. His hair was uncombed, revealing more of his pate than usual. One of the constables waited for him at the bottom.

"Bloody disgrace," he muttered. "Watching me sleep. You should be ashamed of yourself."

"The chief inspector is through here," explained the pale young man. He looked quite shaken, having had to waken the Kraken.

"I'll be having a word with him. You deserve the lash."

He passed me in a wave of bad breath and grumbling complaints. But this was a crime scene and not a battlefield; the police held the upper hand here.

"Fingerprinting," said the one called Stovell, pointing towards the turret cloakroom. I didn't need a blooming escort but I didn't have a choice. As we entered the pentagonal room, I noted the telephone had been removed from the table and placed on the floor. In its place was the equipment for the fingerprinting. This was the sort of thing I enjoyed reading about in a Van Dine novel, not being subjected to myself.

Also on the table was a key; a long, silver one, ornately designed. It was the one for the cloakroom door. I tried to make sense of the sequence of events. With me running off in the wrong direction, Morrow must have doubled back on himself and returned through the front door. How simple, then, to lock Patrick in the cloakroom. There was some white powder on the key, presumably whatever concoction the police used for fingerprint dusting, although it appeared they hadn't found any. Which was rather lucky, as I'd been the last to touch it when I freed Patrick. The parts of a key had all sorts of funny names – the shank and pin (which sounded more like my Friday evening's entertainment) and even a throat. I noticed scratches on the end that did the unlocking, whatever it's called.

"Those marks on the key," I said. "Are they just wear and tear?"

"None of your business, sir."

That was the answer I should have predicted before I'd opened my stupid mouth! Nevertheless, there was something about those scratches, they looked fresh.

The fingerprinting process was uncomfortable and uncouth. While such proximity to a handsome man wasn't entirely undesirable, the constable clearly had no care for me as he manhandled my arms this way and that, pushing my fingers down against the ink, as if I was incapable of doing it myself, and smearing them onto a piece of card. Each digit had its allotted slot.

I tried not to stare at the constable's profile but it kept drawing my eye for reasons beyond its pleasing structure.

"Have you been on the force for long?" I asked.

"A year, sir."

"You like it?"

"Yes, sir."

He wasn't one for small talk. Soon my fingers were done, and now the police had even more personal details of mine. I might as well have just posed in the nude and let them take photographs. I was told it was procedure, so they could discount any prints of mine they might find in the billiard room, of which the chief inspector already knew there would be plenty. But it was as the constable pushed my thumb against the card that I realised I had seen his profile before – a few urinals down at the South End Green toilets! Fortunately, I was too young for a heart attack but I broke into a sweat all the same. He was the exact sort sent to lure unsuspecting men into committing criminal offences in the name of pleasure. How close I'd come to a spell in prison.

"You're done," he said gruffly.

"Right ho," I said, trying not to sound as worried as I felt. "I'll go find a cloth."

He stared at me but said nothing.

"For my fingers," I said, raising them up, as if to draw further attention to myself. Buckle up, Bigge, I commanded. So far there had been no suggestion he'd recognised me and, my God, did I have to keep it that way. Speaking to the murderer was bad enough, being known to share his predilections even worse. I took a deep breath, trying to quell my nerves, reminding myself that I was innocent, after all – of murder if not of loving men.

The turret door closed behind me and I paused to catch my breath. Bloody hell, tonight was proving far too much for me. I imagined Morrow rushing back across the hall, having just locked Patrick inside. Poor Lucy would have been taken completely by surprise. She might have resisted and pushed him back against the billiard room door but her struggle had been futile as he'd had his most gruesome revenge. After that, he'd unlocked the French windows and made his exit, before finding me *wandering* around. And all it had taken was a matter of minutes. The audacity of it was astounding.

"Selby, there you are."

"Bloody hell," I blurted, taken aback. It was Patrick.

"Are you quite all right?"

"Quite, just a little on edge."

I decided not to tell him that only a few feet away was a man who had come very close to arresting me for gross indecency.

"It's a truly awful night," he said. Gone was his stern manner from before and now he looked utterly shagged. My heart went out to him.

"It really is. Has your father been told?"

"He's inconsolable, crying more than when Mother died."

"The poor man."

"Have you any experience of this?"

"Of murder?"

"Emotional fathers."

"The emotions my father tends to show are anger and impatience. I've never known him to cry."

"What should I do?"

"Perhaps Mrs Fairbanks can look after him?" I wanted to

give Patrick a hug and not because I yearned to rediscover his rower's physique but because he deserved some sympathy. No mother to look after him and much too old for a nursemaid. "Or you could call Miss Smythe?" I hated to suggest such a thing but it seemed the most sensible.

"Whatever for?"

"For comfort."

"Oh, yes, well… possibly."

He avoided my gaze. It wasn't becoming for an Englishman to even insinuate that intimacy existed, not that I wished to think about Patrick and his fiancée sharing affection. They would be waiting for marriage, surely, which still gave me time to work my magic.

"Do you think he came here with the intention to kill?" he asked.

"I think he intended your father and stepmother great harm, although I still can't believe he went through with it."

"Well, he did, and right under our very noses!"

"Did you see him come back into the house?"

"No," he replied, shaking his head. "The cloakroom door shut behind me. I didn't hear him lock it either. Damned swine, we never should have let him out of our sight."

I felt awful all over again but I was running out of excuses. I should have reported Morrow to the police the moment he'd mentioned his revolver, even if he had used his hands in the end.

"Now Selby, listen to me." He led me into one of the shadowy corners of the hall, the further from the turret the better, and lowered his voice. "This whole thing is going to kick up a huge stink in the press. There will be journalists sniffing at our door like hounds on the hunt. Whatever you do, don't tell anyone you were here."

"Of course not."

"We have to minimise the scandal."

"I wouldn't dream of telling a soul."

"We want to avoid an inquest at all costs, which is why it's imperative the police get Davenport as soon as possible. Arrest him, hang him and then some other society murder can take the front pages. If the police come back to question you, stick to what you've told them."

"Absolutely, I don't have anything else to say."

"Good. Because the chief inspector was asking some questions I didn't like at all."

"What sort of questions?" I asked, worried they might concern my extracurricular activities.

"About my feelings towards Lucinda."

"Dear me, he doesn't suspect you…"

I might have dodged a bullet, but I hardly wanted Patrick shot.

"It's his job to be suspicious, but we both know it was Davenport."

"We do."

"He was even asking what Lucinda thought of the staff."

"Not much," I said, rather too quickly.

Patrick grimaced. I did have a habit of putting my foot in it.

"That's besides the point," he said.

"Of course it is, but there is the bracelet, I suppose."

"That's nothing," he said dismissively. "Lucinda was always misplacing things and blaming Agnes for it."

"I hope they find it soon."

"What worries me," he said, ignoring my comment, "is that if the police are already considering the household it won't be long before the press do as well. Father is on good terms with the Commissioner at Scotland Yard, so he'll do what he can to limit how much information is shared, but those hacks are a rapacious lot."

"Getting Davenport is crucial."

"Exactly."

His face was very close to mine, I could feel his breath on my ear, yet any frisson of excitement was quashed by our anxiety and the proximity of the police.

"We already know where he works and where he lives."

"I doubt he'll turn up there, Selby. I was thinking there might be other places he frequents, if you know what I mean?"

"No, I..." Then it dawned on me. "Do you mean...?"

He looked at me expectantly, hopefully. Damn those hazel eyes!

"... The sort of places I might frequent?"

"I'll make it worth your while."

At least there was no pretending now, he'd had the measure of me from the off, pegging me as a card-carrying member of the fruity underworld. And he was right to!

"I suppose I could ask around."

The words tumbled out my mouth before I could stop them.

"Thank you! The police might be a bit slower to pursue this avenue, but you did say you have some experience of these things."

Yes, Patrick, but I say all sorts of things to men with eyes as deep as yours.

"A little but nothing like this," I said.

"No, quite. But all you'd have to do is ask, nothing more. And if you find anything, you tell me and I'll tell the chief inspector. We have to find Davenport." He put a hand on my shoulder and squeezed. "I knew I could count on you."

I looked over my shoulder but there were no constables near to hand. Besides, there was nothing saucy in Patrick's gesture and the expression on his face was all seriousness. The task was to contain the scandal and protect the family, and I'd agreed to tag along. And, despite all that, I still didn't know if our kiss at Oxford had been a drunken mistake or something he would wish to repeat.

"There's a bathroom on the corridor nearest the top of the left flight of stairs. You can wash your hands there. And Selby? You will be discreet, won't you?"

"Discretion is my middle name."

Honestly! What was becoming of me?

"You're a good friend."

He didn't sound relieved but certainly a fraction less fraught. We bid one another good night as I climbed the stairs in search of the bathroom. The first floor was as gloomy as the rest of the house but fortunately the bathroom door had been left open, so I didn't have to smudge my fingerprints everywhere. The water was freezing but I scrubbed fast and quick. I wanted to get out of this cursed house atop the Heath and go to bed. I tried not to think of the WC below, where Lucy had dripped blood into the sink. She'd been quick to find a bandage but in the end that had made no difference.

Hands dried, I was ready to make my exit when I overheard

a strange sound emanating from further down the corridor. Guttural, almost animal, but restrained, as if someone was struggling to breathe. Another strangling? Surely not! I rushed to find the source of the cry and threw open one of the doors only to reveal Sir Lionel sitting on the edge of his bed, tears pouring down his face.

"Sir Lionel, I'm sorry, so dreadfully sorry, I didn't mean to intrude, I was worried something awful was happening."

His bed was a four-poster, the curtains pulled back and the sheets in disarray. He wore blue-and-white striped pyjamas and his feet were bare. Gone was his terrifying gravitas; instead he had crumpled into himself, as if he were shrinking.

"Something awful *has* happened," he said, and I regretted my foolish words at once. But his were not said in bad temper, simply in stark, unhappy truth.

"She was an incredibly special woman," I said without thinking, an unfortunate habit of mine.

"She was."

His eyes were puffy and slow tears dripped down his cheeks.

"The man who did this will be caught," I said, thinking this a good way to console the husband of a recently murdered wife. "And hanged."

"Let justice roll like the waters and righteousness an everlasting stream."

I could not place the quote but I appreciated the sentiment.

"Indeed, Sir Lionel, justice will be done."

I backed out the room and his crying resumed once the door clicked shut. I tiptoed away from the scene of despair. There's something so bone-crushingly awful about seeing a man reduced to misery. The teachers at my boarding school always told us boys that emotions were an extravagance reserved for women and infants, a lesson they taught with the cane. I had tried my best to keep a lid on my feelings but every so often it blew off. Tonight someone else had let their emotions run wild, except the consequences had proved fatal.

CHAPTER II

The failings of the Labour government, the fear of the annual influenza surge, anger of the unions, hunger marches from the north, and even the Hatry scandal, were briefly forgotten as the murder on Hampstead Heath hit the headlines. From *The Times* to the *Manchester Guardian*, it was duly sensationalised as all the papers speculated on the precise details of Lucinda Duker's death. There were some points that they all agreed on; namely strangulation as the cause of death and Murchadh "Morrow" Davenport as the culprit (although there was no agreement on the spelling of his Christian name). His guilt was assumed and there was nothing the newspapers liked more than a villainous queer. Since beating the Hun, England needed an enemy and, alongside the foreigner, what better one than that effeminate abomination to mankind who liked nothing more than seducing the menfolk, recruiting the children and, now, strangling the women? Being Scottish didn't help him much either.

Monday morning presented me with a plethora of headlines as I left Bank underground station. Buying only one paper required a considerable amount of restraint, but I paid my tuppence and began to read. There was no mention of Lionel's birthday party or myself and the other guests. Instead it only reported on the strangulation, in morbid detail, and the sudden arrival of Morrow. Nothing of the argument, the chase and my attempted heroics, nor Patrick being locked inside the cloakroom. Presumably Sir Lionel had exerted his considerable authority and the police had done his bidding. Although it was surely only a matter of time before the pesky reporters got their noses into things and started uncovering the details.

I arrived punctually at the office, as I always did, and played the part of the diligent clerk. I flirted with one of the secretaries and listened to my colleagues tell me about their weekends. I told them I'd been to the National Gallery, and only after the words left my mouth did I realise I'd turned Lucy's truth into my lie. Everyone was abuzz with the murder and I did my best to match their levels of morbid curiosity. Sir Lionel was a well-known figure in the banking world as he provided gold to the Bank of England, to keep the pound powerful, as he'd said at dinner. It also transpired he'd served as an expert on government finance committees during the war, which didn't surprise me one jot. My peers seemed to sympathise more with him for his loss of a wife than with Lucy for her no longer being alive. Her demise did not stop them rating her attractiveness and wondering what sort of sordid affair she'd got herself involved in with the nasty Morrow. I thought it best not to tell them that Lucy had been a loyal wife and Morrow's preferences were elsewhere, although one of the chaps was quick to do that anyway and soon the word degenerate was being thrown around with carefree abandon, as were theories concerning said degenerate's mental instability.

"It's Godlessness," said Harold, a short fellow with a receding hairline worse than mine. "People have forgotten the scriptures and strayed from the path."

"It's got nothing to do with God, it's in their blood," countered Anthony, a pale chap with a tendency to speak through his generously haired nostrils. "Perverts are prone to all sorts of criminality, especially homicidal mania."

Quite right, I didn't say. There was nothing I enjoyed more after a nice bit of sodomy than a spot of killing.

"No, no," said Stephen, a regular sop with thick, round glasses. "It's a deformity of the basal ganglia."

I had no idea what that was and suspected my fellow clerks didn't either. Someone then made a joke in reference to the word *basal* and much laughter ensued. Honestly, if I were paid for tolerating my peers I'd have retired long ago. Lucky Patrick never had to endure men like these; he could choose what company he kept while I had to keep my job. Conversation moved from perverts to Harold's engagement by way of Stephen's wife being with child (again), and I was relieved when I finally got to my desk.

At one o'clock, I put the first part of my plan into action. I went for my usual, pointedly solitary luncheon at a small café a few streets away – an inexpensive place with a comforting smell of fried sausage and cigarette smoke. I ordered a cheese sandwich with plenty of butter and a cup of milky tea when...

"I say, Arthur, is that you?"

Oiled, blond hair and a big grin.

"Selby, hallo, what a surprise seeing you here."

It was just the sort of encounter a fellow customer might mistake for chance and not something organised the evening before.

"Do join me," he said.

"I'd really hate to intrude."

"Oh, no intrusion at all."

The fluff and bluster over, I joined him at his table. He'd managed to nab a little one in the corner, which he'd covered in a copy of the *Daily Telegraph*.

"You're looking well today, old chap."

"You're looking very well yourself."

We couldn't suppress our grins. It was nice to see a sympathetic face and his really was most sympathetic.

"This is high drama," he said, pointing at the front cover. "And somehow you're involved."

I hushed him, worried for eavesdroppers, as I usually was.

"That is purely between you and I."

"Right ho," he said, tracing a finger across his lips. "What's your interest?"

"I'm trying to track down the Davenport chap."

"The one with the funny first name? Why?"

"To help a friend."

"A friend, eh?"

"A handsome friend, yes, but I owe him. And I owe her."

"Her?"

I nodded at the grainy photograph of Lucinda, smiling in pearls.

"You knew her!?" he blurted.

"Keep your voice down. This isn't idle gossip, this is serious stuff."

"Very serious."

"I... I tried to warn her, you see, against Davenport, but she didn't listen. I should have been more emphatic..."

"Selby, you can hardly blame yourself for what he did."

"But if there's some way I can help put things right, then I will."

"By going chasing after a murderer! That's hardly your style."

"What's that supposed to mean?"

"It means, stick to chasing after men on the Heath and leave other crimes well alone."

"Arthur, you're not concerned for me, are you?"

His answer was a knowing smile. I was not the only one desiring of Arthur's affections, but men with firmer physiques and more hair than I had failed to capture his heart. A small army of us had, however, captured his eye, and I considered myself most fortunate he still enjoyed our dalliances.

"Look," I said, "I don't intend to apprehend the man, I'm just trying to track his whereabouts."

"And should he discover that's what you're doing?"

"Then I'll take my chances."

"How daring!" he joked but I could tell he was a little impressed. "May I?" He took half my sandwich without waiting for permission and sunk his teeth into the soft, white bread. I ate the other half and, for a moment, we sat in contented silence, surrounded by the chatter and bustle of the little café.

"She liked her precious metals, didn't she?" he said, wiping a few crumbs from his chin. "Says here her first husband's money came from Cornish tin mines. Which she spent and then divorced him when a more lucrative suitor appeared."

"That's not the truth," I corrected. "His name was Rupert Pethybridge and he offered Lucinda Duker a divorce after Davenport threatened to expose his secrets."

Arthur cocked an eyebrow and I nodded.

"He's in Berlin now," I added.

"Lucky him, I'd love to go."

"I'm sure Berlin would love to have you."

He smirked. Arthur liked being complimented and, what can I say, us admirers liked to compliment him.

"First blackmailed, then murdered, doesn't pay to be a wife, does it? What's to say Davenport hasn't hot-footed it to America on the first steamer?"

"He may well have, but it's worth asking around nevertheless."

"My mother always said you couldn't trust the Scots. I'll put a few words in at the usual places."

"Thank you."

"And some of the unusual ones too," he added.

"I don't know those."

"Keep your innocence, Selby, you're much prettier that way."

I blushed.

"What I want to know is how he knew he could get away with it."

"What do you mean?" I asked.

"From what I've read he turns up at the house in the middle of the night, strangles pretty Lucinda Duker without so much as a by your leave, then vanishes into thin air. It's a damned risky thing to leave to chance."

"You think it was premeditated?"

"Don't you?"

Morrow's arrival had seemed very spur of the moment, but the speed with which the ensuing events unfolded certainly indicated forward planning. Something tugged at the back of my mind, something not quite right about the whole situation.

"It was certainly quite the feat to pull off," I said.

"Then you better watch your front as well as your back."

"Why?"

"Because if Davenport doesn't get you, his accomplice will."

"Oh God!" I could have slapped myself for not thinking of that. "You're right."

"Tell me something I don't know, darling."

"I didn't know you were a budding Hercule Poirot."

"Not my cup of tea but I've read *A Study in Scarlet*. That Holmes and Watson, a pair of pansies if ever I've seen one, and I've seen a fair few."

My mind spun through the possibilities and finally what had been tugging at the back of it reached the front – the vanishing key! I'd overheard Mrs Fairbanks criticising Agnes for misplacing the cloakroom key but what if the poor maid hadn't lost it but someone had taken it. Someone who had planned with Morrow to create the most dramatic of distractions while Lucy was left alone and vulnerable.

"Oh dear!"

"What's the matter?"

"It's Patrick."

His name slipped from my lips before I could close them. Someone had locked him in that turret while Morrow had snuck back into the house to strangle Lucy. He'd dragged her body into the billiard room before darting out through the French windows, leaving his accomplice to keep mum. And whoever that someone was, was still inside the house.

"Patrick Duker?" asked Arthur, "Is he the one you're sweet on!?"

I wished I'd kept my big mouth shut.

"You really do enjoy pursuing the unattainable."

That one hit too close to the bone. I'd been the one to fall for Arthur and he'd been the one to make clear the feeling wasn't mutual. I hardly needed to be reminded of it.

"Sorry old chap," he blustered. "It's simply that the article says he's engaged."

"I don't think it's that simple," I replied, trying and failing not to appear rattled. "And if there really is an accomplice, then Patrick is in danger."

"Bigge, you sly dog! He's in danger from what's between your legs."

CHAPTER 12

"Good afternoon, sir."

"Afternoon, Pinks. Not such clement weather today."

"Indeed, sir."

He looked out at the Friday afternoon clouds as I shivered on the doorstep.

"May I help, sir?"

"I'm here to see Patrick."

"I'm afraid that won't be possible, sir."

"Oh really, why ever not?" I asked, affecting nonchalance rather than indignation.

"Master Patrick is not in, sir."

"How odd. I was on the blower to him just moments ago. He invited me to the house. Naturally, I dropped everything at once given how distressed he must be."

"Naturally."

The truth of the matter was that I'd received no such telephone call and, instead, had feigned stomach problems at the office so I could leave early. I'd had the operator patch me through on Monday evening, after my not-so-surprise luncheon with Arthur, but no one answered. I'd tried again at various points throughout the week with little success save for one awkward conversation with Mrs Fairbanks and another with Pinks. Patrick was either absent or unavailable, and for days I'd been worrying about him, spending my nights tossing and turning as I imagined what horrible fates might befall him. In the end, I'd taken things into my own hands.

"Awfully chilly," I said, hamming up my shivers.

"Quite." He couldn't treat me with the same contempt as the gutter press, but it was clear he thought me no longer welcome at the family abode. If only Patrick would appear, he'd be pleased to see me and keen to hear of my latest discovery.

"Funnily enough, I do remember Patrick mentioning he might pop out for a stroll on the Heath but wouldn't be gone for too long."

"Funny indeed, sir. Perhaps it is best you wait in the drawing room."

"Splendid, thank you, Pinks."

I hurried inside, quickly taking my hat and coat off, and thrusting them into the disgruntled butler's outstretched hands. He took them into the turret, which gave me a moment to inspect the door; nothing suspicious – just a large, well-polished door of dark wood with an attractive golden knob. The key was nowhere in sight.

"Are the police still rifling through the valuables?"

"No sir, they're quite finished."

"They haven't taken anything away, have they?"

"Only Lady Duker's body, sir."

He was a droll one, old Pinks.

"No items of significance?"

"No sir, the master would not approve."

"Quite right."

Sir Lionel and the chief inspector really were close.

"I'll take you this way, sir."

We avoided the passageway to hell and went via the dining room. It was grey, the table bare and lustreless, as if the house were also mourning the loss of its mistress.

"Silly me," I exclaimed. "Left my cigarettes in my jacket."

"I can retrieve them, sir."

"Quite all right, Pinks, I'll save you the bother."

He offered another protest but I was already backtracking to the hall. All I needed was a moment to run my little experiment. I pictured the three of us that night, Lucy, Patrick and myself, and then Morrow's arrival. Taking on the role of Patrick, I rushed towards the cloakroom door, swung it open and dashed for the telephone. I feigned picking up the receiver and asking the operator to put me through to the police. He could have stayed standing in this very position, but I was curious to know what he would have seen if he'd turned around. So I did and what greeted me was the door. It had quietly and slowly swung to, ensuring no view of the hall whatsoever. How simple then for anyone to close and lock it.

Footsteps clipped their way across the hall tiles and I quickly retrieved my cigarettes. I opened the door and there was the butler, waiting on the other side.

"Does sir require any assistance?"

"I'd lose my own brain if it wasn't sewn into my hat," I said, waving my cigarettes at him. He looked bemused rather than suspicious.

It felt incredibly odd to return to the drawing room, the site of such recent gaiety and tragedy, but now it too was grey. The golden candlesticks on the mantelpiece had lost their lustre, the carriage clock ticked more quietly and even the fish-shaped spill jar seemed ready to shut its trap. A low fire struggled in the grate and, while the room wasn't as cold as outside, I still shivered. Pinks prodded the coals with a poker.

"Have you worked long for Sir Lionel?"

"Thirty years, sir."

"Gosh, how impressive!" I couldn't think of anything worse. "Happy years?"

"Quite satisfactory, yes, sir."

In Pinks' language *quite satisfactory* probably meant really rather good.

"Sir Lionel must swear by you."

"It is the job of a servant to serve his master with loyalty and honour."

"Quite right." Dear me, he sounded like he was quoting from a manual on slavery. "Are you a Londoner yourself?"

"No sir, I was born in Cornwall. My father was head butler to Lord Ankerton."

"Very impressive." I had no idea who that was. "I imagine your father made a fine butler."

"He did. I worked under him for a number of years. He

taught me everything a good butler should be, it was a most satisfying experience."

I took *most satisfying* to mean quite good. Heaven knew I'd only managed one year in my father's employ, discounting the awful apprenticeship during my adolescence.

"Then you jumped ship?"

"That's not how I would put it myself."

Had he spoken with a trace of humour? Somehow Pinks and humour were not two things I could imagine cohabiting.

"Sir Lionel was a regular guest at Lord Ankerton's and I often valeted for him. He came to admire my service and it wasn't long before he offered me this job. It was a most stirring opportunity to be offered a role in London, our great country's capital."

"Indeed. What did your father have to say?"

"He was disappointed at first but gave me his blessing in the end."

"Yes, I know a little of what it means to disappoint one's father."

It appeared fathers were a pain in all ranks of society.

"I wanted to be closer to the centre of things."

"I beg your pardon, Pinks."

"Sir Lionel is a very important man. He received a knighthood for his contribution to the war effort and has meetings with the Prime Minister. It's an honour to serve him, to add my contribution to the smooth running of our fine Empire."

Aha, so Pinks was insane after all. To think that polishing candlesticks and opening doors could, in any way, affect Great Britain's politics was indeed a sign of lunacy. Still, if it got him out of bed in the morning and gave meaning to his life, I was hardly going to press him on the matter.

"You are a most loyal man, Pinks."

"Thank you, sir."

"It's so awfully sad about poor Lady Duker," I said, testing the water.

"Indeed."

"Sir Lionel must be cut up."

"He is."

"You must miss her frightfully."

He blinked quickly before answering.

"Yes, sir. She brought great contentment to Sir Lionel."

Aha! He might be a loyal butler but he was no actor. He clearly hadn't liked his master's late wife, which hardly surprised me, but how much had he not liked her?

"Did you see Davenport that night?"

"No, sir."

"You checked in the billiard room, didn't you?"

More quick blinking before he provided the expected confirmation.

"It's strange that you missed Lady Duker's body."

"No, sir, her body was concealed by the billiard table and I didn't think to circumnavigate it."

Perhaps he had not deemed Lucy worthy of being married to a man so close to the *centre of things*. Perhaps he thought he was doing Sir Lionel a favour. What a warped sense of loyalty that would be.

"Quite so. I heard Davenport pinched one of the keys."

"I didn't hear that myself, sir."

"What a wicked man. Such a shame you didn't see anything."

I tried to keep my voice steady, realising I might be talking to Morrow's accomplice – not a pleasant thought as improbable as it was. Pinks was taller than I and had a poker nearer to hand, but I had boxed at boarding school.

"I believe you were the last to see him, sir, out in the garden."

Touché!

"And I let him get away. I'll never forgive myself."

"Only God can forgive, sir."

On that he left me alone, the canny old so and so. The next part of my plan would prove a little trickier as it involved entering the garden. I had banked on the room feeling stuffier than it did, to bolster my excuse for wanting to take the air, but if I were quick no one would miss me. I made my way towards the French windows, briefly standing where Lucy had stood some six nights ago, a woman so sure of life and its uninterrupted continuation.

"Good afternoon, Mr Bigge."

"Mrs Fairbanks, hello. Such a grey day."

"Perhaps I could fetch some tea? That might brighten things up."

"That's very kind, Mrs Fairbanks. You remind me of a matron I had at school, a very sympathetic woman."

"Thank you, sir," she replied, blushing, not immune to my charm despite her age. Truth be told, the matron was a harridan of the first order who liked the cane as much as the masters. Still, with her stern face and scraped-back hair, she had borne a physical resemblance to Mrs Fairbanks.

"This must all be very hard on you, Mrs Fairbanks."

"It's Sir Lionel I worry about. Such a terrible thing to happen to such a good man."

Oh dear, was there another ultra-loyalist amongst the ranks? Although I struggled to picture Mrs Fairbanks working hand in glove with the eccentric Morrow; an even odder couple than Morrow and the butler. But if she had, her motive would not have been loyalty to Sir Lionel but loathing of his wife.

"So many reporters, sir, at all hours of the day."

"Are they being beastly?"

"They are, sir. One disguised himself as a milkman and another bearded fellow tried to sneak through the garden gate. Sir Lionel had to shoo him away. I always said he should get it fixed."

Aha, if the gate was broken, that explained Morrow's departure and possibly his entrance too. But had he *cased the joint*, as gangsters liked to say, or been informed by one of the household?

"Journalists are rarely the best of men. And keeping house at a time like this, it must be very taxing on you."

"Mrs Stonehouse is back, which is a godsend, but then there's Agnes…" She checked herself, the curtains of formality twitching.

"I do understand," I prompted. "My mother had a young maid once, a very skittish girl, quite unreliable." My mother had had no such maid.

"Indeed, sir, Agnes is all nerves and agitation."

The curtains had opened! I had to make the most of my opportunity.

"We don't all have your fortitude, Mrs Fairbanks. I'm sure if you'd found the body there would have been no hysterics."

"Young girls these days are so sensitive. If she's not dropping things, she's losing them. She misplaced the teapot and…"

"… the key."

"I beg your pardon?"

"The cloakroom key went missing, didn't it?"

"Only briefly, sir, but that's back in the pantry where it should be."

"Is that where the keys are stored?"

"Indeed, sir, although the teapot remains to be found."

"And Lady Duker's jewellery."

"I beg your pardon, sir?"

"Her bracelet. It's still missing, I assume?"

"Yes, sir."

"Well…"

I let the word hang on the air.

"Agnes had nothing to do with that," she said with conviction. "She may be rough around the edges, but no staff member of mine is a thief."

"Quite right, I didn't mean to imply…"

"I will fetch the tea, sir. Earl Grey."

"Marvellous, thank you, Mrs Fairbanks," I gushed but the moment had passed, the curtains of formality had been drawn.

As soon as the door clicked shut I was unlocking the French windows and slipping out into the garden. I turned left and quickly stepped around the side of the house, swift past the billiard room and not daring a look inside. As I turned the corner to the front of the house, my eye was drawn to a twitching curtain at a first-floor window. That darned Pinks better not be spying on me again. Near enough to the front door I stopped, took a breath and turned around. Back I went, counting the seconds in my head, trying to work out what timeframe Morrow had for his murder. The trouble was I didn't know how long I'd spent looking for him – though it can't have been more than two or three minutes – and I also didn't know how many minutes were required for strangulation. Although, with an accomplice to lock Patrick in the turret and unlock the garden doors of the billiard room, he would have gained a few valuable seconds. I was back at the drawing room French windows in well under a minute. It would have been much less if I'd run. *There you are*, Morrow had said as he'd found me on this very spot. A funny thing to say, come to think of it, as if he'd been looking for me, rather than running from me. I carried on towards the high stone walls of the herb garden trying to make sense of his odd choice of words...

"Dear God," she exclaimed.

So distracted by my thoughts I'd nearly collided with Agnes.

"Oh gosh, terribly sorry. I wasn't looking where I was going."

"No, my mistake, sir, I… I…"

She was stuttering and her face was pale.

"Are you all right, Agnes? You look like you've seen a ghost."

"I'm… I'm… No ghost, sir, just cold."

"It is chilly."

But I did not step out of her way. She looked mighty guilty as well as shocked, as if I'd just caught her doing something naughty. I looked down at her hands and noticed dirt at her fingertips.

"Were you planting bulbs?"

"Picking herbs, sir."

"Ah."

We both looked at her empty hands.

"I... I've forgotten the ones Mrs Fairbanks asked for."

"What's for dinner?"

"Lamb."

"Then rosemary, I suspect."

She gasped but was quick to close her mouth. Perhaps she was allergic.

"Take a moment, Agnes, recover your breath. I appreciate how difficult everything must be."

"Yes, sir, thank you."

Her shoulders relaxed just a fraction and I wondered if anyone had enquired after her welfare.

"Where's your family, Agnes?"

"Lincolnshire."

"Do you have many friends nearby? Anyone to talk to?"

"Not really, sir."

"I can't imagine Mrs Fairbanks and Pinks make the best of confidants."

She shook her head and smiled, just a little. I smiled back.

"They're busy with their own affairs, sir," she said, looking me quickly in the eye before returning her gaze to the paving slabs.

"What affairs are those?"

"That's their business, sir."

"She's a stern one is Mrs Fairbanks."

"She's always chastising me. My work's never good enough for her."

"Perhaps you're thinking of moving on?"

"Oh yes, sir. I'd much rather be a secretary or married." Her pale cheeks turned pink. "Perhaps I'm speaking too freely, sir."

"You're not, don't worry. I quite know what it's like to be regularly criticised."

"She's always blaming me for things that have nothing to do with me."

"Like losing the cloakroom key."

"Exactly…"

Her hand darted to cover her mouth. She looked wounded, as if she'd realised I'd trapped her.

"The police will catch him soon," I said.

"I hope so."

It must be a lonely life, being a maid, and I knew all about that. Loneliness that was. I had no experience of being a maid. It could make people behave most desperately.

"You're shivering, you best get back inside."

"Thank you, sir."

She hurried past and I stuck my head into the herb garden. The bricks had long lost their sheen and some of the mortar between them was coming loose. The desiccated remains of plant stems torn from the wall still clung to the bricks as if they couldn't accept their death. Many of the flowerbeds were barren but what had been planted looked in order, including the rosemary. If only Patrick were here, I could sit with him on the bench and tell him my news. But where was he?

With fingers and toes turning to ice, I returned to the drawing room, whereupon I found Sir Lionel in his armchair by the fire.

"Good afternoon, Sir Lionel."

"Oh, you're here."

He did not look pleased to see me but there was no ire in his eyes. Nor was he crying buckets. If anything, he looked drained.

I was reminded of a fallen hero, Achilles perhaps, torn apart by the death of his lover Patroclus. Not that Sir Lionel would approve of such a reference; I knew he was one to like an ancient Greek allusion but not *that* sort of ancient Greek allusion.

"I came by to see Patrick."

"He's not in."

I closed the French window quietly behind me, spotting a number of small smudges on one of the glass panels. I counted five. Something else Mrs Fairbanks could berate Agnes for.

"I really am most sorry, Sir Lionel..."

"Save your condolences, I've had enough of them. It won't bring her back."

There was still no sign of Mrs Fairbanks and the tea, although I had well overstayed my welcome.

"Any news from the chief inspector?"

"None that I want to hear."

"They'll catch him soon enough."

"He's gone into hiding. He's a cowardly..."

He finished the sentence with one of the insults I expected him to, a two-syllable word beginning with the letter p. I maintained a neutral expression.

"I'll be on my way," I said. "You wouldn't happen to know where Patrick has got to?"

"He's at the Bullion."

"I beg your pardon?"

"The Bullion. It's our club."

"Of course it is."

He continued staring into the fire; his wrinkles more pronounced as were the great bags under his eyes. His whole body, once so firm, was sagging, as if he was slowly crumbling into himself, like the Parthenon.

"I loved her," he said, more to the flames than to me. "She was my second chance at life and now she's gone."

It was dangerous to love too much, that I well knew, but it was impossible not to. The risk of heartbreak was the price one paid for investing in love. How many times had I fallen for a nice young fellow with a strong chin and a forelock only to have him forget me the following week? Although at least none of them had been strangled.

"Was the mystery of the cloakroom key ever solved?" I said, pushing my luck.

"What?"

"Apparently it went temporarily missing."

"I've no idea. Things are always going missing in this house."

"My mistake."

"Lucinda misplaced something at least once a week."

Oh dear, back to his dead wife. He carried on staring at the embers, clearly better company than I.

"It's a mortal sin, isn't it?" he said eventually.

"I beg your pardon?"

"Suicide, it's a sin."

"I believe so." Dear me, was the man really contemplating the abyss? "But Sir Lionel, you mustn't... not even for a moment... it's not right."

"What counts as *right* in a world where justice proves so slippery?"

"I don't know," I replied quite honestly. "But there is always the truth."

He dragged his eyes away from the fire and looked to me. "I've always tried to be a good father to Patrick."

"I'm sure you have, Sir Lionel, I know he regards you most highly."

"What was it you studied at Corpus?"

"Classics. At Fitzalan."

"And who's your father?"

"Arthur Bigge."

"It's funny, I only first heard your name just the other week and now here you are – right at the centre of things."

He closed his eyes, which I took to be my exit cue, so I beat a swift retreat via the dining room. Bloody hell, I didn't know whether to fear the man or fear for him. As long as he didn't plan on doing anything silly. Mrs Fairbanks was in the hall carrying a tea tray, including a plate of freshly toasted teacakes. Agnes was a few paces behind, closing the door to the turret cloakroom, her hands now clean.

"That looks divine, Mrs Fairbanks, but I'm afraid I have to be on my way."

"Oh, that's a pity, Mr Bigge," she replied without much pity in her voice.

"But Sir Lionel's come down. Perhaps that will cheer him up?"

"Perhaps."

She sounded doubtful. Who knew if the house on the Heath would ever recover from this tragedy. The two women passed me, Agnes' eyes glued to the floor, and I returned to the cloakroom to collect my hat and coat, thinking again on the key. Pinks and Sir Lionel hadn't heard anything about it, whereas Mrs Fairbanks and Agnes had been decidedly shifty at its mention, which tallied with the conversation of theirs I'd overheard that evening. It would be odd, though, for the housekeeper to draw attention to it if she'd been the one to take it, unless she was employing the double bluff and trying to put herself above suspicion.

But could any of the household really have been in cahoots with Morrow? It was quite a stretch of the imagination. Still, someone had locked Patrick in the turret and I had to find out who. Lost in my thoughts, I almost tripped on something. Looking down, I saw an envelope lying on the floor next to the table with the telephone. That hadn't been there when I'd arrived. I knelt down to retrieve it. It was a small thing, a bit crumpled, and previously opened. There was no name on the envelope but there was something inside. Foolishly but true to my nature, I removed the letter and began to read...

My love, my forbidden love...

Footsteps echoed on the hall tiles and I quickly stuffed the letter back into the envelope, then stuffed the envelope into my pocket. I could regret that later but, for now, I wanted rid of this damned house. I slipped back into the hall and let Pinks open the front door. If he hadn't been the perfect butler, he might well have slammed it behind me.

CHAPTER 13

London was grey, cold and wet as October took the leaves from the trees. I'd walked from the Duker household down into Hampstead village and hailed a taxi, driven by an overly friendly Cockney chap who had all manner of dire predictions about the state of the nation and its finances. I decided not to tell him that I worked at a bank and the British economy was doing rather well, despite the recent blip. No one had liked Cassandra.

"Nanti bona for old Blighty," he said as we skirted the Regent's Park.

"I beg your pardon?"

"*Not good*, things are going to get worse before they get any better in fair Albion."

I feigned ignorance of the Polari vernacular, even though I knew it well; the language of gypsies, Jews, perverts and sailors. Many a time had I conducted my affairs with the aid of this surreptitious tongue. Nevertheless, vigilance was my watchword and I wasn't divulging any of my secrets to some cocksure cabby. The roads became busier the deeper into the city we got: red buses lit up top and bottom, black cabs and the odd horse and cart, one struggling under a load of coal. Unhappy pedestrians huddled into their coats, umbrellas ascending as the drizzle worsened. Soon we were nearby, or *ajax* as the cabby put it, and I wondered if he could sense my difference. Some normal men could, but only because they had it in themselves, regardless of whether or not they knew it.

The Bullion Club was located amidst the warren of roads behind Goodge Street. It stood taller and prouder than its Victorian neighbours, a grand building of yellow brick with ostentatious pillars either side of the front entrance. I eyed it from the far side of the street, umbrella up and feet cold. It was the sort of place I'd love to be a member of. I'd be on first-name terms with the doorman and turn up at any hour I fancied, whether it was for a leisurely breakfast or an evening tipple. I would have a number of favourite chairs; an armchair near one of the fireplaces that was usually taken by some cantankerous old bore, and a sturdier, leather affair in the library, for when I wished to read a novel, but definitively not *Last Train To Death*. Although what would Octavia's creation, the dogged Inspector Glover, do in my situation? He always got his man in the end but he did have the Metropolitan Police force to hand and, in some of the worst novels, a ghost. The entirely real Chief Inspector Lisle came to mind and I wondered if he was any closer to tracking down Morrow. I shuddered at the thought of my interrogation in the study and the penetrating stare of that constable of his; Shovel or something similar. Providing the subordinate's facial recall proved worse than mine, I hopefully would never have to see them again.

Someone emerged from the club, an older chap with a beard and a sour look about him. The doorman sorted his umbrella and off he went. All I had to do was cross the road, head inside and request to speak with Patrick Duker. I did not move. What if he was avoiding me? It was an unpleasant thought, but he hadn't responded to any of my telephone calls. I could understand him wanting to put some distance between that fateful night and the people associated with it, but he'd entrusted me with an important task. Of course he'd want to see me.

A quick stroll would quell my nerves as I paced my way up the street and crossed over to the other side. Back down I went, turning my head as I passed the club to spy the doorman and the warmly lit lobby beyond. Why shouldn't I just step inside? Yet off I went down the rest of the street before crossing and heading back up. Something was holding me back and, if I knew any better, it was my sense of tact. Barging into a private members' club and accusing someone in Patrick's house of complicity in murder would hardly win me any favours. I took to traipsing up and down, eventually deciding that now was as good a time as any for reading the rest of that letter.

I located myself under a lamppost and fished it from my pocket. The envelope was a little damaged following my manhandling and I held it close to my chest to avoid the drizzle. Why I'd taken it I wasn't sure, but a Holmesian sense had tingled – this was the sort of clue that solved a mystery (or proved entirely irrelevant to it). Umbrella in one hand, I retrieved the letter with the other and brought it close to my nose. Just a short note of swirling handwriting on a small piece of paper, but its contents got my heart racing:

My love, my forbidden love.

How I yearn to be yours again. But, for now, we must be quiet, nothing too loud, no cries or screams. Until we are away and can make all the noise in the world.

Forever yours,

X

I say! Forbidden love chez Duker, this added a twist to the tale. My train of thought took me immediately to Agnes, who'd been loitering at the cloakroom door not long before my departure. Perhaps she was its recipient or author for that matter. Although I struggled to imagine her writing such a thing, all that talk of cries and noises seemed much too passionate for a maid, but then it was her job to be unobtrusive. Who knew who she really was?

I looked back to the club and...

"Blast!"

It was Patrick. Having dithered with the note, I'd missed him make his exit. He was at the bottom of the steps already, his distinct profile caught in the orange glow of the street. He glanced in my direction and my heart juddered, caught as I was in the gaslight reading a love note I'd just stolen from his house. But he didn't appear to recognise me and set off in the opposite direction. A lone taxi drove down the road and I assumed he'd hail it and then disappear entirely, rendering my afternoon's work a complete failure. But he kept walking, taking a right at the end of the street.

All I would have to do was speed up my pace and tap him on the shoulder. I could tell most of the truth – that I'd gone to the house and been told he was at the club – and not mention the hanging about for such a time. I turned right and saw him further along. He didn't have an umbrella but was wearing a long coat and hat. Come on, Selby, hurry up. The longer I waited, the more suspicious things looked. My heart rate increased but my pace did not. Even if he were to be had, that kiss was a long time ago. I had changed. Perhaps he was more attracted to the Arthurs of the world. Or perhaps I should bloody well give it my best shot!

The drizzle spattered against my face and I rubbed my eyes. The letter was back in my pocket with its many mysteries still to be unravelled. X for a kiss. X marks the spot. X for a secret name shared between lovers. X for a murderer's accomplice. He stopped to look up and down the road before crossing to the other side and vanishing down a side street. I stepped out, putting my foot in a puddle and receiving a blaring honk from a passing autocar.

"Bugger," I swore as the damp seeped between my toes. I hurried on and caught up with his shadow once again. This wasn't the direction for Goodge Street underground. We twisted and turned our way through a few more streets until I was forced to stop because he'd turned into a place called Wilkington Mews. It was a dead end and if I followed he'd know it. I watched surreptitiously as he walked a little further before stopping. He looked back over his shoulder and, for a heart-stopping moment, I thought he'd seen me but then he was knocking at the door of one of the squat terraced houses. Soon after it opened and he vanished. Now what? I could hardly march up to the house and announce myself: *Patrick, I just happened to be stalking you, any chance I could come in for a cup of tea.* Go home, Selby, you're making a fool of yourself!

I entered the mews and walked past the house. The door was painted a dark green and there was a light on in one of the ground-floor windows. Was Patrick conducting an illicit affair with a guardsman or was this where one Theodora Smythe lived? I scuttled away and found a dingy little café at the end of the adjoining street. There were a number of empty tables. I was rather peckish as a matter of fact; a ham sandwich would do. Three minutes later and I had a seat by the window which, if I pressed my face close to the glass, afforded me a glimpse of the turn off into the mews. A cup of milky tea was warming my fingers and the love letter was open before me.

"Who are you, Mr X?" I whispered, assuming it to be a man. I'd received and written a number of love letters in my time, and was just as capable of overly sentimental romantic twaddle. What if Morrow had written it to Agnes, deceiving her so as to acquire an accomplice? I could picture him seducing her with his bright eyes and cunning smile. She wasn't a worldly sort of girl and wouldn't know a normal from a fruit. She probably thought she'd found her Prince Charming. But he'd had no intention to bed her, let alone marry the poor thing, he just wanted to get close enough to Lucy so he could get his hands around her neck and...

This time I didn't miss him. I'd been checking the mews exit regularly and I was looking up when Patrick reappeared, hat down and raincoat collar up. His gait was different; straighter, less slouched, he must have sobered up. He walked my way and passed the café on the other side of the street. I was quick to leave my table and return to the wet gloom. It was much too late for elaborate explanations; I'd have to feign surprise this time. *Patrick! I didn't expect to see you here.* Or perhaps, *I say, is that you, Patrick?* Maybe even, *Gosh, Patrick, have you been following me?* Yes, that would work if I got ahead of him and it was he who accidentally bumped into me. This trick had worked before on an Irish accountant I once bedded – his lingual skills as advanced as his numerical.

The convoluted game of cat and mouse took us onto Wells Street then across Oxford Street. The shop windows offered their tantalising wares as the buses rumbled past. I was careful to avoid the puddles and not get run over, and on we went down Berwick Street into Soho, familiar territory. Patrick walked quickly as if he knew where he was going, although whether he walked furtively or confidently, it was hard to tell. Then Peter Street, this couldn't be! There was only one reason a man like Patrick would come here and that was for the River Styx, one of the few clubs that provided for a most unconventional night. Bohemians, artists, musicians, all were welcome, providing they could afford the entrance fee and didn't make a scene. He was one of us after all! I felt delightfully vindicated. The door to the club opened up and Patrick vanished inside. Fortunately, bumping into him here wouldn't require an explanation and he need never know the reason for my damp shoes. I knocked. No one answered. I knocked louder.

"What's the word?" came a gruff voice from behind.

"Good evening?"

The door creaked open a little and an unfamiliar face peered out at me.

"You're not a member."

"No, but I have been before."

"Two shillings."

"Two shillings!" I exclaimed but managed to get my foot in the door before it was slammed in my face. "Right you are, just a minute."

"I don't have a minute," answered the man.

I fished in my pocket and retrieved a handful of coins. There was a shilling, that was a good start, but I wasn't sure I'd have enough pennies. One, two, three... where was the usual doorman... four, five... he was much friendlier and often gave me a discount... six, seven... if only I hadn't bought that ham sandwich... eight, nine, ten... not enough mustard. I felt the door being pushed against my shoe.

"Excuse me," I said, "I do have the money."

"If you could take a step back, sir."

"Look, here's a shilling." I waved the coin in his face but he didn't look impressed. "I'll have the rest in a tick."

"I don't do with ticks."

My foot was back on the pavement and the door almost shut.

"Wait," came an unfamiliar voice from further within. "He's with me."

"Oh yeah?" asked the impertinent doorman. "It's still two shillings."

"Gosh, you aren't having a good night, are you, Charlie?" replied the voice.

"Can never be too careful with the new customers."

"But you can be nice."

I heard the clink of coins and suddenly the door opened wide.

"Come on, then," said the one called Charlie.

"This is no way to treat a semi-regular," I said as I huffed past him into the gloomy corridor. My saviour was up ahead – head bowed, hat still on, but the coat I recognised at once.

"Patri…" I began but he grabbed me and pulled me quickly along the corridor. We ascended a narrow set of stairs, lit by a single lamp on the wall. Voices and music issued from above. I'd been to the Styx a few times before; one particularly memorable night had involved most of the members taking their tops off, including the women!

"Really, Patrick, is everything all right?"

He ignored me until we reached the top of the stairs, stopping in front of the door that led into the club proper. Slowly he began to turn and I, a few steps below, looked up to him in anticipation. By Jove, I couldn't believe my eyes!

"Theo…"

She put her finger to my lips.

"Exactly. In here, that's all they call me."

CHAPTER 14

"Bottoms up!"

We clinked glasses, champagne no less, at the expense of family Smythe. The chilled bubbles slipped smoothly over my tongue, tickling it into a brief frenzy of gustatory joy.

"Thank you, Theo…" I forced myself to cut the final two syllables. "This is divine."

So far, we had only covered so much – tonight Theodora Smythe was one Theo, a young man of the musical persuasion dressed impeccably in a tailored suit, with his already short hair slicked back to appear more masculine, a natty moustache and a bodice of sorts to reduce the size of his, well, his breasts. Fortunately for him they were already quite small. I assumed a little make-up had been applied to accentuate the cheekbones and darken the jawline. The change was remarkable and, for those who hadn't met him under more feminine circumstances, I don't think they would have been any the wiser.

"I do like a drop of Mumm," he said, his voice huskier than usual. "Tell me, Mr Bigge, do you make a habit of stalking people?"

"Stalking?" I exclaimed, "Do you make a habit of dressing as you do?"

"I do, as a matter of fact but, tonight, I shall be the one asking the questions. If it weren't for me, you'd be back on the street getting wet."

"I really am most grateful."

"Good. Patrick was worried someone was following him and, when I walked past the caff, you were the first thing I saw."

"Oh."

"I was tempted to lead you astray and lose you down a back alley, but you do not strike me as the reporter type. I've seen the way you look at Patrick, that cannot be feigned."

"No, I... I..." I hid my mumblings in another sip as my cheeks turned pink.

"No need to be embarrassed. He's a most beautiful man."

"I can assure you my motivations are innocent."

He indicated he believed nothing of the sort.

"Innocent enough," I protested. "I'm no reporter. Patrick and I were at university together."

"He did mention that."

"Oh, he mentioned me, did he?"

He smirked and my pink cheeks went scarlet.

"You were at Corpus with him."

"Fitzalan. Classics."

"Bully for you. I'd have liked to have gone to university but my father wouldn't stand for it."

"How unfortunate."

Women at university were a rarity. I hadn't known many in my time, confined as they were to a small number of all-female colleges. My own tutors took rather a dim view of it; they were the sort to think women better suited to the kitchen or parlour. One particularly bellicose philosopher had described women as lesser-men with shrivelled testes and shrunken penises – God's leftovers and Darwin's joke. I refrained from telling him I thought that a better description of himself.

"We've strayed from the point, Mr Bigge. Why were you following Patrick?"

"There's a very simple explanation. I went to the house but he wasn't in and Sir Lionel told me he was at the club."

"You went to the club?"

"I did, yes."

"And?"

The ensuing silence was filled by the chattering of the other guests and the clinking of glasses. I liked the River Styx with its over-abundance of Turkish rugs on the floors and walls, and lots of little benches and seats hidden away in nooks and crannies. There was a number of hookah pipes, which I believe is the correct name, and the place was suffused with a sweet-smelling smoke. It was like Ali Baba's cave, except instead of thieves hiding in baskets, it was buggerantos.

"I got cold feet, metaphorically and literally. I was worried… well, I…"

"You were worried?"

"That he might not care to see me."

"Oh, Mr Bigge."

His voice became soft, accompanied by a kind sort of look

on his face; one I believe is called pity.

"Patrick is very easy to fall for."

"Y… yes," I admitted, somewhat humiliated to be confessing my secrets to my rival in love. "You're very lucky."

"Me?"

"To be the true object of his affections."

"Ha! Please be under no illusions, our engagement is decidedly one of convenience."

I had to put my glass down very carefully, ensuring it didn't shatter against the polished wood of the tabletop. Did my ears deceive me?

"You mean to say that Patrick and you are not in love?"

"Come, Mr Bigge, you can ask me more plainly than that."

"This is a most unconventional conversation."

"We are unconventional people."

"Is Patrick unconventional as well?" I held my breath. The door that had been so firmly closed and locked hinted it might again be opened. The key was held before me.

"He is."

The key fitted!

"And you are his…?"

"Alibi. As he is mine. We can't have the wrong people knowing our secrets."

"But you've told me yours."

"As have you. Call it a stalemate. Or grounds for an acquaintanceship."

He downed his glass and signalled for a refill. The waiter who topped us up was a saucy number, wearing only a waistcoat on his top half. I could see two of his abdominal muscles, his belly button and a rather suggestive trail of hair descending from said belly button. He caught me looking and winked. Unlike some of the pubs I frequented, the Styx appealed to the sort of man who knew what he was looking for. There was no chance I'd accidentally proposition a normal here. No one batted an eyelid to see two men dancing cheek to cheek. There were a few women too and for all I knew some of the other men were like Theo. It was a place I felt comfortable, somewhere I could loosen my wrist and slacken my jaw, relieved to be amongst my own kind for a change.

"Did Patrick not want to come?" I asked once the waiter had gone.

"Not when he was worried he had a shadow."

"I am sorry, that was very foolish of me."

"If truth be told," Theo said slowly, "Patrick doesn't really go in for places like this."

"Does he prefer the Turkish baths?"

"No, he's yet to venture too far from his own front door, or mine for that matter."

"Oh, he's an innocent?"

The key didn't just fit the lock, it positively glided in! To find a man unsullied by the underworld was most rare.

"He would never come to a place like this. He doesn't like the clientele. He doesn't like himself for that matter."

Ah, sullied by the overworld instead.

"Does he dislike himself very much?"

"Very much," he replied gravely.

I knew of men like Patrick, who hated the very essence of themselves. They saw their perversion as a grave affliction, bravely borne, and something they wished they could be without. Often God, a psychiatrist, an overbearing father or some combination of all three was to blame.

"We met a number of years ago at a drinks party; Susan Goodley, do you know her? She's so much fun."

I shook my head as I imagined the delights of one of Susan's drinks parties. I bet all the right people were invited and they got to drink all the best cocktails.

"We were the last ones standing and terribly drunk. We traipsed off into the garden and as the sun came up so all our secrets came out. He's scared, you see, of who he truly is, and he couldn't stand a scandal. It would kill his father, especially after everything that's happened."

As much as I wanted to know the ins and outs of Patrick's inner torment, I knew that he was one of us and that was what mattered. I'd been with self-loathing men before. After enough drinks they tended to open up, so to speak. But now was the moment to ask something else entirely.

"You must have seen it in the papers," I said.

"It's impossible to miss."

"It's good none of our names have been mentioned."

"Very good."

"You didn't see him that night, did you?"

"What do you mean?"

"When you left. Perhaps you saw a strange figure lurking on the pavement?"

"I was driving, Mr Bigge, I was hardly looking out for potential murderers."

"Perhaps Mrs Stubbs did?"

"Not that I know of."

"How was she, by the way?"

"Meaning?"

"She wasn't acting strangely on the way home?"

"The only thing that's strange is the nature of your questions."

Someone guffawed on the far side of the room and I was pleased to have an excuse to look away from his critical stare. A pair of eyes was watching us, a sly-looking chap caught in a haze of hookah smoke. There was always the risk of a police officer in disguise, alerted to the latest den of inequity by some overly vigilant, God-fearing neighbour. As far as I was concerned, the officers jumped at the chance to enter our clubs and associate with the likes of us. Hypocrisy was a favourite of England's pastimes.

"It was a strange evening," I said, trying to regain my composure. "I wish I could make some sense of it."

"The sense has been made. Morrow Davenport turned up drunk and strangled Lucinda."

"You think it's as simple as that?"

"Don't you?"

"I struggle to believe he did it in such a short space of time."

"I'm not familiar with the typical length of strangulation."

"If truth be told," I said, trying to regain the upper hand, "Patrick asked me to enquire into Morrow's whereabouts, given he'd rather be murdered than frequent a place such as this. And I've been thinking a great deal about him."

"Patrick or Morrow?"

"The latter. My first thought concerns the fact he strangled her."

"Is that odd?"

"It is. Because, when he turned up that night I distinctly remember him threatening to shoot Lucy – and Lionel for that matter."

"Was he brandishing a gun?"

"No! But I know he has one." I briefly explained my prior visit to his flat. "And he might have had it on him that night, tucked away in a holster perhaps."

"Either way, he used his hands and not a bullet."

"Then why make such a thing about shooting them? It was a very specific threat to have made."

Theo tilted his head, neither agreeing nor disagreeing. "Your second thought?"

"That Morrow had an accomplice."

"What makes you think that?"

It was a risk, a decided risk, but then my entire life was one of those. I reached into my pocket and passed him the letter. He read it quickly.

"Where did you find this?" he asked.

I explained the curious case of the dropped letter.

"You really think it belongs to Agnes?"

"I did see her coming out of the cloakroom."

"You actually saw her emerge from the room?"

"Strictly speaking, I saw her closing the cloakroom door."

"The two are not the same, Mr Bigge."

"I am aware of that, no need to be pedantic."

"She'd hardly go into the cloakroom simply to drop a letter for you to conveniently stumble upon."

"She is known for dropping things."

"And then you took it for yourself."

"I did."

He shook his head and tutted. "Don't you think that was a stupid thing to do?"

"I have no intention of keeping it. I was thinking of passing it on to Patrick. He might be able to shed a little more light on it."

"I doubt it. He's currently nursing a bottle of gin in my bedroom. This week has torn the stuffing out of him."

"Then what do you suggest I do?"

He slipped the letter back across the table. I was quick to return it to my pocket, worried the man at the hookah pipe might still be watching.

"I suggest you tighten your hypothesis. Do you have any further evidence to incriminate Agnes in all this?"

"I caught her coming out the herb garden this afternoon," I replied. "She looked positively frightened. What if she'd been burying the phoney engagement ring Morrow had given her?"

"Any proof of said ring?"

"Um..."

"And if she were so fearful of disclosure, why did she hold on to this letter when she should have burnt it?"

"Because love is rare," I replied quietly, thinking on the times I'd held on to such a letter, greasy and creased from much fingering, only to burn it a few months later.

"You're clutching at straws, Mr Bigge."

"I'm investigating every angle."

"Are you sure you're not a policeman?"

"Of course I'm not. I knew Lucy was in danger, you see, and I tried to warn her but she dismissed me..." I suddenly paused as a memory returned – Lucy standing by the window in the drawing room telling me of her suspicions. "But she did say she thought Agnes might poison her one day."

"She really told you that?"

"Yes, and that Agnes rather liked her jewellery."

"And you're sure she was being serious?"

"Yes she... well... I think so."

"It's a strange thing to mention to a guest she hardly knew, don't you think?"

"Or she was confiding in me because she couldn't trust anyone else. A quiet plea for help but I didn't act. And now she's dead."

"You blame yourself?"

"I do," I confessed, nodding my head in shame.

"Don't be silly," he replied curtly. "The only one to blame is Morrow."

"Who is still on the loose while Agnes busies herself dusting the chandeliers. If I can stop them striking again, that will count for something."

"This isn't one of my aunt's books, you know. I don't think any of us who were there that night has an evil twin, let alone a triplet. She truly broke the bounds of credibility in *Smoke Up The Belfry*. But don't tell her I said that. As far as she knows, I'm her biggest fan. Nevertheless, having read enough crime novels for three lifetimes, I can inform you that you are making one very big assumption."

"Oh really?" I replied, trying not to sound indignant.

He took an indulgent sip of champagne and then another, just to wind me up no doubt.

"You are assuming that Morrow was the one that did the strangling."

My mouth gaped and no words proved forthcoming.

"Come on, it's obvious," he said, sounding just like one of my Oxford tutors. "It defies logistical sense for Morrow to run out the house, creep back in and lock Patrick in the tower, thereby achieving ten more impossible things before strangulation. Much simpler that he was the distraction designed to lure you from the house, a task he achieved with ease, while his accomplice did everything else."

"So... so... he was a decoy!"

Now Morrow's words made sense – *there you are* – because he really had been looking for me, simply to keep me as far from the billiard room as possible.

"I have to admit that's rather good," I confessed, noting the smug grin on his face, "but there is one flaw in your theory. Agnes's hands might lend themselves to administering poison, but they are much too small for strangulation."

The grin vanished and I found my eyes moving down to the table. Theo's hands were resting either side of his champagne glass; he had long elegant fingers with neat nails. As a man's hands, they were ordinary enough, but for a woman's they were rather large. I started to get hot under the collar thinking that Morrow's accomplice might be sitting opposite me. Theo started to laugh. He didn't stop; his face creasing, shoulders jostling and tears forming at the corners of his eyes.

"Oh dear," he said once he'd calmed down, "These!" He held his hands up for me to get a better look. "You think a woman capable of such a grisly thing?"

"But you aren't always a woman."

"Touché! But I was the night of the murder."

"You are tricksy!"

"I'm multitudinous."

He would have been a devil in a tutorial!

"You're still assuming Agnes is involved in the murder because you saw her standing outside the cloakroom," said Theo.

"And because of what Lucy said."

"Which may well have been said in jest."

I didn't deign to dignify that with a response.

"But don't you see, Mr Bigge?" he said. "It doesn't have to be Agnes. It could be anyone in that house."

"Which means Patrick isn't living with the accomplice, he's living with the murderer! Don't you think we should warn him?"

"He's fragile enough as it is, but if you want to be the bearer of such news... And you can explain your theft of the letter. To be quite honest, you're the one acting suspiciously."

"Says the baron's daughter in man's clothing."

"My father is a baronet and tonight I am a baronet's son in man's clothing. I am not a woman who dresses as a man, I am a woman who dresses as a woman and a man who dresses as a man."

"You're multitudinous."

"Exactly! See, sometimes your wit can be as sharp as your tongue."

Down went the champagne and up went Theo. I followed him to the little hole in the wall that led into the cloakroom. Inside, a middle-aged chap with pince-nez was huddled over a small desk reading something. He looked just like a mole as he scurried off to find our items. I glanced at his reading material and blushed when I spied the black-and-white photographic image of a man wearing only a garland of flowers.

"A fine model," said the mole as he handed over our coats and hats, still damp. "And such a big one!"

"Rather," I concurred and Theo laughed. "Say, I have a question for you?"

"Tuppence," he said.

"I beg your pardon?"

"Tuppence for the photograph or thruppence for two."

"Oh no, that's quite all right," I replied, blushing more deeply. "I wanted to ask about that Hampstead murder."

The chap leaned forward, readjusting the pince-nez on his nose. "I'm all ears."

"I was simply wondering whether he'd ever been here."

"Who?"

"Morrow Davenport."

"A murderer, here! That would be some news." He shook his head and chortled. "Never seem him, never want to. The only thing that's ever been murdered here is fashion."

Coats retrieved, we descended the stairs.

"It was worth a shot," I said defensively.

"If you say so."

Downstairs, Charlie the doorman was having another heated conversation with someone outside.

"Not tonight."

"But I've got my two shillings," came a high-pitched response.

"I said, not tonight."

"Excuse me," announced Theo boldly as Charlie stepped aside to let us through.

On the pavement stood a most striking chap with bright-red lips, smudged blue eyes and powdered pink hair. There was a touch of effeminacy, then there was a whole smothering of it; the effect was quite stunning. It took great risk to present in such a style, even a place like the River Styx could be unkind to more feminine men. The underworld had its hierarchies and they could be policed just as strictly as those of the overworld.

"Stop being such a rotter, Charlie, and just bloody let them in."

The beauty gave Theo a little curtsy as we dashed away into the drizzle.

CHAPTER 15

I first touched a penis that wasn't my own when I was thirteen, three years after the outbreak of war. I can still picture the soldiers and the uniforms they wore, with ironed trousers especially tight around their buttocks. I remember their families waving them off with smiles and tears, and how those smiles faded over the years and the tears were kept for private moments locked in the water closet or shut in the larder. My father didn't fight due to his health, and oh, how that shamed him. He took it out on the rest of us and my canings came more often and more fiercely. The supply of butter and cheese diminished with time, as did the amount of meat in the cook's stew. My friends lost brothers, fathers and uncles. I prayed God would send me to the front and let me shoot a Hun or two, to make up for my father's shame. I wondered sometimes what the soldiers might get up to in those trenches far from their wives and sweethearts.

Despite the war, West Sussex retained its rural charm; it was a place of rolling downs and fields, farmed by the same families for generations, many of whom stored what little wealth they had at the local banks – including the one at which my father worked. He made a point of attending the various agricultural fairs and markets in his bowler hat and suit, thinking himself some minor honorary, and even then I knew enough to be embarrassed. I'll never forget that overcast Saturday afternoon. The market stalls were lacklustre, including the butcher's, who had a few ropey cuts of pork on offer. That's when I caught his eye. A pretty young lad my age with dark brown hair and blood-smeared cheeks. What excited me the most was that the catching of eyes was mutual. I made a point of remembering the name of the farm the pork belonged to and, later that summer, after a number of hikes in wrong directions and some nasty scrapes with brambles, I finally found him. He was pleased to see me and we enjoyed a brilliant half-hour tugging each other off in a hay barn. He even kissed one of my bramble scratches to make it better.

If my fate had been sealed from birth then that was the moment the hot wax was stamped. I liked girls well enough and knew one day I would marry one, but that summer, stinking of sweat and with the taste of his mouth in mine, I discovered I liked boys too. I was too young and politely bred to have heard the words invert or pervert, and had no idea that men who played with other men were a whole subcategory of moral disdain. I had no idea that penal servitude and hard physical labour could be the consequences of such an act. It was hardly the thing my family discussed at the dinner table. Nor did I pause to think whether it was in my nature to be inclined to the same sex or if

I had some horrible disease. I knew God condemned pleasure and that sex was strictly for conjugal procreation but in that barn, with our cocks out, nothing seemed depraved at all. It was just jolly good fun.

Looking back, I considered myself lucky to have discovered that truth when I was an adolescent. I wasn't a criminal guilty of perversion, I was just a lad enjoying his summer. It was that innocence, untainted by the moral dictums of the adult world, which ensured I did not grow up to become one of the many, many men who hated themselves for such desires. Unfortunately, Patrick had. I was looking down at him, curled up in bed, clutching a half-empty bottle of gin.

"That was full when I gave it to him," said Theo.

We'd returned to the squat house with the green door but the fact he owned a house went unexplained. Oh to have been born into wealth!

"He looks dreadful," I said.

Patrick was pale-faced and huddled up like a foetus, still in his shirt and trousers, with the bedsheets rumpled around him. Yet, despite the disarray, he retained his angelic charm. His tousled hair asked to be patted back into place and that creased brow simply begged to be smoothed with a stroke. As for those soft lips... I pulled myself together and surveyed the rest of the bedroom. It was typically artsy with ill-matching furniture, large fans mounted on the walls and a painting above the fireplace of a woman reclining naked (fortunately it wasn't Theodora). Ashtrays and dog-eared paperbacks littered the floor. I spied a number of Stubbs and a Conan Doyle for good measure.

"We'll have to wake him up soon," said Theo.

"We can't let him sleep?"

"And insinuate sex before marriage!"

"But you're bohemian."

"And my parents are Victorian."

"He can't stay at mine," I said. "The insinuations would be even worse. I swear my landlady puts glasses to the walls."

"Darling, I was hardly suggesting that. He'll go home."

"Back to the lion's den!"

"Shh, keep your voice down."

Patrick stirred on the bed, letting out a childish whimper.

"Look, Agnes isn't going to strangle him in his sleep and Morrow, if he has any sense, is as far from that house as possible," said Theo. "That letter might have nothing to do with all this. Maybe Agnes has an entirely different lover?"

"Which would be rather the coincidence."

"Life is full of them."

He stared at me. His eyes were brown and knowing, and I wondered how I must look from his perspective. I had tried to play the charming, aloof chum of Patrick, but I feared he saw straight through that to the boy from Horsham.

"Selby?"

"Patrick, oh gosh, I'm so dreadfully sorry, I didn't mean to wake you."

"What are... you... here?"

His voice was slurred. He tried to prop himself up into a sitting position but didn't have much luck.

"I, um, I bumped into Theo at..."

"We met at the Styx," said Theo calmly. "Don't worry, Pat, he's one of us."

"I already knew that."

I sometimes wondered if there was a sign above my head, written in big lavender letters.

"We're going to take you home."

"We are?" I said, trying to sound calm.

"I'll whizz us up the hill in my new motor, but you'll have to take him to the front door. I can hardly be seen escorting my drunken fiancée back to his house."

"But what should I say?"

"That you two were having a few drinks at the Bullion, weren't you?"

"If you say so."

"That's the ticket."

"I don't want to go home," complained Patrick, closing his eyes and dropping his head back onto the pillow.

"Oh no you don't."

Theo and I manoeuvred Patrick into a sitting position. It was tough going and much more physical exertion than I cared for after ten o'clock in the evening. He wasn't exactly a dead weight but he wasn't much help either. Once we had him upright with his legs over the side of the bed, Theo went off to get his car out the garage while I laced his shoes. It seemed a strangely intimate act, the sort of thing I might do for an ailing lover, if it weren't for the reek of gin and Patrick's irregular hiccupping. I wondered if similar things had happened to him at university: wild parties, lots of drinking and waking up with a terrible hangover, next to someone. I dismissed such thoughts. Patrick wasn't the type to let himself run wild. No, his secret was kept, the wildness ran riot within.

"I don't want to go home," he repeated.

"I'm sure you've got a nice cosy bed waiting for you."

"It's not safe."

I looked up at him and he looked genuinely scared. The events of the last week had clearly taken their toll.

"Why is it not safe, Patrick?"

"Because they'll find out."

"Who?"

"The police, the journalists, they'll find me out."

"They won't, I promise," I said, trying to sound reassuring. "You've got to keep your cards close to your chest and hold them there, come what may."

I wondered if I was talking more to myself than to him. A short while later Theo re-entered the room, looking every bit the son of a baronet, albeit a decidedly queer one.

"You ready, boys?"

"No," said Patrick petulantly.

"None of that, it's time to get you home."

I walked away from the bed towards Theo, deftly navigating the paperback obstacle course. I stopped between *The Valley of Fear* and *Decapitated In Devon*, the latter a sequel to *Coshed In Cornwall*.

"Theo, are you quite sure this is a good idea?"

"Quite sure."

"We'll be driving through the dark to the scene of a murder."

"Then how about some protection?"

He went over to the bedside table, opened the top drawer and produced a pistol – a dainty thing with a mother-of-pearl handle.

"I say," I exclaimed. "Does everyone own a gun these days?"

"Yes. Don't you?"

"I don't, as a matter of fact."

"You must ask Saint Nick."

"I don't believe in him any more."

"Poor Selby. Shall we?"

"We shall," I replied, finding his enthusiasm both irksome and infectious.

We looked to the drunken chap on the bed. He groaned and flopped back onto the sheets.

"Up you get," commanded Theo. "We've got a criminal to catch."

"We *are* criminals," he moaned.

The stairs proved the unwritten thirteenth labour of Hercules as I went in front and Theo behind, but somehow we got Patrick to the bottom without landing in a heap of tangled limbs and broken bones. We paused to catch our breaths in the narrow hallway, Patrick's arms slumped over our shoulders and our arms around his waist. Theo opened the little front door and out we shuffled. The motor was near to hand – a Crossley, I believe, as dark green as the door. We stuffed our charge into the back seat and took ours in the front.

"I am grateful for your doing this, Selby," said Theo, his voice lowered.

"What, delivering Patrick to his death?"

"Gin will kill him before the parlour maid does. And while I know it was you who found us tonight," he said pointedly, and I hoped Patrick was too far gone to catch his drift, "I'd appreciate it if no one else were to find out what you have."

"Your secrets are safe with me," I replied solemnly. "As I'm sure mine is with you."

"It is."

The car juddered into life as we bumped over the cobbles of the mews. Soon we were winding our way back through the city's dreary streets. The rain splashed against the windows as I marvelled on the night's turn of events – Theodora's second identity, the sham engagement, and now risking life and limb to put Patrick to bed. I turned in my seat and saw him slumped awkwardly in the back seat, his eyes closed and head lolling against the window. The things I did for the hope of a kiss!

"Where are your digs?" asked Theo.

"Pimlico."

"I'll drop you home once we've dealt with our luggage."

"Right ho."

"And how can I get hold of you should I need?"

I told him the telephone number of the house. "It's Miss Wickler who'll pick up," I said. "She's a nosy old bat, you'll have to be discreet."

"Discretion is my watchword."

"Touché!"

The lights of London dimmed as the houses and gas lamps were replaced by the great, murky expanse of the Heath. For many, the darkness was threatening but for those like me it was an opportunity, even on a night such as this. We were beetling down Spaniards Road when Patrick groaned.

"Everything all right back there?" asked Theo.

He groaned again, louder.

"We're almost there."

"I'm going to be sick," he announced.

"Not on my upholstery, you're not."

The car came to an abrupt halt and, by some miracle of physical dexterity for a man who was most parts gin, Patrick opened the door and leapt out. The ensuing retching noises were rather disgusting so I shall not describe them but, suffice it to say, what was down remained so.

"Everything all right, Pat?"

There was no answer.

"Pat?"

More silence. Theo stuck his head out the car.

"Bugger. Where is he?"

We leapt from the car into the gloom. Theo kept the headlamps on, but Patrick had vanished. We called after him but to no avail.

"Selby, you go up the road. I'll go down. Call if you find him."

"Yes, sir."

A chilly gust of wind blew rain into my face as I set off up the road. A voice in my head reprimanded me for being such an utter fool but I'd long ago learned to ignore it. Why would he disappear like this when he knew he was in danger? A noise sounded from up ahead and my jog became a run. I heard lumbering footsteps.

"Patrick, is that you?"

The footsteps quickened but I was soon behind him. I reached out and my hand touched his shoulder. He shrugged it off and veered away from the road, crashing through the foliage. Beyond was the Heath extension and, if he wasn't careful, he'd fall down a nasty slope. He wasn't careful.

"Patrick," I called as I stared into the gloom. "Patrick!"

I could hear him swearing as I ambled, very slowly, down the decline that led from the road into the woods. Dead leaves squelched underfoot and a wet branch almost took my hat off. I guided myself between the tree trunks and eventually reached what I assumed was some semblance of a path. Along with Golders Hill and the Heath proper, this was my usual hunting ground, except my prey usually wanted to be caught. I heard Theo calling my name.

"I'm down here," I called. "He's run off."

My eyes were slowly adjusting, according me a view of varying shades of darkness.

"Patrick?"

A loud retching was the reply. I followed the sound and spied a moving shadow not too far away.

"Patrick, are you all right?"

"I… I'm…" He retched again without any success.

"We need to get you home."

"I am going home." He spoke with the usual petulance of a drunkard.

"You don't live in the woods."

"Yes I do."

He was right, as a matter of fact; his father's house backed onto the extension. But how the devil he'd find it in this state, I did not know.

"You can't go alone, it's dangerous."

Off he went, staggering through the undergrowth. Brambles and bushes impeded our progress and my shoes were soaked through. There was nothing worse than soggy socks. And I had no idea where I'd left my umbrella.

"Ow," I exclaimed, bumping into Patrick's back.

"Selby?" he asked, as if suddenly aware of my existence.

"Come on, back to the car."

"You must go." His words were sharper now, tinged with panic.

"Don't be an ass. I said I'd help."

The night ate his silence. I wished I could see his face, to be able to read the look there and provide a reassuring one of my own.

"I never should have got you involved in all this."

"But I wanted to help," I said. "You know that."

"Because you remember that bench by the pond."

My heart sang and suddenly his hands were at my jacket lapels and he was pulling me towards him. I was startled but only for a moment as his warm, moist lips pressed up against mine. His kiss was strong and tasted of gin. I kissed him back, trying to match his vigour. There was desperation in his gesture too, like a thirsty man finally able to slake his thirst. I thought of all those long, lonely nights and cold, empty mornings; the walks in the park and all those happy couples arm in arm, and my own entirely empty. Until finally, I had someone to touch and hold and squeeze, even if it was in the dark.

"Patrick, are you sure?" I asked, tilting my head back.

His answer was to find my lips again. His hands moved across my chest, almost clawing at the layers of jacket, shirt and vest, as if he hoped to tear them away to reach my skin. What I did in response was, in hindsight, foolish, but as we'd gone from zero to fifty in a matter of seconds I'd assumed he was game. I forgot he was an innocent and not one of the many cruising gentlemen who knew what he was looking for. Nevertheless, I let my hands go wandering and, more adept at these things than he, I quickly unbuttoned the front of his coat and jacket. His lips pushed harder, surely as encouragement. I had easy access to his belt, which I loosened, and to his fly, which I unzipped. Then I was groping within, trying to find the opening in his underwear. He bit down on my lower lip, which really rather hurt. Then I had it!

After all this time and all my fantasising, I finally had Patrick Duker's member in my hand and it was as soft as an uncooked sausage. I had to confess to being disappointed, given mine was as hard as a stick of rock, but I gave it a squeeze and a tug and still nothing happened. He just needed some encouragement, it was a cold night and I doubted he'd ever partaken of such an alfresco activity in the woods. For a flaccid one, it was decently sizeable, and I gently navigated the foreskin up and down in the hope of stimulating some pleasure. That's when he gasped.

"Patrick, are you all right?"

Perhaps my icy hand had given him a shock. And it was raining. Nothing worse than a cold, damp cock.

"I… I can't," he stammered. "Father wouldn't approve."

"Let's not think about him."

"The family's in enough trouble as it is. I can't bring more."

"No one needs to find out."

"I can't!"

His words were quieter as he turned around and started walking away.

"Patrick, please…"

His walk became a run and the darkness was quick to gobble

him up. I tried to follow the sounds of his crashing footsteps but promptly banged my knee against something unrelentingly hard.

"Bloody hell," I moaned. I kicked out at whatever it was, managing only to stub my toe. By now I had no clue where I was and Patrick was all but gone. My heart deliberated between racing for the finish line or quitting the race. Too much had happened in such a short space of time, but I could still feel the warm skin of his penis in the palm of my hand, as well as the taste of gin in my mouth.

"Patrick?" I called, but to no avail.

"Selby!" came another reply.

"Theo!"

"Where are you?"

"Over here!"

We traipsed our way through the undergrowth, navigating by the sounds of our voices, which seemed to be bouncing off the trees with carefree abandon. At one point I approached a human-ish sized slab of darkness only to have my fingers pricked – a damned holly bush. A pair of lights floated through the distance, either angels come down to take me to heaven or a pair of headlamps. The former proved unlikely given I was destined for hell and the latter briefly lit the trees and bushes.

"There you are," said Theo, closer to hand than I'd realised. "Did you find him?"

"I did, but he ran off again."

"Damn him. Which way?"

"I have no…"

Something loud interrupted me, tearing through the drizzle

and the night. It fell silent as quick as it had sounded, leaving only my echoing breath to fill the void. I had no idea what direction it had come from but it had been bloody loud, like a small explosion.

"Crikey, what was that?" exclaimed Theo.

"A firework?"

"It's October, too early for Guy Fawkes."

"A car backfiring?"

"Or smacking into my motor."

We hurried through the woods until we stumbled upon the slope leading back up to the road. Walking closely to one another, so as not to get lost again, we guided ourselves back by the headlamps of the Crossley.

"Thank heavens she's all right," said Theo, getting back into the driver's seat. "I'll take you home."

"What about Patrick?"

"Pat be damned. If he wants to play silly buggers, he can do it alone."

CHAPTER 16

I was semi-erect. I'd fallen asleep thinking of Patrick and I woke thinking of him too – the brush of his lips against mine, the grip of his hands and the feel of his cold, flaccid member. My juices stirred as I slowly slipped my hand under the blankets. I was lying in my narrow, single bed in the attic, the flimsy curtains not much protection against the grey light of morning. I struggled with the buttons at my pyjama trouser fly but once they were undone I got hold of my person. At Bledwood, one particularly devout vicar had sermonised on the dangers of onanism and how it resulted in all manner of ills, including blindness. But for those of us who'd put it to the test, we found our sight remained intact. I had been caught off guard the first time I'd ejaculated, not realising that was the result of said activity, but I soon got the hang of it. The trouble with my attic bed was the hinges, which squeaked at the mere thought of my shifting position. My member stiffened in my hand and I began to rub, very slowly. Patrick returned to my thoughts and I tried to forget his erratic behaviour and enjoy the feel of his hands against my chest. It had not been the most auspicious of starts but he remembered. I finally had something to hold on to.

"Mr Bigge?"

Bloody hell!

"Yoo-hoo, Mr Bigge?"

My hand darted from under the covers, the hinges positively shrieked.

"Yoo-hoo!"

"Good morning, Miss Wickler," I called, trying not to sound too alarmed.

"Oh yes, it is still morning."

I heard her ascend the narrow wooden stairs that led from the first floor to the attic. I willed my erection to subside but the thing was rather stubborn. She wouldn't come in though; it would be unbecoming for her to enter my room.

"There's someone on the telephone for you. A woman."

She spoke the final word as any woman raised during Queen Victoria's reign would.

"Perhaps it's a wrong number," I said, stalling for time.

"I don't think so, she was most insistent she speak with you."

Blast! In our great war of attrition, Miss Wickler was always the victor. There'd be no avoiding this one. I pulled back the sheets, mortified at the sight of my own penis.

"My sister, perhaps?"

"I don't believe so."

I leapt from the bed, narrowly avoiding sticking my right foot in the chamber pot, and reached for my dressing gown.

"Must be the lady at the library about an overdue book."

"On a Saturday?"

My cock was still hard as a rock, and I pushed it up against my tummy and restrained it with the cord of the pyjama bottoms before wrapping myself in the dressing gown and using that cord for further reinforcement. If the thing leapt free it would give Miss Wickler a heart attack.

"Did she give a name?"

"She did, yes."

My mind boggled. Who would be ringing me here?

"And it was?"

"Miss Smythe."

"Ah, yes, sister of a dear friend. He's in bad health."

I had given her the number last night but why on earth was she ringing me? I'd told her only to call in emergencies.

"Oh dear, your poor friend."

I put my cold feet into my slippers, gave myself the once over and emerged from the room. Miss Wickler was the sort of nondescript older woman who could be anywhere between forty and seventy. There was grey in her hair but still plenty of black, and the lines on her face were the result of frowning, which she often did when conversing with me.

"Oh, you're not decent," she said, quickly averting her gaze and scurrying back down the stairs. "Really, Mr Bigge, you might have told me."

Each word was like a woodpecker striking bark and, talking of wood, mine was thankfully beginning to subside.

"Terribly sorry, Miss Wickler, I've got an awful head you see, barely slept a wink."

"You were out rather late last night," she replied, quickly forgetting my lack of suitable attire.

"Trouble at the office. We're down a few men and, you know how it is, money never sleeps."

"So you've told me before."

I crossed her on the landing, passing through a waft of lavender and flour. One thing in her favour, aside from the lower rent than other places, was her baking. She made a drop scone to die for and her Victoria sponge was pure nectar.

"She sounded quite upset," she twittered, following me down the stairs.

"Her poor brother might have taken a turn for the worse."

"It's not the flu, is it?"

"Tuberculosis."

"How dreadful! You haven't seen him recently, have you?"

"No, he's been cooped up in a hospital for a long time."

My lies came as fast as her questions and, given she was prone to asking so many, I had, over the time I'd lived with her, acquired two aunts, a dead uncle and a number of acquaintances in far-flung places. *How's that friend of yours in India?* she'd asked the other day. *India?* I'd said. *The one who went to work for the consulate.* Fortunately I'd been keeping tabs on my lies in a notebook I kept hidden under the bed. *Oh, Marcus*, I'd replied, before regaling her of the two entirely fictitious children he'd had with a local woman. That had shut her up, momentarily.

"Good. I wouldn't want you bringing any nasty diseases into my house."

"Quite right, Miss Wickler. Health and sanitation are my watchwords."

The hallway was a long corridor with a floor of clay-red tiles. The telephone was on a little wooden table just next to the door that led into the living room, ensuring Miss W a prime spot to listen from. Once, I'd foolishly given the number to a staggeringly beautiful young man (an opportunity I simply couldn't miss), who'd proceeded to phone during one of my landlady's weekly games of mah-jong. That took some explaining.

"Thank you, Miss Wickler. I'll take it from here."

I lifted the receiver but waited a moment for her to scuttle down the corridor towards the kitchen, which had a door that led into the dining room, which had a door that led into the living room. All the doors had very well-oiled hinges. As for that which had recently been standing to attention, it was now hanging at ease.

"Hullo, Theodora, everything all right?"

"Who on earth was that woman?"

"That would be Miss Wickler, my delightful landlady."

"She was most impertinent."

"She loves getting to know people."

"She enquired into my marital status."

"Delightfully friendly."

Theodora coughed her disapproval. Setting her against Miss Wickler would make for an interesting match. The latter had age but the former had entitlement.

"Selby, something awful has happened."

The tone of the conversation immediately took on a darker turn.

"Oh dear, not Patrick?"

"No, Davenport."

"They've found him?"

"They've found him dead!"

I managed to pinch myself before bellowing the word *dead* down the hall.

"What happened?"

"I shan't explain on the telephone. Meet me at the National Gallery café at half past twelve, their Earl Grey is sublime."

She hung up without waiting for my reply. I looked to the grandfather clock that took up too much space in the hallway and it read ten minutes to eleven, plenty of time.

"Your friend has taken a turn for the worse?"

Miss Wickler materialised behind me like some phantom apparition. She must have heard the receiver click, ears like a hare.

"Drastically so, I must be off at once."

"I'm making blackberry and apple crumble if you'd care for some."

"I would, but I don't have a moment to spare. When I'm back."

"If that could be a little earlier than last night, I would most greatly appreciate it. Those attic stairs do creak and you know I'm such a light sleeper."

Liar. She went to bed with a brick tied to her back so she could stay awake listening for my footfalls.

She was pretty enough, with flowing auburn hair and a dash of colour on her smooth, pale cheeks. The green scales on her lower legs were less attractive, but they were necessary. Other than a lyre, she was completely naked. A single hand covered most of her breasts as she plucked at her instrument's strings;

there was only a suggestion of nipple, but those Victorians had to get their pleasures somewhere. Too artistic to be considered pornographic, I liked it not for the nudity but for the drama. While she sat on a rock, so there was a man at her feet, almost entirely submerged in water. A young sailor, whose ship had run aground, lured to its fate by her sweet playing. He too had long hair, dark, and a gold ring in one of his ears. If he weren't drowning, he would have been quite pleasant to look at. A bit of broken wood from his ship floated nearby and in the distance loomed great cliffs.

I'd arrived at the National Gallery long before Theodora and taken myself to the paintings. It was a regular pastime of mine, especially good for escaping the chill of an autumn afternoon. I had trailed the parquet floors of the gallery rooms, passing through the grand pillared doorways and under the vaulted ceilings, some of which contained glass to let in the natural light, or what was left of it given the thick clouds. Couples walked arm in arm, and clusters of women huddled together. I wondered how many animals had been slain to line the trims of their coats; at least a schooner's worth of mink. There was the odd solitary figure such as myself, some military codger with a walking stick and a bad cough, and a middle-aged sort of man with a neat beard. He had given me a nod as he passed by and I'd returned it.

My weekends in London varied. Sometimes I was invited to luncheon by my colleagues, other times I made the fateful trip home for a Sunday roast, but I regularly found myself alone. It was difficult keeping friends in the fey world, a mercurial place that was never allowed to stand still. The occasional cinema visit proved distracting from my loneliness, especially if it was the Trocadero, when the distraction was much more stimulating. But there was only so much Charlie Chaplin I cared for, likewise the imminent threat of arrest. Today's purpose was different; I had come to find *The Siren*. Lucy had said she'd seen it when she visited the gallery and here it was, in all its splendour. I loved the mythic stuff: beautiful nymphs and alluring naiads; strong heroes and vengeful gods; battles of epic proportions as Zeus rained lightning from the sky and Roman warriors fought for glory.

I seated myself on one of those funny oblong sofas that are much too close to the ground and have incredibly low backs. *The Siren* was dead in front of me. Looking at it now, I thought of Patrick's disparaging remarks about his late stepmother. For him, she had been a harpy ruining his father's life, but her intent had never been malevolent and now she too was a tragic figure, a true Eurydice. She had spoken to me of a shadow, the sense that someone had followed her to the gallery. She even thought it might have been Patrick, so desperate to find proof of her supposed adultery. What if it had been Morrow, stalking his prey, before he too became the quarry? I started as I felt something press briefly against my back. The person on the other side had clearly leant back too far and brushed up against me.

"Terribly sorry," said the other, and I turned to see the man with the neat beard. The look passed between us again.

"Not to worry."

"Such wonderful paintings."

"They are, but I really must be on my way."

"Must you?" he asked.

"I must."

To a passer-by our conversation would have appeared formal and nothing of note but my heart was thumping as I assumed his was too. It would have been simple enough to wander off into another gallery, looking back at the opportune moment to encourage him to follow. We might have ended up admiring the same painting, standing a few yards apart, and then worked our way back downstairs and outside to somewhere more suitable. And at every step we would have been looking over our shoulders to make sure no over-zealous member of the public was watching, an awful diehard from the Purity League or the National Vigilance Committee, ready to write a letter to the management of the gallery and another to the police.

Avoiding one temptation, I headed for another, the café. Theodora had not needed to tell me it did the best Earl Grey in town because I already knew. With its high ceilings, huge sash windows and marble-topped tables, the restaurant was a splendid one. The scones were motive for murder in themselves, served with gooey strawberry jam and crusty clotted cream. I found Theodora tucked away in one of the rare corners, a pot of tea already on the table with two cups. She wore a rather fetching cloche hat with a little feather tucked into it and her lips were redder than usual. If I didn't know better, I would have mistaken her for a normal.

"It's been brewing for four minutes," she said as I took a seat. "Should be ready."

"I leave it for five."

"Really."

She poured us both a cup and left me to choose between milk or a slice of lemon. I opted for the former and she the latter. The amber turned ochre as I stirred the brew with a teaspoon.

"It's a shame they don't do a smoky one," said Theodora after her first sip. "Because then they might be able to give Fortnum's a run for their money."

"Do you go to Fortnum's often?"

"On occasion. I find one can overdo a good thing."

"I couldn't agree more."

She gave me a withering look of appraisal, accompanied by the chatter of the other guests and the clinking of crockery, and I dreaded to think the conclusions she was drawing. Theo hadn't been quite so prickly. She leant forward and indicated for me to do the same.

"I found out this morning," she said.

"How?"

"Patrick rang. He sounded dreadful. Chief Inspector Bile arrived at some godforsaken hour to inform Sir Lionel of the news."

"It's Lisle, I think."

"I prefer Bile."

"What else did he tell you?"

Her cup paused halfway from its saucer to her lips, the tendrils of steam gathering around her face for dramatic effect. She had quite the piercing gaze.

"He told me how he died: a gunshot to the temple. The police are calling it suicide."

"Suicide!?"

"He'd been staying in some awful guesthouse in Limehouse,

which is reason enough to take one's life. The chief inspector thinks he did it out of guilt. Overcome by a most convenient fit of remorse, he returned to the scene of the crime and offed himself."

"He went back into the house and shot himself?"

"Not quite, his body was found by an early morning dog walker on the Heath."

My fingers tightened on the handle of the teacup and I was quick to let go in case I snapped it off. Something between dread and panic started in my belly and worked its way up to my throat. I dug my nails into the leather of the seat and tried to keep my breathing steady.

"On... on the Heath you say?"

She nodded ever so slightly.

"Did... did we hear the shot?"

"I think we did."

Her deep, brown eyes were wide and she looked as shocked as I did. Gone was the aloof child of a peer; now she looked simply worried.

"Oh God," I said. "What if Patrick had been shot and we'd just abandoned him to the killer. I warned you!"

"Don't make a scene. Patrick is alive and well."

"What if *I'd* been shot?"

"Then I'd give a most moving eulogy. How were we to know Morrow was hiding in the trees, busily killing himself?"

"You can't really believe it was suicide."

"I don't. Far simpler to take a number of pills at home or do the deed in the bath with a..."

I winced, holding up a hand to stop her going on. "I'm well aware of how people kill themselves."

Suicide amongst my kind was not uncommon. While the chosen methods tended to differ, the motivations were always the same – the avoidance of exposure and complete social ruin. Some thought suicide an honourable way out; I wasn't one of them. There had been someone at Oxford, a chap I was friends with, and his death had revealed to me quite how tragic it all was. I preferred not to dwell on that aspect of my time at university.

"I'm sorry if I spoke too flippantly," she said, a little cowed. "I'm afraid flippancy is how us Smythes survive."

"It's quite all right," I lied. "Much more important is working out what on earth happened last night."

"I shan't for one second believe it was an accident. That would be a most monstrous coincidence. So there's only one thing it can be."

"Oh dear God..." I couldn't bring myself to finish the sentence.

"What's the matter, tea too hot?"

"Patrick."

"What about him?"

"What if he shot Morrow?"

"Hardly," she replied dismissively. "He was as drunk as a fishwife and had no gun on his person."

"But you did."

"And I was standing right next to you when we heard the shot. I'm many things, Mr Bigge, but a magician is not one of them. How about you stop accusing me and my pals of murder?"

"Good idea." I took a ruminative sip of tea. "Someone else we know who owns, well, owned a gun, was Morrow."

"So he brought it last night. Why?"

I tried to imagine things from his perspective – on the run, wanted for murder and with the entirety of the Metropolitan Police force out looking for him. Returning to the scene of the crime was a dangerous risk, he must have been desperate…

"That's it!" I forced myself to keep my voice down, as excited as I was by this new chain of logic. "He was after his second victim."

"He was?" Her neatly sculpted eyebrows rose in surprise.

"Yes! He was tying up loose ends, or at least trying to."

"What loose ends?"

"Silencing the only other person instrumental in the death of Lucinda Duker."

"His accomplice."

"What if they'd arranged to meet on the Heath, Morrow having spun some lie about running away together for warmer climes. Then he takes out his gun, ready to commit a second murder, but something goes wrong, there's a tussle in the dark and *bang*, goodnight Morrow."

"Very good, Father Brown, but why would they arrange to meet on the Heath? It's too conspicuous."

"Maybe they had no choice. Maybe the accomplice couldn't be too far from their place of work, the Duker household."

"Surely even a servant would travel further afield for that," she replied, quick to dampen my enthusiasm. "Hiding amongst the trees for a moonlit chat with a fellow murderer does seem a little conspicuous."

"Or it was the other way around and the accomplice had lured Morrow up to the house."

"Why?"

"Perhaps they were threatening to expose him."

"At risk of exposing themselves too?" She checked herself. Our voices had risen in the heat of the moment, but no one seemed to be eavesdropping. "There are too many holes in this, Selby. We can't even be sure he had an accomplice."

"But the letter."

"Could have been written by someone else."

"Precisely, *to* Morrow *from* the accomplice."

"You still have no proof that letter has anything to with these ghastly deaths."

"What about the strange marks on the cloakroom key?"

"What about them?"

"Oh, I don't know," I said, a little exasperatedly, hoping something would have clicked into place by now. "We might as well go back to square one."

"Would that be such a bad idea?"

My tummy grumbled, protesting at the lack of breakfast and the large quantity of alcohol the night before. A teacake would have gone down a treat but I thought better of summoning a waiter. A rather alarming idea occurred to me. "Actually, it's a very good idea," I said, leaning even further across the grey- and black-streaked marble table. "Because there's an even bigger assumption everyone is making."

"What's that?"

"That Morrow had anything to do with Lucy's death."

I had stunned her into silence. I was quite pleased with myself.

"The police are full of it, the newspapers too, even my colleagues at the bank. It's the logical conclusion, after all. He turns up drunk, hurling insults at the woman he hates and a few minutes later she's dead. But what if he had nothing to do with it and there wasn't an accomplice either?"

"You're suggesting she strangled herself?"

"What if someone else used Morrow's arrival as cover to commit the crime? An opportunist of the highest order."

"What a risk!"

"Indeed, but the opportunity might never have arisen again and all they'd need would be a few minutes alone with Lucy."

The Duker household flashed back into my memory – the grand billiard room, the unlocked French windows and Lucy's bloodied eyeball winking at me. I pictured her alone in the water closet, tending to the cut on her hand, and the door slowly opening behind her. The assailant wrapping his hands around her neck, a struggle, staggering backwards into the corridor and then into the billiard room, the curtains opened...

"What if he saw?" I said, feeling rather excited.

"What?"

"Morrow snuck up on me that night but, before he did, he must have passed the billiard room."

"Must he? I thought the police found a footprint in a flowerbed on the other side of the house."

"They did, but he might have doubled back on himself."

"He might have, emphasis on the word *might*. Then what?"

"Then he might have paused to look through the billiard room French windows, the curtains open, and within he might have seen Lucy..."

"... and whoever it was strangling her."

"Exactly."

"Then what?" asked Theodora breathlessly, coming around to my hypothesis.

"What would you do if you saw a murder taking place?"

"Telephone the police!"

"But you're a reputable citizen, more or less."

"Takes one to know one," she retorted.

"If you were Morrow, facing a court case and possible financial ruin at the hands of Sir Lionel, what would you do?"

"Blackmail!"

"Exactly. A few days later, he gets in touch with Lucy's strangler, reveals his fee and they arrange to meet for the relevant exchange of funds, and *bang*."

"Curtains for Morrow."

"Two bodies, one killer. But the question remains…"

"Who?"

We sat back in our chairs and eyed the high ceiling, as if the murderer's name might conveniently be written there in red paint. Half a dozen pigeons – the rats of the sky as I called them – flew past one of the windows.

"Let's be methodical."

"Let's," said Theodora sarcastically.

"Who had a motive for killing Lucy?"

"*Who didn't* is probably the easier question."

"Sir Lionel," I said.

"Hardly, husbands murder their wives all the time. He's our most likely suspect."

"But he loved her and that love was reciprocated."

"Then that makes him the least likely suspect, which also means he did it."

"I thought you said this wasn't one of your aunt's novels."

She grinned and I was glad to have scored a point.

"Do you know, he's the only person to mourn her death," I said. "No one else seems to care tuppence."

"Do you?"

"I do, as a matter of fact. In the brief time I knew her she was kind to me. She understood, a little, of what my life is like."

"If you say so," she said, not bothering to hide her scepticism.

"Not everyone is a heartless aristocrat, Theodora."

"I am not heartless," she protested.

Now it was my turn to not hide my scepticism.

"A woman has been murdered," she said. "And although I did not like said woman, I find our kind are killed much too often in this city. Our deaths are either ignored or treated as a spectacle. I've read what the journalists are saying. All they care about is what lesson her murder has to teach other loose women."

"Yet you thought her a gold-digger."

"I did and I was right to. But unlike the journalists, all male I can assure you, I didn't blame her. Isn't it the dream of every Englishman to be rich? But when an Englishwoman achieves such a feat, they hate her for it. We aren't all born to wealth and I can hardly blame her for wanting more. Tell me, Selby, if our country's laws permitted and Patrick offered you his hand in marriage, would you turn down the Duker kingdom?"

I almost spat tea all over one of the nearby tables. "Honestly! Even if such a thing were possible, I would only marry Patrick for love."

"Please! I know you're far more taken with his pert posterior."

"Let us go back to the matter in hand," I said, rolling my eyes. "Who else wanted Lucy dead?"

"Well," replied Theodora, moving on from teasing me, "we know Agnes hated her and you're all for pinning it on the maid."

"I had her down as the accomplice, not the murderer."

"Either way, perhaps she'd had enough of being humiliated by her mistress. The worker's revenge, the Russians are all about it. She might have been awake when Morrow turned up, and snuck out of the servants' quarters to see what was going on and then, finding Lucy alone, seized her moment."

"With those slight hands?"

"Never underestimate what a woman can achieve with her hands, Mr Bigge, however slight."

I avoided looking down at hers and just nodded gravely.

"A similar scenario could apply to Mrs Fairbanks: Sir Lionel's dutiful housekeeper for umpteen years," she continued. "All of a sudden threatened by the new, upstart wife. Who's to say she's not a light sleeper?"

"But that's the thing," I said. "We weren't making lots of noise precisely because we didn't want to wake anyone. Patrick, Lucy and I were in the hall when Morrow knocked and the ensuing conversation was all whispers and hisses, a bit like one of those bedroom farces."

"What about Pinks?"

"What about him?

"I never trust a man above suspicion," she replied. "Especially a butler."

"He did say he heard Morrow and I talking in the garden. What's not to say he'd heard us from the billiard room?"

"Colonel Price?"

"He was obsessed with Lucy. I saw him grope her on the stairs."

"The letch!"

"She clearly didn't like it, but he is the persistent sort."

"Then he finds her alone but she spurns him and…"

"… Unable to take no for an answer, he takes it one step further."

This quite horrific set of circumstances played itself out upon the theatre of my mind. I could see his fingers reaching out to pat and pinch. I could see her trying to avoid him, pinned into a corner.

"Poor Lucy," said Theodora. "So many reasons to kill her."

"The Colonel might even have sent her the love letter."

"Florid prose and Colonel Price don't strike me as the best of chums, and the letter implies reciprocal affection rather than one-sided obsession."

"Golly, what a puzzle this all is," I said. "Just like a jigsaw."

"I hate jigsaws. Mother's quite potty about them."

I wondered what sort of a woman Theodora's mother was. Presumably quite a terrifying one.

"There is one angle we haven't considered," I said.

"Which one?"

"The bracelet. Perhaps Lucy found out who'd stolen her bracelet and was silenced for it."

"Where does that put Morrow?"

"He was exactly what the thief needed: a perfect distraction and a scapegoat for murder."

"I doubt that very much."

"How can you be so sure?"

"If we are to use my aunt's books as a reference point then you'll know that stolen jewellery always turns out to be a red herring."

"That's not true. Last year's Christie hinged upon it."

"Last year's Christie also involved a ghost," she retorted.

"Inspired by Aunt Octavia, no doubt. Although I do think she might be able to shed a little light on this case."

"Agatha Christie?"

"No, your aunt!"

"Oscar! However can she help?"

"I got lost that evening trying to find the water closet and, as it turned out, so had she. I heard Agnes say to Mrs Fairbanks that she'd been wandering around upstairs."

"I wouldn't make anything of that," she said curtly.

"I'm not. I'm simply suggesting she might have seen something suspicious on her first-floor escapade. She strikes me as the sort of woman with eyes in the back of her head and a third ear concealed somewhere on her person."

"You're not far off the mark there, but if we talk with her, we'll have to exercise considerable tact."

"Tact is my middle name."

"It would have to be, given your hobbies."

I had the decency to blush.

"Selby, you do realise what we're doing, don't you?"

"What's that?"

"Trying to solve a murder."

"It's a double murder actually and I've been on the case for days. Do catch up."

If looks could kill, mine would have been the third corpse.

CHAPTER 17

Octavia Stubbs' house was just as one would expect the house of a published writer to be: a shrine unto herself. The bookshelves were groaning under the weight of her books and each individual title came in multiple forms, including hardback, paperback, special edition and a variety of foreign languages. There were dog-eared copies and untouched ones, those with bent spines and those without. I spied the odd Dickens and Shakespeare, and one Dorothy L Sayers, but any other writers in crime fiction were significantly lacking.

Theodora had hailed a taxi from Trafalgar Square, which drove us up past Primrose Hill, and she'd crashed the knocker against the door with great gusto. A timid maid led us into a chintz-heavy parlour at the front of the house, where we were brought yet more tea and a few Peek Freans. We sat next to one another on a faded gold sofa. Halfway through biscuit number two, Octavia arrived dressed in some billowing affair and a sparkling turban on her head – she played the part of the eccentric perfectly. She enthroned herself on a vast armchair with a pouf at her feet. Aunt and niece made the appropriate noises at one another and I'd said how much I admired her bookcases then promptly put my foot in it by asking if she'd read the latest Poirot.

"How could I read that?"

With your eyes, I did not say.

"Such lifeless prose. Not a literary flourish to be seen. What is wrong, may I ask, with a metaphor?"

"I… I don't know…"

"Nothing! There's nothing wrong with a metaphor. *The foggy chill of the graveyard crept up her stockinged legs like the clammy hand of death itself, as if to pull her down to rest with the skeletons below.* That's from chapter three of *A Funeral To Die For*, my fifth novel."

"I do like that one," I said. "The vicar did it."

"No he did not."

"It was the vicar's wife."

"No," repeated Mrs Stubbs, and God knew she probably wished clammy old death would drag me away as well. "It's the third cousin twice removed who's disguised himself as the curate. He's the one that'll inherit the fortune."

"I thought a curate was a vicar," I muttered under my breath.

"Her books are so dry, so lifeless. What of the fourth dimension and the voices of the other planes? Minerva is most critical."

"Minerva?" I asked.

"Minerva Temple, my medium. A most gifted woman, she has the second sight. Everyone should consult a medium as often as they consult their doctor. The fourth dimension is a place of unparalleled inspiration for me. Numerous chapters in *The Clue of The Crystal Gazer* take place in the land of dreams and prove vital to the solution. Many admirers have sent me letters applauding this feat of literary daring, but do you know what *The Times* said?"

I dared to ask.

"*Soporific!* As for *The Fearful Phantom and Other Stories*, they said it was *Ghast-ly!* The cheek of it. I do so hate reviewers; failed novelists the lot of them, taking pot shots at those of us who succeed in reaching publication. And they're all men. I was born decades before Christie when everyone was falling head over heels for Conan Doyle and his pair of bachelor pansies. Holmes and Watson could have shared a passionate embrace and the public would have cheered while my dear, married Glover solved the most beastly of cases and was lucky to get a mention in the Much-Deeply monthly gazette. And my publisher told me no one would read me if they knew I was a woman. So Oscar Trolloppe was born and, despite everything, I got my foot in that door and heaved it open. Then along comes Christie, skipping in my wake, unaware the door had ever been closed and able to publish under her own name! And what thanks do I get?"

I swallowed my mouthful of biscuit, unsure whether it was wise to say anything at all.

"Now to what do I owe the pleasure of your visitation?"

The change of tack quite threw me off guard but Theodora was quick to step in.

"As a matter of fact, Aunt Oscar, it's this horrible murder business."

"I've been taking notes. Oh, don't look so surprised."

I reddened, clearly having failed to hide my look of surprise.

"Art imitates life, after all."

I thought *art* quite a generous word to describe her books but I was hardly going to challenge her on the matter.

"They've found Morrow Davenport's body," added Theodora.

"I thought they might."

"Shot last night not far from the house."

Her left eyebrow twitched but that was it as far as shock went. "Did Patrick tell you this?"

"He telephoned this morning."

"The police are saying it's suicide, I assume."

Theodora nodded and I concentrated on keeping my jaw muscles clenched. Anyone would think she was a detective and not a novelist of variable ability.

"That's the case solved, then."

She leaned back in her chair and stroked her chin. If Sir Lionel had a leonine aspect to him, then here reposed a tiger.

"You really think it that simple?" I asked.

"I do. They rarely have it in them."

"Who?"

"Sissies. They're a weak breed. Morally compromised from the off and most unmanly. I'm surprised he had murder in him, let alone strangulation, what's more suicide. A surprisingly honourable coda to all that went before."

A strange chain of logic, I thought, to accuse Morrow of weakness and then note three acts which all required quite a degree of strength. This was always the case with the sexually perverted, either he was feeble and effeminate and worthy of scorn, or he was violent and vicious and worthy of scorn. Which one depended on the point his critic was employing him for. We fey men were made of straw as well as tainted blood.

"It's for the best," she said. "The police can close the case, the journalists can have their fill and, as for those of us who were present that night, we can forget it ever happened."

"Apart from Sir Lionel," I said.

"I do feel sorry for him," she conceded. "But could he really expect a love like that to last?"

"He could hardly have expected her to get murdered."

Perhaps I should have said nothing. Prodding a tiger was inadvisable after all.

"In a few years' time," she said, "I'll incorporate the details into another opus, but don't worry, Mr Bug, I'll change the names."

"Bigge."

"No, my novels tend on the shorter side. Would you care for some more tea?"

She rang a little bell by her chair before either of us had had time to answer, and the flighty maid reappeared and topped up our cups, without spillages, in record time.

"Terribly efficient," praised Octavia.

Terribly terrified more like!

"I do wonder, Aunt Oscar, if it all ties together so neatly."

"Like a ribbon on a Christmas present." She paused to remove a small notebook and pencil from within the folds of her voluminous dress and quickly scribbled something down. "A ribbon on a Christmas present, I like that one."

"Did you not notice anything odd that night, before we left?"

"Nothing odder than usual."

"Not even when you went looking upstairs."

"I see."

What exactly she saw I did not know but her squinting gaze settled on me, causing all my organs, inner and outer, to shrivel.

"I thought you might have been looking for clues," replied Theodora tactfully. "Did you not suspect foul play?"

"Hardly, my dear," she replied, not fooled for a moment. "I simply enjoy looking around people's houses, as you well know."

"It is a habit of yours, yes."

"Much simpler to describe places I already know rather than have to make everything up. My good friend Harold's estate in Gloucestershire ended up in *Slaughter In The Stables*. He was very upset, but that was because his wife was in it too. Her head gets chopped off by the lusty gardener she's having an affair with."

"How ghastly!" I said before I could stop myself, remembering too late that Octavia might not appreciate that particular adjective.

Her withering stare confirmed my supposition.

"I could hardly foresee Lucinda's death," she said. "Besides, by the time it happened, I was long tucked up in bed. The matter has nothing to do with me, nothing to do with me whatsoever."

Her repetition of the point served only to make me doubtful of its veracity. She was hiding something all right.

"That Agnes should be sacked, casting aspersions on my good nature."

"Agnes?" asked Theodora.

"She was the one who found me upstairs…" She suddenly stopped herself and a wicked grin came to her lips. "Look at that, I've done what the most foolish of suspects do in my novels, revealed too much. How did you know I'd been upstairs?"

Theodora simply turned to me with a smile, reminiscent of Octavia's. I felt like a man before the gallows.

"I... I... overheard Agnes mention the fact."

"Stupid girl, she should know better. Servants' gossip is an ugly thing. I wouldn't be surprised if that Mrs Fairbanks goes in for it too. You know what these old maids are like, stuck in those houses with nothing better to do than tattle and chatter. All those repressed sexual urges. Yes, Belby, I said *sexual* urges."

"Er, Selby," I timidly corrected.

"I have read Freud, you know. I doubt Mrs Fairbanks would know sex if it ravaged her down an alley. Hers would be some squalid little affair with whichever man was to hand. I do so hate it when servants fall in love, the dusting takes the hit."

I struggled to ascertain what was truth and what was tirade. Did she have it in for servants in general or did she have something on Mrs Fairbanks?

"But, Aunt Oscar, can we be sure it was Davenport? Might someone else have had it in for Lucinda?"

"They all did as far as I could tell, but he was the first to her throat, so to speak."

My sip of tea glugged uncomfortably down mine.

"What if he wasn't?" asked Theodora. "What if someone else used his arrival as cover to commit their own murder?"

"Oh, that is rather clever, I hadn't thought of that. It would take some daring."

"It would."

"And quite some seizing of the moment."

"Quite!"

She closed her eyes for a moment, ruminating on the possibilities and looking ever more the feline predator.

"If only Lucinda Duker had put more effort into ingratiating herself with others and less effort into supplying people with motives to kill her," she said. "Women like that regularly die in my novels, it's what they have coming. Now, if you don't mind, I have a chapter to be getting on with. Glover's found the bullet but not the gun."

I quite sympathised with his predicament. We were ushered from the parlour and back into the hall. I paused to admire a display cabinet. Inside were all sorts of rarities, including a jewel-encrusted dagger, what could well have been a blowpipe (or just a piece of wood for that matter), and an array of necklaces and rings.

"I do like my trinkets," Octavia explained, sidling up next to me to admire the items. She smelt of attar of roses. All sorts of predators were capable of masking their scent.

"Aunt Oscar's a collector," said Theodora. "She has things from all over the world."

"That knife is from Ancient Persia, alleged to have killed a king."

"What's that?" I said, pointing to a dirty piece of old leather.

"A holster for a revolver, found in the mud of Ypres. It's important we don't forget the past."

"Quite so."

"We lost far too many good men. You're too young to understand such things, but I'm not, nor is the Colonel."

"That dreadful man!"

"Now now, Theodora, he is witness of the past." She stopped to make a jotting in her notebook. "*Witness Of The Past*, I can see it on the front cover, with a pair of eyes beneath, crying blood. Very good! The Colonel and I will never forget, just like elephants. We must be forgiven our foibles, not that I have any, but that man's drinking is verging on gluttony."

On that rather sombre note, we were returned to the pavement and I took a deep breath of fresh London air.

"What a beastly woman," I muttered. "A harridan of the first order."

Theodora said nothing as we set off for the brow of Primrose Hill, her gait somewhere between expected femininity and promenading masculinity. I wondered if she was two people in one or just more of a person than her body could fit. She eventually broke the silence.

"Have you ever written a novel, Selby?"

"No," I replied, somewhat confused at the question.

"And are you a woman born in the final quarter of the nineteenth century?"

"Most certainly not!"

"Then may I suggest you walk a mile in my aunt's buckled shoes before you go calling her a harridan, or any sort of woman for that matter."

Oh! I was being reprimanded, how utterly humiliating.

"Can I at least call her a dragon?"

Theodora glowered, at which point I spotted the family resemblance.

"She was at Fortnum's once, having tea, when she overheard two people laughing about her latest book of the time, *Decapitated In Devon*. The words 'awful', 'preposterous' and 'laughable' were particularly audible. And who did those two people turn out to be?"

I was tempted to reply with something rude but settled for a civil, "I don't know."

"Anthony Berkeley and G. K. Chesterton. None of the other crime writers take her work half as seriously as she takes it herself, especially the ever so logical men. The trouble is many of her early works were glorified ghost stories with the odd murder thrown in. She much prefers the supernatural to the criminal. She's derided for it even though some of her straight crime stuff can be very good."

"I imagine that must be tiresome for her," I said, trying my best to sound sympathetic. "But the things she says about us chaps of the Greek persuasion, that's hardly nice, nor women of the Sapphic order."

"I couldn't agree with you more and, by all means, dislike her for those opinions, but do not dislike her for being a woman."

"How do you put up with her?"

"Because she's my aunt and family matters. Let me be the one to put arsenic in her tea when the time comes and you can worry about your own relatives."

I felt that all too familiar sinking feeling in my tummy. Despite the occasional visit, I had put a county and a half's worth of distance between my family and I. Perhaps if my aunt were a famous-ish writer and my father a baronet, things would be different. Theodora was staring into the middle distance and still looked a bit upset. An apology might have smoothed things over but the word *sorry* was always such a difficult one to say. A dove cooed in one of the trees.

"Do you really think her trip upstairs was motivated by curiosity?" I asked, trying to pull us back to the case in hand.

"I do," she replied, a little too quickly. "She's a very inquisitive person. You have to be careful what you say around her, otherwise you'll end up in a book, most likely a corpse."

"I noticed she didn't much care for Mrs Fairbanks."

"I don't blame her."

Her response was much too flippant for my liking, but she said no more. We watched as the dove flapped from the tree and flew out across the park.

"Is that it then?" I replied, my tone verging on frustration. "The case is closed."

"Absolutely not. I'm disappointed in you, Selby."

"You are?"

"Solving the case, I thought you had it in you."

"I'm trying my best."

"To be honest," she said. "I rather saw myself as solving it with you assisting me."

"I'm to play the Watson to your Holmes, am I?"

"Or the Sergeant Mumble to my Glover." She spoke of the dreary chap who played second fiddle to Octavia's chief detective. He spoke in monosyllables, loved roast chicken and was a thoroughly two-dimensional character. "We both know things aren't as simple as they appear and Patrick needs our help."

"He does?" My heart fluttered at the thought of being Patrick's knight in shining armour, even if our parting on the Heath had been less than promising.

"He likes men, so do you, and I occasionally am one. These are secrets that can never come to light. And, while I hope the police will be satisfied with Morrow's supposed suicide, I wouldn't underestimate that Chief Inspector Bile."

"Lisle."

"Just what I said. He came to my house and asked all sorts of prying questions. He's tenacious if not exactly intelligent. The last thing Patrick needs is more scandal in his life and I have no intention of being slandered by the gutter press. It would destroy us."

"You really think we can outsmart the police?"

"We don't have a choice. Our reputations depend upon it."

We were at the top of the hill now and could easily have passed for a happy couple out on a morning stroll. London lay innocently before us, hiding its secrets well.

"Who's next on the list of Lucy-haters then?" I asked.

"The Colonel. We need to find out the extent of his obsession with her."

"Obsessed enough to kill," I mused.

"Men do not love, they possess."

"That's rather damning."

"And women do not love, they fear."

"You've seen it from both sides, I suppose."

"Exactly. And I don't know which I prefer."

"Where does he live?" I asked.

"Patrick will know. I'll ring the house and arrange to see my fiancé and, once we've got the Colonel's address, we can plan our line of attack."

"I doubt he'll want to see us."

"You bring a bottle and I won't dress in trousers."

"You are fiendish!"

"I am, rather."

CHAPTER 18

"Loyalty, that's what the young lack these days, loyalty."

The evening had arrived and I was sat in a huge, red leather armchair in the Bullion Club. Polished brass, sparkling chandeliers and the murmur of male conversation – every self-respecting Englishman belonged to a private members' club such as this one. Opposite me was Colonel Price, with a third double whisky in hand. I was still struggling with my first.

"And respect for their elders."

After Primrose Hill, I'd returned to Miss Wickler's for a lunch of beef casserole and under-boiled potatoes with a dessert of far too many questions. Theodora eventually rung, saying she couldn't find Patrick anywhere. She had telephoned the club, acting as the distressed fiancée, but hadn't any luck, although she did learn Colonel Price was there. *Carpe diem*, we decided, and I donned my black tie and sped to the Bullion just in time to catch the Colonel after one of his WC visits. I became the excuse he needed for another drink and also someone to direct conversation at.

"What you lot need is a war. Nothing like a good war to shape one's character."

"You've fought in a number, Colonel."

"I have! The glory of the Empire has much to thank me for."

"But surely the peace is what you fought for."

"Peace, yes, but not impertinence."

He took a gulp of whisky and I took a tentative sip, my throat aflame. Regular tests of one's masculinity were the mainstay of my sex, from drinking each other under the table to beating each other up. Fortunately the Colonel was too squiffy to notice my below-par performance.

"One of the batmen I had in the trenches was a lad from Shropshire, George Baker. Took him on because I liked a challenge – scruffy boots, terrible grammar and an accent like shrapnel. Ignorant beggar, thought war a game. I taught him a lesson or two. Had him polishing boots noon and night, emptying the piss pots, running messages up and down the trenches. He hated me at first, mumbling under his breath and taking the Lord's name in vain, but by the time I finished with him, he could have passed for a gentleman."

"He must have been most grateful to you."

"He was. I taught him his place in the world."

"I imagine he still sends you a card at Christmas."

"He got shot the day he went over the top. But he died an honourable death and that's what matters."

I offered a solemn nod and withheld my screams.

"He was good at heart if rough around the edges. I sanded

him down. Not all the men were like him. Some came back with ideas in their heads, thinking themselves entitled to more than they had. The Communist disease, spread worse than the Spanish flu and just as deadly.

"You won't remember the riots of '19. All over the country – Liverpool, Glasgow, even Luton. One thousand mutinous soldiers marched on Downing Street. Lloyd George declared a state of emergency and that young chap Churchill had warships, tanks and regiments sent to quash the uprisings. We'd be a Soviet Republic if it weren't for the military. I was damned if I'd beaten the Hun only to see England fall to the Reds. I did my bit, shot at crowds of rebels in Manchester. It's the moral order I was protecting, each man allocated his rightful place, a true gentleman knows that. George knew."

His voice cracked at the name of his late batman. I wholeheartedly disagreed, but thought better of telling him. After being forced to return to Horsham after Oxford, my rightful place felt most wrongful, so I came to London to build a better life for myself.

"Sir Lionel's a true gentleman, isn't he?"

"One of the best."

"You two go back a long way."

Again came the obligatory anecdote about the Second Boer War and various criticisms of the Dutch and men with dark skin.

"You must have known the first Lady Duker," I said, cutting him off during a lengthy description of Kitchener's Scorched Earth policy.

"She was a great woman," he assented. "They don't make them like her any more, especially not after the War. We should never have let them into the factories in the first place and now they want to go back. And vote... And divorce! We're fighting a war on the home front now."

He downed his glass and ordered another. I quite marvelled at his ability to imbibe alcohol and, as of yet, not keel over. I thought I'd push home my advantage while I had the chance.

"What of the second Lady Duker? She struck me as the sort of woman who knew her place."

"Ha!" the Colonel barked. "Daughter of a doctor married to a knight, her motivations were as plain as day."

"Money?"

"Exactly."

"You really think she didn't care for Lionel?"

The anticipated Lucy diatribe ensued and he did little more than repeat what I'd already heard and read a number of times. I nodded in the right places and on he went. Sir Lionel was likened to a dog and Lucy his master, then there was some garbled metaphor about the dog's lead.

"She was quite pretty though," I said.

"Pretty as any painted tart." His purple nose and cheeks purpled somewhat more as he shifted in the chair, the leather squeaking against his suit.

"I thought her a bit prettier than that," I said. "A face to launch a thousand ships."

The Colonel just mumbled into his tumbler.

"I could imagine any man she spurned getting quite envious, just like Menelaus," I said.

"Mene-who?"

"She must have inspired jealousy in the hearts of those who

didn't possess her," I said, avoiding an explanation of the intricacies of the Trojan War.

"It's not jealous men you need worry about," he said curtly, perhaps cutting wise to my gist. "It's the women."

"The women?"

"What does any woman hate more than a woman prettier than her?"

"You think Mrs Stubbs?"

"Not the old toad but the young one."

"Theodora! But she's engaged to Patrick?"

"They're all the same, all they want is money. Why settle for the son when she could have the father?"

"You think she'd ditch Patrick and murder Lucy for a shot at Sir Lionel?"

"Never underestimate the wickedness of women."

I felt for his wife and actively willed her to sample adultery.

"George had a wife, you know? And three children. He spoke about them sometimes when we couldn't sleep for the sound of German artillery. He painted a pretty scene, out in the Shropshire hills, but a difficult one, close to poverty. He cried once. It's a terrible thing to see a man cry. I'd wanted to shout at him, order him to buck up, but instead I did a most strange thing, I hugged him. I held him like a father might hold his infant son. He was like a son to me, come to think of it, for a short while." He spoke his words to the wall behind me, as if the ghost of George might be standing there. "After the war I sent her a letter commending her husband's bravery. I included some money. I knew she needed it. She sent the letter back with the money. Never underestimate the wickedness of women."

For a moment I saw an old, unhappy dipsomaniac, one who had been given a gun, a high-ranking position and an Empire to protect. I saw the teachers I'd had at school and the sort of men my peers would grow into. I saw my father. And I didn't like what I saw at all. They were given the world, only to crush it underfoot. He snored. The old brute had fallen asleep, my exit cue from the Bullion Club. It was a grand place, yes, but it needed better company. When all this mess was tidied up I would return with Patrick and we'd toast our budding friendship with champagne.

"Mr Bigge?"

I'd just reached the bottom of the steps leading back onto the pavement when someone recognised me.

"Sir Lionel, good evening."

He was dressed as smartly as ever and I assumed he had a whole wardrobe of suits, whereas I had one black tie left over from university days which required regular dusting and the odd stitch.

"What are you doing here?"

Conducting my own investigations into the murder of your wife and the death of a gossip columnist, I could hardly say.

"I was having a drink with Colonel Price, as a matter of fact."

"I didn't know you knew him."

He took a step towards me and, while the effect verged on menacing, I saw the fatigue in his eyes. I assumed nights of little sleep and repressed tears. He was no longer the domineering man I had met at the Ritz. He appeared on the edge of breaking.

"I don't, but I'd stopped by, looking for Patrick, when I bumped…"

"Why are you still looking for my son?"

"I... I'm concerned for him, after all that's happened."

"Your concerns are entirely unnecessary."

"Then where is he?"

My question achieved the desired result as Sir Lionel was briefly lost for words – a state in which I'd never seen him. So, he didn't know where Patrick was either.

"Your enquiries into my son's whereabouts are proving most tiresome," he said, quick to regain the upper ground. "And they are verging on the unseemly."

He might have been a grief-stricken man but that didn't stop him scoring a victory over me. So he left me standing at the bottom of the steps, looking up at a club to which I had no membership.

CHAPTER 19

It was Sunday morning. Robed in dressing gown, pyjama trousers and slippers, I was enjoying the brief freedom when Miss Wickler was at church. I'd made sure she believed me a God-fearing man, but I drew the line at worshipping with her. I preferred private communion with God in the privacy of the bedroom. One of my lies that I don't think she'd believed, but at least it distracted from the other ones. Buttered toast, jazz on the wireless and dancing with myself around the kitchen, I needed some distraction from all that was going on. If I stopped for too long, my head began to spin, and if I stopped even longer I worried whether I was next on the killer's list. Up went my hands and up went my ankles as I did the Charleston around the breakfast table, not caring for the crumbs that fell to the floor. I was about to do a twist when the doorbell rang.

"Bugger."

Tying the dressing gown cord tighter and smoothing my hair

down I shuffled down the corridor. It can't have been one of Miss Wickler's acquaintances because they would be at church with her, keen to share the gossip over stewed tea and bourbons. A long-lost son, perhaps, or secret lover. It would be nice if the scandal shoe were on the other foot for a change. I opened the door to a very pleasant surprise.

"I've come to fix your pipes, guv'nor."

It was Arthur, the cheeky rascal!

"You'd better come in then."

"Yes, sir."

I was swift to shut the door behind him.

"Did anyone see?"

"Street was empty."

"Good. Twitching curtains?"

He shook his head and took off his flat cap. He was even wearing overalls.

"Was this disguise all for me?"

"I'm driving a van down to Dover this afternoon. Thought I'd drop by to wish you farewell."

"Farewell? Dover isn't too far."

"I've got to cross the Channel to deliver the goods."

"What goods are those?"

"The less you know the better."

Arthur was one of those Jack-of-all-trades types; one day he'd be telling me about an antique Spanish chest he'd located for a collector, and the next he'd regale me of a life drawing class for which he'd modelled. How closely his work was tied to the more criminal parts of the underworld I didn't know and thought better than to ask.

"You heard what happened to Morrow Davenport?" I asked.

His answer to my question was to push me up against the wall and start to kiss me. I worried the hallway was not the most appropriate place for such an act. Every wall of this house was so bloody thin, perfect for the nosy neighbours. His kiss only but intensified; here was a man who knew what he wanted. Thinking of thin walls took me back to Morrow's flat and how I'd heard his voice from outside. Worrying he had a gentleman caller, I'd hidden in the stairwell only to discover he'd been practising his greeting for me. Such a silly thing to do, but one with which I was familiar. Arthur's lips moved from mine to my cheek, then down my neck to my collarbone. My body thrummed. Morrow must have been incredibly nervous; talking about our predilections was dangerous enough, let alone acting on them. The kiss I'd given him had been brief but in that moment we'd both been criminals. And now here I was again, breaking the law. Still kissing my neck, Arthur untied my dressing cord and then undid the buttons on my pyjama shirt. His dexterity spoke to his experience. Shirt opened, he squeezed my nipples. His fingers were cold and that added to the thrill. His mouth found my right nipple and gave it a friendly nip.

"Arthur, I say..."

"Best you say nothing, Selby. It's a long drive to Dover."

Truth be told, I was erring on the side of Morrow having not strangled Lucy. The act required a ferocity that went beyond his bluster and threats. Social annihilation via gossip column was one thing; cold-blooded, well-planned murder quite something else. While the man on the street liked nothing better than blaming perverts for the ills of the nation, what if, this time, said pervert was innocent and a stooge in someone else's plan? Foolish Morrow. If he'd just kept the lid on his poisoned pen, he might still be alive. Arthur's mouth was at my navel now as he kissed and licked the vicinity before following the thin trail of hair that led to my pelvis. Suffice it to say, I had long been standing to attention, and with a few more undone buttons, out I sprung.

"Patrick!" I blurted.

"What?"

"N... nothing, terribly nice."

"Did you just call me Patrick?"

Arthur rose back to his feet to look me in the eye, a mere erection's length between us.

"Slip of the tongue, I'm afraid."

"That's the posh chap, isn't it? The one you're sweet on."

"He... he's just a friend," I said, as my mind raced to that damp, dark night on the Heath.

"And here I am giving you a jolly good send-off before I head for France."

"It's most thoughtful of you."

"Thoughtful!" he echoed, taking hold of my shaft and pulling back the foreskin to reveal the head. How I wanted to moan, but the less the neighbours heard the better. "It's more than bloody thoughtful, it's romantic."

"Quite so."

"I'm only visiting three chaps before I go. You should feel honoured."

"I do!"

Back and forth he worked his hand and I had to bite the back of mine to cover any further moans.

"What's this Patrick got that I haven't?" he asked.

"An empty address book for starters."

He rubbed harder.

"Selby the bank clerk thinks he can do better than a handyman."

"You are very good with your hands."

On that, he stopped his rubbing and tucked it away inside my pyjama bottoms.

"It's no use," he said. "I can tell when I'm not wanted."

"It's not that, Arthur, but so much has happened in barely a week."

"You've fallen in love."

"It… it's hardly love."

"And your other chum's just died."

"He wasn't my chum," I retorted.

"I did as you requested and you'll never believe what I heard."

"What?"

"Nothing."

I repeated the word and he nodded.

"I asked punters at the pubs, waiters at the bars, renters on the Dilly, even some bleeding waitresses at Lyon's, but no one ever saw hide nor hair of that Davenport until he was all over the news."

"How odd," I said. "Surely he'd have frequented at least one of those places. If you ever read his gossip column, you'd know he wasn't the most subtle of chaps. Anything from Hyde Park?"

He shook his head. "It's like he never existed."

But before I could reply, I heard the creak of the gate outside the house.

"Shit," he whispered. "Church isn't over yet."

"Get under my bed," I commanded. "I'll deal with this."

He obeyed his orders and hot-footed it up the stairs, knowing them well enough to avoid the creaky ones. Footsteps approached the front door and I made sure my bedclothes were tidy enough. The door-knocker knocked ominously. I waited a few seconds, trying to calm myself and hoping Arthur would be quick. Another knock, louder. I opened the door.

"Good morning, Mr Bigge."

"Go... Good morning," I stammered, sounding just like a guilty man with secrets to hide.

"I've caught you unawares," he said, eyeing the inch of chest I had failed to conceal. "They do say the early bird catches the worm."

"That they do. Come in?"

"Don't mind if I do."

So Chief Inspector Lisle of Scotland Yard entered Miss Wickler's Pimlico abode while I had a man upstairs. I'd played it close to the line before, but never this close. If Arthur had any sense, he'd climb onto the roof and shimmy down the drainpipe. The constable was with Lisle too. He sidled past me, pausing to sniff the air. I just hoped it was Miss W's potpourri he could smell rather than anything fruitier.

"You're quite alone, aren't you?" asked Lisle.

"Yes."

"Landlady at church, presumably."

"Yes." How did the bugger know that!? "Would you care for some tea?"

"I want to ask you some questions."

"Perhaps I should dress."

"No time for that."

Propriety was as offended as I was but there was little use protesting. We passed into the living room. The chief inspector moved a wooden chair in front of the seat by the window and pointed for me to sit. My interrogation had begun and I wasn't even wearing a tie.

"How is the investigation going?"

"I'll ask the questions."

"Quite right."

The deference he'd shown the night of the murder was gone. No longer was I a friend of aristocrats, just a bank clerk.

"Are you a keen gardener, Mr Bigge?"

"Me, a gardener? No, can't say I am."

Was I to be accused of burying a third body in a vegetable patch somewhere?

"How curious." He took a notepad from one of his jacket pockets. "It has come to my attention that you have taken an interest in the herb garden at Sir Lionel's house."

"It has?"

"It has." He thumbed through the pages of the notebook, but I think that was to inspire dread rather than find a particular piece of information. "On Saturday the twelfth of October, you were seen entering the walled garden with Patrick Duker."

"Quite so. He wanted to show me the garden."

"He did, did he?"

"Yes."

Though my heart wished to exit my body via any available orifice, I was not going to let this man know it.

"And two days ago, on Friday the eighteenth, you returned to the house and were seen entering the walled garden again."

"Was I?"

Agnes, she'd blabbed!

"You were, and I would like to know why."

"I was waiting for Patrick."

"In the garden?"

"In the house, but it was stuffy."

"I don't believe Master Patrick was at the house at that time."

"You're quite correct."

"So, if you had gone to the house to see Master Patrick and he wasn't there, why were you in the garden?"

"I had to go to the house in the first place to learn he wasn't there."

"And felt the need to digest this information in the herb garden? Perhaps you find the smell of rosemary soothing?"

The constable sniggered. But better him in the room to witness my humiliation rather than off sneaking about the house. So far there was no suggestion he'd recognised me from our near brush at the South End Green toilets, but that was nothing compared with what was waiting for me upstairs. Photographs, letters and other such pieces of incriminating evidence I had long burnt, after having committed them to memory, but a man under my bed was something else entirely. I knew two men imprisoned for holding one another in their living room.

"Rosemary?"

"That's what I said."

An image came to mind – Agnes' hands. They'd had dirt on

them when I caught her leaving the herb garden on my second visit.

"I'm afraid I didn't bury the revolver in the vegetable patch, if that's what you're thinking."

"The revolver?" the constable blurted, only to receive a look of utter fury from his superior.

"Not a revolver then?" I risked.

"What makes you think something was buried in the garden?" asked the chief inspector, still furious.

"Isn't that what gardens are for, burying things in. Bulbs and the like."

"I'd advise you not to be clever with me, Mr Bigge. If you have any secrets, I can assure you we'll find them."

"Quite so."

Why I was pushing my luck, I did not know. It wasn't just my neck my impertinence risked this morning, but Arthur's too. Our affairs were far better saved for the bushes than the jail cells.

"I can assure you that my interest in the walled garden is entirely innocent. The drawing room is over-heated and the garden makes for respite, like one of those plunge pools at Swedish saunas."

"I don't know anything about Swedish saunas," he replied as if they were the sort of place frequented by sadists and sodomites, which they were – or so I'd been told. My foreign adventures never got much further than France, but I'd regularly been regaled with the exotic escapades of the Oxford upper sets. I bet Patrick had been to Sweden. The chief inspector rose to his feet and the constable snapped to attention.

"That will be all for now, Mr Bigge, but Constable Stovell and I may well return."

It sounded like a threat.

"Are you any closer to finding out who did it?"

"That's not for me to divulge."

He shoved past me and his lackey followed, giving me a reproachful look as he went.

"Do you think there will be a third?"

"A third what?"

"Murder."

"For there to be a third, there needs to have been a second."

"But Morrow Davenport…"

"Was a suicide. Don't you read the papers?"

So he was taking that line too.

"Unless there's something else you're not telling us?" he said.

"I've told you everything I know. It just… it just seems an odd thing for him to do – kill himself at the scene of the crime."

"I think *odd* a good word to describe your behaviour as well. After all, you were the one who stopped to chat with him shortly after he'd strangled Lady Duker."

"I hardly knew he'd done that!"

"What did you talk about? The weather?"

"I told him he shouldn't do anything he'd regret."

"He clearly ignored you."

"Clearly."

Bugger it to hell, these policemen were slimy numbers. If only Pinks had kept his usually shut mouth shut. At this rate, I'd be put down as Morrow's accomplice.

"What about those scratch marks on the key?" I said defensively. "Have you got to the bottom of that?"

"How would you know about those?"

"I saw them. The key had been left on the table in the cloakroom by the finger-printing device."

"Yes, Constable Stovell drew my attention to those marks."

"He did, did he?"

The damn swine! He'd never have noticed them if I hadn't said something. Someone should sew my lips together.

"Old keys get scratched, it's as simple as that."

"Quite," I replied, trying not to goad him any further.

Constable Stovell opened the front door for his superior, who passed through. But he stopped on the front step and turned to face me.

"I have to say, Mr Bigge, this whole case strikes me as decidedly queer."

"Decidedly," I concurred.

"And if there's one thing I'm good at, it's putting an end to a queer case."

Stovell made sure to bang the front door shut on their way out. The concertina of glass above shook and I feared the day it came shattering down as a rain of many coloured shards. I stayed standing in the hallway for a while, trying to catch my breath in the wake of the inspector's questions. I was accustomed to not living far from the edge of the abyss, but that didn't make the abyss any less terrifying. I waited for their footsteps to recede before I climbed the two flights of stairs to my room.

"It's me," I said, as I opened the door. "The coast is clear."

Arthur's handsome face appeared from under my bed. I helped him to his feet, whereupon he hugged me. I appreciated the gesture and I could feel his heart beating in his chest, just like mine.

"Bloody hell," he whispered. "Who was that?"

"The police."

"Shit, Selby, what have you done?"

"Been present at the scene of a crime."

"They don't bloody suspect you, do they?"

"I bloody hope not."

We hugged for a little longer until I had to step back lest my member get excited all over again. He smiled. We traipsed back down the stairs, a little stunned from our near-brush with the law. At the bottom, I gave his shoulder a friendly squeeze.

"Thank you for asking after Morrow."

"Pleasure. Sorry I couldn't be of more help. A mysterious chap, eh?"

"That's not the half of it. And next time you think of popping by, do telephone in advance."

"Yes, Mother."

"When will you be back from France?"

"Not sure yet. I've got a friend in Calais, arse like a peach and cock like a cucumber."

"A veritable fruit salad!"

"And you should head to the Dilly for some fun and stop pining after Earl so-and-so's son."

"His father is just a knight."

"Oh, just a knight, is it? You know what I've told you about getting attached to unavailable men."

That one hit rather close to the bone, but I did my best not to let him see.

"Bring me back a croissant," I said.

"I'll bring you a whole baguette, if you're lucky."

He kissed me briefly on the lips before letting himself out through the front door. He closed it without a sound, waited a moment, then took off down the street. Strange to think the skills of being a good burglar went hand in hand with those of being a lover.

Batting aside thoughts of Arthur's plump lips, I went over my conversation with the police. Lisle knew far more about me than I was comfortable with and seemed intent on scaring me, which he'd achieved most successfully. However, I had learned something from him – that the herb garden possessed a strange significance. I'd certainly got a reaction when I mentioned something being buried, but if it wasn't the revolver that killed Morrow, then what?

"That's what I fought for. Gold and diamonds."

Sir Lionel's words echoed in my mind and I saw him, sitting at the table at the Ritz, and next to him, Lucy. She was holding up her hand and on her wrist was a band of gold and diamonds. Of course! I rushed for the telephone and got the operator to patch me through to Theodora, a reverse charges call, mind, so Miss W wouldn't suspect.

"Hullo, fourteen Wilkington Mews."

"Thank God you're there."

"Selby! Whatever's the matter? You sound like you're being chased by a herd of cows."

"Worse. Lisle was here, asking about the herb garden."

"The herb garden?"

"I think Agnes buried Lucy's bracelet under the rosemary bush."

"You what? How on earth...?"

"It's too long to explain but I'm highly confident I'm right."

"*Highly confident,* you say?"

"Listen to this for a solution: Agnes is routinely bullied by her mistress, so she gets her revenge by stealing her favourite bracelet. But Lucy knows how much the maid likes her jewellery, so suspects her immediately and threatens to end her career once and for all. This could be the end for Agnes, but then Morrow turns up, giving her the perfect opportunity to off Lucy, except he sees her through the window. Morrow comes back to get his blackmail money, but Agnes gets him first."

"And convinced him to bring his gun to his own murder?"

"What?"

"Selby, haven't you looked at the newspapers?"

"That's just what Chief Inspector Lisle said," I grumbled.

"Morrow's suicide is front-page news and, what's more, the gun was his, given to him by his..."

"... father!"

"Yes! A souvenir from the trenches, standard British military revolver, darn sight heavier than my little thing. Pater Davenport was all too happy to talk to the press and tell them his story. Said he'd never known his son was a sodomite, but he blamed, and I quote, 'That city of sin'. Can you believe?"

"London! The buggers' capital."

According to rural folks, London was the birthplace of all depravity, from pre-marital sex to incest. A childhood in Horsham had put paid to that theory.

"But look," I said, "regardless of how Morrow got that gun, it still doesn't prove he shot himself."

"Of course not, but nor does it make little Agnes a strangler and a shooter!"

"I just need to find more evidence."

"You can't find evidence to prove someone's guilt if they're innocent."

"The police do it all the time. It was quite a fright getting a visit from them this morning."

"All the more reason to lie low for a bit."

"But I have to get to the bottom of this herb garden business."

"Could you at least do it discreetly?"

"Discretion is…"

"… one of your many middle names, yes, I already know."

"Top marks," I said. "I've already got a plan."

"Go on then, what is it?"

"If I'm quick to Hampstead, I might catch some of the servants before they get back from church."

"Oh, that's actually a good idea."

"It is! All my own. Any news from Patrick?"

"No. I've rung a few mutual friends but even Sammy didn't know."

"Who's Sammy and why should he know where Patrick is?" I asked, jealousy kindling at once.

"Honestly! Sammy is a she who finds men decidedly unattractive. Call me when you know more and do be careful."

CHAPTER 20

It was a glorious autumn morning, the sky clear of clouds and the sun shining brightly. Damnably cold, of course, but the sort of day when it's easy to forget that winter is just around the corner. I couldn't afford to hang around for a bus, so I threw my tea money at the nearest black cab. The Sunday traffic wasn't too bad and we made quick progress up to the Heath. The taxi drove through the village and I looked to the South End Green toilets, a place of worship for men like me. My first trip to the Heath had been summer last year, when I was still an ingénue to London's northern delights. I'd swum a few shaky laps of breaststroke around the bathing pond before towelling off, hoping to catch a gent's eye. With no success on that front, I strolled down into the village thinking to stop for a cup of tea, but a saucy chap looked my way and I'd followed him to the toilets: a veritable cornucopia of surreptitious glances and creaking cubicle doors. While some trekked to the Holy Land, others made pilgrimage to shrines like this, where the flesh was made manifest in other ways. That some of the worshippers were in fact police officers was an ongoing concern for the faithful.

The taxi dropped me off outside Christ Church, its grey tower pointing to the sky, like a schoolboy with his hand up at the front of the class. For many, God was the greatest teacher of all and passing his examinations was crucial. An organ was giving a rousing rendition of some hymn as I slipped through the vast wooden doors. Inside was magnificent, all columns, stained-glass windows and intricate patterns of stone in the eaves. A few judging eyes noted my late arrival, but I went quietly into the back row and took the hymnal. Bledwood had been this experience endlessly. So many mornings, us boys would traipse to the chapel to sing the praises of our Lord. Doctor Froggatt, master of Certus Hall, my boarding house, would tick off our names in a little booklet and if ever a boy missed a service, the backs of his legs would suffer the consequences. Punishment was not always so violent. Sometimes it would be a long cross-country run before the sun had risen and at other times a *Times Leader*, namely copying out, word for word, the entirety of a front-page article before breakfast. Froggatt chose the longest of articles on the most boring of topics. He'd make us wait in his office as he read our efforts, making sure we hadn't skipped out any bits in the middle. If we had, then back we went to do it again. He was a deeply religious man, and I sometimes wondered if his excessive fervour had encouraged my questioning of the existence of the divine creator. If God really was love, as it said in the Bible, then why had he created that sadist of a housemaster?

The church was well attended this morning and I scanned the pews to see if there was anyone from the Duker household. The hymn finished before I'd had a chance to examine everyone, although identifying people from the backs of their heads was quite difficult. The vicar took to the pulpit to bemoan the sins of modernity. The cinema and jazz were duly criticised, as were the Irish and other such godless folk. Paganism came in for a good beating. I was more a Heathen these days, given my love of outdoor activities. Then a woman a few pews in front turned her head to one side to sneeze quietly into a small lace handkerchief. Mrs Fairbanks! More hymns, plenty of praying and a few psalms for good measure, until finally we were set free. I congratulated the vicar on his rousing sermon and shook his clammy hand on my way out. He was none the wiser.

"I say, Mrs Fairbanks, is that you?"

"Oh, good morning, sir."

"What a marvellous surprise. I hadn't realised you're a regular at Christ Church."

"Yes, sir, every Sunday."

"Please, it's Mr Bigge when we're not at the house."

She didn't look too pleased by my informality. Housekeepers like her rarely were. Questioning hierarchy tended only to end in communist revolution or an anarchist bombing. Nevertheless, I had to seize my moment. We were on her home ground, but I could play the card of social superiority.

"This is Mrs Stonehouse," she said, introducing the lady next to her, whose existence I had barely registered.

"Pleased to meet you, sir."

She was short, pink and wore a simple hat.

"The pleasure's all mine. Are you the cook?"

"I am, sir."

"I hear your roast potatoes are scrumptious."

"Thank you, sir."

"Sir Lionel must be so pleased you've returned."

"I hope so, sir."

Not one for loquaciousness.

"Mrs Fairbanks, I'm glad I bumped into you because I have a question."

"You do?"

"A delicate one."

I looked suggestively at the cook.

"Mrs Stonehouse, you go ahead to Miss Beggum's and I'll join you there."

"Right you are, Mrs Fairbanks. Good day, sir."

I touched the rim of my hat to her as she gave an awkward little wave. For the mite of a moment her gloved hand was suspended in mid-air and I saw quite how large it was. Then it was gone, tucked behind her back. All the better for whisking eggs.

"It's a frightfully silly thing, but it was just last week when I realised I'd misplaced a lighter. Terribly old thing, but a gift from my father and I do treasure it so. I've been racking my brains as to where I might have left it and I think, perhaps, I left it at the house."

"At the house?" She sounded alarmed.

"It's the only possible solution, unless I dropped it into the Thames when crossing London Bridge."

"I don't think so, sir."

I let a silence linger, hoping to make her feel uncomfortable.

"The trouble is, Mrs Fairbanks, I think we both know where it might have ended up."

The dart hit the bull's eye or near enough. She tried to restrain a gasp.

"Look, I have no intention of getting her into trouble, especially with the police investigating two deaths, but I do want my lighter back."

"Sir, no lighter has been discovered at the house."

"Not even buried next to the begonias."

Her face paled. We were still in sight of God's house and, as far as she was concerned, He was watching her from the sky as well. Now was the moment to push home my advantage.

"You mentioned a few things had gone missing, I believe."

"Only a pair of pliers, sir."

Missing pliers. This was news to me.

"When did that happen?"

"Not too long ago, if I recall correctly, but they'll soon turn up."

"What of the teapot?"

"Only temporarily misplaced. It was found under one of the beds."

"Indeed."

"Agnes may be clumsy, sir, and forgetful, but she's no thief."

"Maybe she has forgotten she has my lighter? I'd hate to have to mention this to Master Patrick."

"You needn't do that, sir. I can assure you she doesn't have it."

It was hard to tell whether her pleading was to defend the guilty or the innocent but, either way, it seemed genuine enough.

"I am like you, Mrs Fairbanks, I hate a scandal, but I hate theft all the more. You mentioned other items had gone missing?"

She avoided my eye and sought guidance from the pavement, a lamppost and a nearby poplar tree.

"The odd silver teaspoon, sir, and a cigarette case."

"Oh dear, this is bad." I wanted to keep her on her toes, but also didn't want to give her a heart attack. "When did these things go missing?"

"Over the last few months, sir."

"Can you be any more specific – the day, perhaps, even the time of day?"

She looked back at the church, hoping for a sign from the Almighty. The vicar waved; that ought to do it.

"Come to think of it, it's funny you should ask that, sir, because I do remember the days. Well, not the exact days, but I always remember being worked off my feet attending to the guests and then, to cap it all off, something goes missing."

"So the vanishing items coincided with the presence of guests."

"Yes."

Clever girl, that Agnes, using the guests as cover for committing her petty crimes. She could even blame one of them if necessary.

"Do you remember who the guests were?"

"Oh no, sir, I can't remember all that."

"Not even one of them?"

"Not who was there on what day, but we've plenty of regulars at the house."

"Such as?"

"That tall woman with the square face – the young master's fiancée."

I withheld laughter at this rather apt description of Theodora.

"That famous lady too, the writer. She's ever so kind, you know. She came back to the house last week to offer her commiserations to the master. She even came through the servants' quarters to enquire into our wellbeing, most kind."

"That is very kind."

First she was seen upstairs on the night of the murder and a few days later she's scuttling around the servants' quarters. Something was starting to smell decidedly fishy about the famous writer.

"And Pinks," I asked, "how is he taking things?"

"Quite well, thank you, sir."

We started heading down the hill. I thought it best to shift my tack. I wasn't sure she could take much more interrogating.

"I do admire a man like Pinks," I lied. "A true gent."

"Quite so, sir. He's the best head butler I have ever worked for."

She sounded positively gushing, which was quite something for the housekeeper.

"I suppose you've told him about the missing items?"

"I had to," she said rather solemnly. "He was most disappointed."

"He didn't blame you, did he?"

"Oh no, but it isn't doing to have items go missing."

"Other than that, he's lucky to have such a marvellous housekeeper to work with. In fact, the evening of Sir Lionel's birthday I remember him saying such a thing to me."

"You do?"

Her voice rose an octave and she sounded like a schoolgirl

with a crush. I felt awful to lie to her, but I needed to understand how all the pieces of the puzzle fitted together.

"He was most complimentary."

"It's impossible…"

"I beg your pardon?"

Her hand went to her mouth, as if to stuff back in the words that had fallen out.

"Nothing, nothing," she floundered. "I'm this way, we've run out of potatoes."

She took the first available road.

"But the shops will be closed, Mrs Fairbanks."

"Miss Beggum will have some, she's ever helpful in a crisis. Good day, sir."

Off she trotted, as fast as etiquette allowed, confirming her role as housekeeper with a guilty secret. Except it wasn't Agnes' kleptomania she was covering up, but her own passionate yearning for Pinks! What a match. I would have laughed if it weren't for the rather dark thought that came to mind. The housekeeper threatened with excommunication and the butler believing his master's wife most unsuitable. Who's to say they didn't use Morrow's arrival for their own nefarious ends? Pinks had been in the billiard room, after all. He'd flatly told me there was nothing to see, but that's exactly what someone rearranging the position of a corpse would say. I shivered in the cold light of day, the steeple of the church still visible. Unlike God, I wasn't all-seeing, but I was trying my best to see more.

CHAPTER 21

Once again the skittish maid permitted me entry into the lair of Octavia Stubbs. I walked past the display cabinet full of her much-loved trinkets – the ornate knife, the empty holster and the many jewels. How easily I had assumed Agnes guilty of the theft. But it was after a Sunday lunch of Miss Wickler's speciality: overdone beef with almost-roasted potatoes and wilted greens followed by a quite remarkable lemon syllabub (she was much better at desserts), that I wanted to follow up on my suspicions. What if those items in the author's overloaded display cabinet hadn't all been purchased at auction? What if some had been purloined? Theodora had been dismissive of the stolen jewellery angle, which is precisely why I'd gone without her. Family loyalty often meant keeping family secrets.

Will you walk into my parlour? said the spider to the fly flitted through my head as I entered the dusty parlour full of books. I could quite easily see Mrs Stubbs as the spider spinning her devious plots and, sometimes, enacting them in real life. I settled onto the sofa and awaited my latest suspect.

"To what do I owe this pleasure?" she asked mockingly as she entered the room. "I'm in the middle of a chapter, you know."

"I had the police visit my house this morning."

"I hadn't thought clerks owned houses."

"The house of my landlady."

She settled into her grand armchair, a wicked smile on her face. Her words were her web and if I wasn't careful I'd get stuck in them.

"Get to the point, Mr Bag. I'm entertaining you purely on the basis that this might prove material for a future chapter."

Being immortalised in her fiction would prove the end of me, but at least not many people would read it. If she'd ever achieved a high quality of literature, those days were long past. *High Atop The Altar* was considered her best, the twist both surprising and poignant as the scandals of the church were revealed in all their sordid glory. It had caused considerable controversy, which doubtlessly aided the sales figures. One wondered how much of it was taken from real life.

"The police were implying I have something to do with this sordid affair."

"You do," she said bluntly. "You were there at the time of the murder. And I wasn't."

"How convenient for you."

"Hardly. I have no crime to hide."

"Don't you?"

She stared at me, her watchful eyes surrounded by a generous border of wrinkled skin. Theodora had said she'd been quite striking in her youth and some of that power remained, even if too much time bent over a typewriter had stooped her shoulders.

"Go on then, this ought to be fun," she said.

I swallowed the saliva in my mouth as I prepared to knot the rope that would hang me.

"I think you went to the first floor that evening to look through the bedrooms and, in one of them, you found Lucinda Duker's bracelet. You took it. After you heard about her murder, you realised it wouldn't be a good thing to hold on to. I think you returned the bracelet to the house a few days ago under the guise of offering commiserations. Except you didn't put it back where you found it, you hid it in Agnes' bedroom, most likely under her mattress."

I allowed myself a quiet breath.

"I know the Red Queen can believe six impossible things before breakfast," she said. "But I've just had lunch and am disinclined to entertaining fancy."

I tried to forget that the Red Queen was renowned for chopping people's heads off.

"I caught Agnes coming out of the herb garden with dirt on her fingers. I think she'd found the bracelet and, terrified of the implications, buried it."

"You think an awful lot, Mr Bug."

"You exploited the animosity between Lucy and her maid, and employed a well-known device from your genre – thieving staff. A device, I'm afraid to say, I fell for, and if the police do too then an innocent woman might be hanged for double murder."

"Little Agnes! Please, she can barely hold a teapot, let alone get her hands around someone's neck." She said the last few words with alarming relish. "Forget the maid. I have you down as my number one suspect. I should telephone the police."

"You won't."

"Won't I?"

I must admit that despite the terror, the thrill was considerable. Her plots might be lacking in sense but her wits were about her. I was reminded of those dreadful tutorials at Oxford when some old curmudgeon would obliterate my essays on Plato and the like. I'd learned how to argue my case, eventually.

"Because you'll have to explain a thing or two to them, as well."

"What, that on one occasion I went upstairs and on another deigned to speak with the staff? Neither of those things make me a criminal."

"Unless…"

"Oh ho," she chortled, "you're not suggesting!" She stopped again to laugh, a deep sonorous sound and I immediately thought of dark caves full of cobwebs. "You're right! I stole the bracelet and regretted it at once. I had Theodora drop me home, or at least she thought she did, and then I hotfooted it back to the house to put the bracelet back. I slipped in through the billiard room French window, conveniently unlocked, only to bump into the late Lady Duker. Naturally, I strangled her. Inconveniently for me, that prancing pansy was in the garden and he saw. Next stop blackmail. So I lure him to the Heath, with his own gun, mind, get it out his hands and *Bang!* The crime writer commits two crimes in one week!"

She clapped her hands together gleefully. She was having much more fun than I.

"As far as solutions go, that is worthy of an Anthony Berkeley or one of the better Sawyers. I would never be so crude."

"I imagine you kill your victims with words."

"Quite right. A number of former acquaintances, tiresome relations and hated teachers have been murdered by my pen."

"You might not be a murderer, Mrs Stubbs, but you've still been acting suspiciously. I'm sure the police would be interested in a further lead."

She looked me dead in the eye, sizing me up, but suddenly her face fell.

"I couldn't bear it," she whispered. "It's not what you think at all."

"Then what is it?" I asked, seizing my moment.

"I... I... never meant to frame her. It was a gift."

"A gift?"

"For sweet, sweet Agnes..."

"I... I see."

Now that was a twist I had not seen coming, Mrs Stubbs with the lesbic inclinations! Agnes was pretty, I could easily see her as the recipient of the older woman's affections.

"You do, Mr Bigge?" she asked, her eyes wide and frightened.

"I do, as a matter of fact."

"Oh, it's like that for you too?"

My silence was my way of an answer. Busy as I was pursuing men, I knew the odd woman who liked pursuing others of her kind. Although it wasn't as easy for a lady to enter a public convenience, not least because of all the skirts and undergarments to navigate.

"Perhaps this is yours?" I produced the love letter, rather

crinkled now, from my jacket pocket and crossed the room to give it to her. She snatched it from my hand and quickly read the note.

"You think I wrote this to Agnes?" she asked. "I wouldn't be so unsubtle. People like us can't afford such grand declarations. Think of the scandal."

I did, regularly.

"Where did you find this?"

"Er, in the cloakroom."

"Of the house where you rent?"

"Not quite."

"Sir Lionel's cloakroom, then."

"I'll be sure to put it back."

She passed the letter back to me and wrapped one of her hands around mine.

"I can think of someone else in that house with an *impossible love*."

"Who?"

Her grip tightened.

"The person who hated Lucinda Duker the most."

"Who?" I repeated.

"Her son-in-law."

Her grip was vice-like and I did my best not to flinch.

"Patrick? Absolutely not!"

"Are you mad? He hated her. He was my number one suspect from the off."

She let go of my hand and I stumbled back a step.

"I know he hated her," I said. "But he wouldn't resort to murder."

"Oh, I see," she said. "You don't *want* to see."

"It's not like that at all…"

"It's exactly like that."

Oh bugger, now she knew I liked Patrick, but at least I knew she liked Agnes. Call it a stalemate.

"It can't have been him."

"Why?"

"Because he was locked in the turret."

"As simple as that, then?"

I didn't know what to say. Patrick could hardly have leapt out the window, run after Lucy, then leapt back into the cloakroom, having locked it from the outside. He was no magician. Besides, why involve me in any of this if he'd always been planning to kill her? The fewer witnesses the better. No, it wasn't him. I wasn't attracted to a murderer.

"You do know there are ways to lock yourself in a room."

"But the key was on the other side."

"Precisely," she replied enigmatically. She rose to her feet, and though she was smaller than I, she still seemed so much bigger. The veritable spider and I the proverbial fly. "It's time you went."

We left the parlour and passed the display cabinet, filled with her pirate's hoard of valuables, no doubt all of them stolen from unsuspecting acquaintances. I spied the old holster, still specked with mud from the trenches.

"Do you think Davenport's revolver had a holster?" I asked. "There's nothing in the papers about the police finding it."

"He might have thrown it into one of the ponds for all I know."

She chivvied me down the hall, not caring for my observations.

"You must promise me something," she said in a lowered voice.

"What's that?"

"You must keep my secret."

"I will."

"And I will keep yours. We are alike, you know, in our little perversions."

She opened the front door and ushered me through. It seemed odd to have something in common with a woman I really didn't like, but then there were so many of us in London. And all across England's green and pleasant lands, even if most normals refused to believe it.

"So many people in that house have secrets, Mr Bog, and it's best we keep ours."

I agreed quietly but fervently and made my way down the steps. I crossed the road and as I reached the pavement on the far side I turned. She was closing the door and there was a horrid grin on her face, as if she'd been laughing behind my back.

CHAPTER 22

"Are you sure you don't want something alcoholic? It is after six."

I negatived the offer and took the proffered cup of Earl Grey.

"Suit yourself."

I did as Theodora fixed herself up a vodka, soda and lime. She used silver tongs in the shape of bird's feet to transfer a few cubes of ice from a small silver bucket. We were in the living room at the front of her house – home to a chaise longue, a rocking chair, two poufs, a garden chair and nothing approaching a settee.

"It must be expensive, a house like this?"

"I presume so. My father bought it for me."

"Lucky you."

"More a bribe than an act of generosity. He wants me kept out the way. I consider myself less the black sheep of the family and more the ewe that's also a ram."

She sat down on one of the poufs as I tried to remain stable in the rocking chair.

"Your father doesn't approve?"

"He doesn't know the specifics but he knows I don't behave as a woman should. I'm not timid and acquiescent like my elder sister Cecily. She thinks London a pit of vice and decadence."

"She's not far wrong."

"Indeed! I'm not married either, which makes me a blight on the great family name. At least I got a house out of it."

She raised her glass with a laugh and I raised my teacup in return.

"This place is my sanctuary, you see. Somewhere I can put brilliantine in my hair and comb it back. Where I can put on a trilby and suit, and leave the front door as Theo. Here, I can be the man that I am as well as the woman. It's somewhere I can escape to when the burden of my secret gets too big. How do you manage yours?"

"My burden?"

She nodded and I tried not to flinch. A lifetime's worth of dissemblance had long taken its toll, and every day I had to put the pieces together, hoping they would hold.

"The Ancients were a balm when I was younger – imagining all the things those sandalled men got up to. Now I get up to some of them myself, with men in public conveniences."

"Is that enough for you?"

"N… no," I stuttered, surprised to find myself answering the question so quickly. "I do yearn for something more but I think you already know that."

The smile she gave was neither ironic nor caustic.

"It's hard," she said. "Keeping secrets."

An image came to mind quite uninvited: I was fourteen or so, in my rugger kit, standing in the middle of a playing field at school. Shivering and covered in mud, I was doing my best to appear unafraid of the opposing team. Feigning fearlessness was just as vital to the game as catching the damn ball.

"I was fiercely competitive as a boy," I continued. "I tried to be a sportsman but didn't much make it, so I compensated for it in the classroom, working hard at school and even harder at Oxford. But the older I got, the more I realised how different I was to the people around me. So I had to work doubly hard, just to stay one step ahead. Not winning is one thing but being seen to lose is quite something else."

"It is tiring, trying to keep up."

"It's exhausting."

"And lonely."

"Yes," I replied, foolishly baring a small piece of my heart. "For so long I've wanted to share my life with another but it's so damned difficult."

"I quite understand."

"Someone with whom to sit atop Parliament Hill and admire the view."

"A partner in crime."

"No," I said. "Ours is no crime. I want to meet a fellow detective."

We smiled at one another and it felt nice to share this moment, brief respite from all else that was going on. I took a sip of the tea, quite delicious, and then placed the cup on the back of a small, wooden elephant – there was nothing so much as a table in sight.

"Where's Patrick?" I asked.

"I wish I knew. I even tried the Styx."

"He could be at one of the pubs."

"Patrick doesn't go in for pubs unless it's full of old-world charm and situated somewhere in the middle of the countryside, as far from other perverts as possible."

"I'm afraid the countryside is full of perversion."

"Personally acquainted, are you?"

I blushed, choosing not to recount the stories of my youth.

"You know," she said with a laugh, "I do rather like you, Selby Bigge, you're full of surprises."

"You're most surprising yourself."

This got another laugh of approval.

"Now, Theodora, there is something I have to tell you, something that might prove distressing."

"Oh dear, another body?"

"Nothing like that, it's about your aunt." I braced myself, not knowing quite the best way to break the news.

"Go on then, out with it."

"Um, you see, your aunt is… er… well, she's one of us."

"A *homo sapiens*?"

"Yes… but no… I mean she's one for tribadism."

"She what?"

"I believe the current medical term is lesbian." I pronounced it as best I could. "A female homosexual."

"I'm perfectly aware of what a lesbian is."

"Your aunt is of the Sapphic inclination."

The silly chair rocked back and forth, revealing my discomfort. Theodora said nothing for at least fifteen seconds.

"How did you discover this?"

"She told me this afternoon when I visited her after lunch."

"You visited her alone?"

I nodded.

"That was most unwise. And she shared this secret with you?"

I nodded again and Theodora went back to silence, closing her eyes to indicate deep concentration.

"My aunt, a female homosexual?"

"I'm afraid so."

Her eyes burst open and a huge grin spread across her face, followed by howling laughter. This went on for a good half-minute as I hid my embarrassment in the cup of tea.

"Oh dear, I'm afraid you've been had. My aunt is about as Sapphic as a doorbell."

"It gets fingered a lot," I replied defensively.

"Very good. Tell me, when she revealed this surprising secret of hers did you, perhaps, reveal yours?"

"I think she knew it already, if I'm honest."

"But you confirmed it once she'd told you about her *tribadism*."

"I believe so, yes."

"Had you accused of her anything beforehand?"

"As a matter of fact, I think your aunt is the one who stole Lucy's bracelet and later planted it in Agnes' room to implicate her, even though your aunt told me it was a present for the maid."

"My aunt in love with the maid! Dear Selby, you must be careful."

"Me? But your aunt is the thief."

"Something for which you have no evidence, but which did result in you disclosing your inclinations."

"As did she."

"She was lying to you to encourage your confession."

"Then it's a stalemate."

"No! Because she's not actually a lesbian, but you're as queer as margarine. I'm afraid it's checkmate to Aunt Oscar."

"Bugger."

She leant forward to pat me on the knee. "Don't worry, I won't let her hurt you. You're safe so long as you're a friend of mine."

"Am I your friend?" I asked, failing to hide the hope from my voice.

"A new acquaintance, yes," she said with a sympathetic smile.

"Still, if she's not a lesbian, she is a thief."

"Quite so."

"Quite so!? How can you sound so blasé?"

"If you must know, I was the one who suggested she return the bracelet."

"You knew all along?"

"No, but I deduced there might be a connection between its vanishing and Aunt Oscar's predilection for trinkets. I had no idea she was going to frame Agnes for the theft. The poor girl must have been at her wit's end, I quite understand her burying it in the herb garden."

"You didn't think to tell me?"

"Why ever should I? I do have some loyalty to my family, you know."

"Because it might have a bearing on the case."

"Oh, tosh, it's just one of her foibles."

"A foible she might kill for?"

This initiated another round of laughter.

"We must consider every angle," I interrupted. "You weren't there when your aunt quite vividly described what might have happened if she'd gone back that night to return the bracelet only to bump into Lucy in the billiard room."

"You accused my aunt of murder as well as theft?"

"I intimated."

"Pulling a trigger is something she might do, but she doesn't have the stamina for strangulation."

All of a sudden, another image flashed to mind – one of Theodora returning to the house by way of the billiard room, clutching her aunt's recent theft.

"But a niece keen to hide her aunt's secrets would."

"Selby, you must stop accusing me of murder, it's most tiresome."

"Every angle," I muttered.

"You're just as likely to have done it as I, and you have a much better motive."

"I do?"

"Patrick."

"Why would I kill for Patrick?"

"Because you're a deranged pervert, like the lot of us. Lucy found out your secret and you silenced her. As for Morrow, he knew you were a Mary Ann from the off. Takes one to know one, after all. He put two and two together, so you shot him in the head."

"But if Patrick is my motive, then surely you're my number one victim."

"The rival in love, yes, a common theme in my aunt's books. But you don't have to kill me now you know it's all a sham."

"What's to say *you* didn't kill Lucy to hide *your* secret?"

She rolled her eyes.

"I met Mrs Stonehouse, by the way," I said, changing the subject.

"Who?"

"The Dukers' cook. She was at church with Mrs Fairbanks."

"The cook, you don't think…?"

"… That she wasn't up north at a funeral but hiding in the toilet waiting to strangle Lucy? The thought had crossed my mind."

"It's the sort of solution Philo Vance would arrive at."

"You really are your aunt's niece! And nephew for that matter."

"Family loyalty, darling." She winked as she took a gulp of vodka and soda.

"There's still something off about this gun business," I said, returning to the less ridiculous.

"How so?"

"If Morrow had taken his revolver to the house the night of the birthday there must be a reason he didn't use it."

"He lost it?"

"Conceivably. It might have fallen out of his pocket."

"And then someone else found it before the police arrived."

"Or what if he didn't have the gun on his person," I mused, "but had hidden it in anticipation."

"Maybe they'll find a holster hidden in a flower pot."

"You could be right! The police said they found a footprint in the flowerbeds. He may well have been sneaking around the house beforehand."

"There's something we're missing, isn't there?"

I nodded sombrely. The pieces of the puzzle just weren't fitting together.

"We do really need to find Patrick," I said, drawing my mind away from this revolver business.

"I've tried everywhere," she replied. "And I've telephoned the house far too many times. He's gone into hiding."

"*Into hiding*," I repeated slowly. "I've heard those words before."

"Where?"

"One moment!"

I let the words echo in my mind and they quick acquired a voice – Patrick's. He must have spoken them to me not so long ago, but when…?

"The Ritz!" I said, the memory returning, "Have you tried the Ritz?"

"Whatever for?"

"Sir Lionel has a favourite suite. Patrick told me when I dined with them there. He said he used it as bolthole every now and again."

Theodora was on her feet at once. I wasn't so quick on the other hand, trying not to fall off the rocking chair and land flat on my face. The telephone was on a pile of books nearby and, as soon as she had the operator, she asked for the connection. She acted the part of the worried fiancée with practised ease and we soon had what we wanted.

"Selby, you're very good at this!" she said, looking as if she didn't know whether to hug or kiss me. "We must be quick, before he chokes on his own vomit."

*

Under different circumstances it would have been a pleasure to return to the Ritz. After dining at great expense, I might have treated myself to a trip downstairs to the Long Bar in the hope of catching the eye of an illustrious gentleman keen to buy me a drink. But those pleasures would have to wait. Naturally Theodora had us take a taxi (I doubted she ever used the underground, let alone a bus) and soon we arrived in that splendid hallway. The saucy footman was there but I didn't catch his eye this time. It pained me to think what had happened in little over a fortnight. Back then I had been excited and Lucy and Morrow had been alive. Theirs had proved a fatal dispute in the end.

Theodora did the talking, mentioning her family name a number of times, and soon we were in the lift heading to the fourth floor.

"We'll take it from here," said Theodora to the porter, placing a coin in his palm, before setting off down the thickly carpeted corridor. To think what exotic and rich guests were preparing for dinner behind these very doors. We stopped at suite number seven and Theodora rapped quickly. No answer. She knocked again.

"Patrick," she hissed. "It's me."

Something groaned from within and something else crashed to the floor.

"Patrick," she said more loudly. "Let me in."

There was another groan and then shuffling towards the door, more like an animal than a human. The door opened and there he stood: hair dishevelled, shirt creased and opened to his belly button, and beneath that he wore only underpants and socks. He had strong legs with a pleasant down of fur on his calves while his thighs were completely hairless. I forced my gaze back up.

"Patrick, you look awful."

Theodora barged her way inside, taking me with her, and Patrick lurched back to the four-poster bed, crashing onto it in a tangle of predominantly naked limbs. I spied a number of empty champagne bottles on the bedside tables and one on the floor.

"You're drunk," announced Theodora.

"You're stating the obvious," he retorted, not too far gone for wit.

"I've been worried to death about you. Now is not the time to vanish."

"Now is the perfect time. Why is he here?"

It hurt to be referred to as *he*, no better than the cat's father, but I put it down to the drink. Then again, the last time I saw Patrick was when he'd fled from me and my wandering hands.

"Because Selby is worried too, Patrick."

"I want a Bloody Mary."

"You've had more than enough."

"I *want* a Bloody Mary."

I'd never seen this side of him, the petulant and rude little boy used to getting the things he wanted. I didn't much like it at all.

"Have some water."

"I want a Bloody Mary."

"Patrick!"

"A Bloody Mary or I shall scream and wail and cause a scandal."

"You've done that already," she hissed, but there was resignation in her voice, as if they'd been in this situation before. "I'll go downstairs to the bar and get you a tomato juice, nothing else, and while I'm gone, Selby can help you get dressed."

"He'll do no such thing."

"Please, Theodora," I said, embarrassed beyond belief. "I'll go to the bar, it's no bother."

"I might be engaged to him, but I have no desire to see him out of his clothes."

She about-turned and was swift to leave. I turned apologetically to Patrick but made no advance.

"You can keep your hands to yourself this time."

"I believe you made the first advance."

The silence that followed was not a friendly one. I stood close to the door, surveying the gargantuan room with its own three-piece settee and chandelier. The bathroom door stood open and through it I could see a marble bathtub. One night here probably cost more than a month's at Miss Wickler's. I looked back to Patrick, moving into a sitting position on the edge of the bed and looking quite the worse for wear.

"Patrick," I said, slowly crossing the space between us. "About that night…"

"I don't want to talk about it."

"I… I got the impression you don't particularly like who you are."

"I like myself very well, thank you."

"I do not think that's true." I took the risk of sitting next to him, leaving a sufficient gap in between. "Many men like us don't like who they are."

"What's a man like us?"

"One who likes other men."

He turned away from me and I saw his hands grip the golden coverlet. I saw his wonderful rower's thighs as well.

"I'm not like you." He turned back to me and there were tears in his eyes. How I longed to take him in my arms and tell him it would all be all right.

"You are, Patrick, and I knew from the moment I met you on the Heath."

"Rubbish. I was going for a walk."

"Which involved asking a single, young man for the time, even when you have your own watch?"

"It's faulty."

"I struggle to believe the son of Sir Lionel Duker owns a faulty watch."

"Stop it," he hissed. "I'm not a sodomite."

"The words don't matter," I said. "What matters is how you feel."

"I… I feel awful." I could hear the pain in each word as if he'd dredged them up from some dark space hidden deep within. "There's something in me, something infected, that's rotting me from the core. But there's no cure and, trust me, I've looked for one. Nothing can scrub this canker from my soul."

The tears fell down his cheeks and it would have been quite pathetic if it weren't so sad. His hand still gripped the coverlet in the gap between our bodies and I so wanted to reach down and touch it. To squeeze his hand in mine and will love from my body to his.

"You remember that bench overlooking the Worcester

College duck pond, don't you?" I asked. "Where we sat and talked?"

"I... I do."

Such simpler times, I thought, when essay deadlines were the greatest threat and murder was something reserved for Agatha Christie paperbacks.

"And we kissed."

He slowly nodded his head.

"We can have that all again, you and I."

"I'm not like you, Selby."

"I think you're more like me than you care to acknowledge."

"I can change."

"You don't need to. There's nothing wrong with loving another man," I said, trying not to show how desperate I felt.

"I love no such man."

"Then how do you explain this?"

I fished into my pocket and produced the letter. He snatched it from my grip and read it quickly.

"I found it at the house," I said by way of explanation.

"You think I wrote this?"

"Or received it?"

"You think I was interested in that painted cockatoo!"

He shoved the letter back in my hand, our fingers brushing for the briefest of moments.

"But you do have a *forbidden love*?"

"It's not love, it's perversion, and for so long I have tried to rid myself of it."

"You don't recognise the letter."

"Of course I don't."

"Do you think anyone else knows your secret?"

He wiped the tears away and tried to sit up straight, but the alcohol made him slump.

"Perhaps Lucinda?" I suggested.

"She knew all right, with her hints and insinuations. She always implied she would tell my father unless I treated her well. A cuckoo in the nest if ever there was one. I'm glad she's dead."

"You mustn't say that."

"Mustn't I? Why not? She was a gold-digger and a hussy. Our lives are better without her."

I gasped, unable to hide my shock.

"Do you think I killed her?"

"I... I..."

He shuffled closer to me on the bed. His body was hot and his sweat pungent.

"You think me an invert *and* a murderer."

"I... I think you utterly hated her, yes."

All along I had denied the possibility. I had never wanted it to be true, yet from the very start Patrick's hatred of Lucy had been clear. One of the first things he'd ever told me was how he was planning her murder. I'd chalked it up to hyperbole. And ever since she died, he'd been the one acting the most suspiciously, unravelling like a dropped ball of yarn.

"How did I do it?"

"There are marks on the key to the turret cloakroom, marks that could have been made by a tool, a small pair of pliers perhaps? Like the ones that went missing."

"And?"

He inched nearer to me, putting his face close to mine.

"The key could have been on one side and the tool used from the other, through the keyhole."

"So I locked myself in the cloakroom after having strangled Lucy?"

I managed a single nod.

"And Davenport?"

"Was a distraction from the real crime."

"Coincidence?"

"Accomplice. The cloakroom key had gone missing earlier that day, which implied premeditation."

"And he wrote me that letter?"

"It's a possibility."

"Before I turned on him to keep my secret."

"And shot him with his own gun."

We were so close to one another, a hair's breadth away from a kiss, or something more violent. His bloodshot eyes searched my own as he wiped the remaining tears from his cheeks.

"Who are you, Selby?"

"I… I'm your chum."

"Chums don't accuse one another of murder."

But the pieces fitted, more or less. Patrick's soul was a battlefield, as hate fought love, abetted by shame. We all struggled with that internal war and then along came Lucy, fuelling the flames with such blithe ignorance. And who's to say that very same hatred hadn't run from me that night on the Heath extension, ripped the gun from Morrow's hand and fired the bullet through his head?

"I didn't kill her, even though I wished her dead. I was locked in the turret, plain and simple."

"And the letter?"

"I haven't a clue."

"Then someone is trying to frame you."

"What?"

"Those marks on the key, they're too recent, too suspicious. It's only a matter of time before the police put two and two together."

"To get what?"

"To get you as their prime suspect. There is the inheritance angle, after all."

"What do you know of my inheritance?"

"Nothing, but presumably you lost a significant amount of it once your father remarried."

"That's none of your business."

"You made it my business when you approached me on Parliament Hill. You said you were worried he might disinherit you."

"He was never a fool before she arrived."

"And suppose that your father and Lucinda had had a son."

"The thought sickens me."

"Who in that house hated you enough to frame you for murder?"

"The only person who hated me was Lucinda and she's dead."

"She didn't hate you."

"She did, make no mistake of it. I stood between her and all my father's fortune."

"She can hardly have strangled herself to frame you for her murder!"

He lurched to his feet and went off in search of his trousers.

They were lying in a heap on the floor and, when he bent over to retrieve them, I received a front-row view of his behind.

"I think she liked you, Patrick. She spoke with me that evening, before she was killed. I think she was fond of you."

"Please, if that woman weren't a full-time gold-digger she would have been an actress. You shouldn't have believed a word she said."

He aimed one of his feet into the trouser leg and missed.

"She spoke so kindly to me and she was so understanding of our... our unique position in society."

"She was a first-class fraud."

"Then why did you confide in her?"

"I did no such thing."

He had both feet in now and was wiggling the trousers up his legs. In a different life, this could have been happening after we'd made love, rather than after I'd accused him of murdering his stepmother.

"You must have done, Patrick. She implied you rather liked me."

It sounded so pathetic now but deep down there was a part of me that still hoped for a happy ending. I've always said I'm a top-notch liar, I practise on myself.

"Do you really think I'd have talked to that harlot about personal matters? Never. She was lying to you, as simple as that."

"But you told her about Oxford."

"No I didn't."

"She said you did. She was the only one who remembered I was at Fitzalan."

"I've already said, she was lying."

"Then how did she know which college I was at? She never actually asked me, nor did your father, or anyone for that matter."

"You must have told her at some point."

"I never got the chance to tell her and if you didn't, who did?"

"Where's my belt?"

"It's under the pillow. Who told her, Patrick?"

He ignored me and took to failing to thread the belt through the loops of his trousers. There was a knock at the door and I opened it to let Theodora in. She was carrying a tray with three glasses of tomato juice on.

"Drinkies!" she announced.

"Oh my god!" I gasped.

"They're all virgins, don't worry."

"*That's* how she knew!"

"How who knew what?"

"How Lucy knew I was at Fitzalan."

"I thought you were at Corpus."

"Of course you bloody did. That's what everyone thought, except him."

"Except who?"

I rushed past her out into the corridor.

"Selby, where are you going?"

"To get the evidence."

I didn't hang around to hear her protests and ran for the lift instead. The pieces of the jigsaw whirred around my head, stubbornly refusing to fit together. So I did what I had to – I threw them away. All along, I'd been trying to solve the wrong puzzle.

CHAPTER 23

"Good evening, Pinks, is the master in?"

"No, sir, he's dining at the club tonight."

"How splendid."

Once again, I stood on the steps leading into the house on the Heath, except there were no birthday celebrations waiting on the other side. But there might be the final clues I needed.

"Master Patrick is not in either, sir."

"That's quite all right, I came to see Agnes."

"Agnes?"

The unflappable Pinks was surprised. One point to me.

"Quick as you can."

"Sir, this is most uncommon, perhaps it would be best if..."

"I know what's best, Pinks," I said, striding into the hall. "Where is she?"

Pinks' polite revolt in the face of the indignant, posh man who won't stop until he has what he wants was futile. I knew how to act this part; I had encountered enough of them at Oxford.

He led me through a door in the far-right corner of the room, not one I'd been through before, and soon we were in the warren of the servants' quarters. The walls were greyer and the lights dimmer; it was a place where expense had been spared. Agnes was in a small cupboard, polishing cutlery. She looked shocked to see me.

"Don't worry," I told her, which only made her worry more. "I have a simple question to ask."

"Yes, sir," she said hesitantly, looking to Pinks for reassurance.

"I'd like to ask you in private."

Pinks coughed.

"It's nothing like that, Pinks, you can wait outside. No eavesdropping."

He did as he was commanded and now Agnes looked even more frightened. It wasn't becoming for an unmarried woman to be left alone with a man, especially if they were of different classes.

"I don't want to frighten you, but I have to ask you about the bracelet."

Her hand went to her throat as she restrained a gasp.

"I believe you buried it in the garden."

She looked ready to faint.

"I know a scandal like this could terminate your employment."

"I didn't take it," she whispered.

"I know that too. I think someone put it in your bedroom as a nasty trick and you hid it the second you had the chance. I don't for one moment think you're a thief."

Defiance, fear and relief vied for space on her pale, young face.

"I couldn't have the police accusing me of all sorts," she said. "I'd lose my job and never get another. It's bad enough with Mrs Fairbanks on my back."

"Like the missing teapot?"

She nodded.

"And the missing cloakroom key."

"That wasn't me," she said defiantly.

She looked over my shoulder and I turned to see a narrow cupboard attached to the wall. Its doors were open to reveal a corkboard full of hooks. On each hook hung a key and above were small labels with the names of various rooms and cupboards. I spotted the long, silver cloakroom key quickly enough. Anyone in the house on the day of the murder could have popped into the larder and slipped it off the hook. That very same person could have made the scratches as well. But who would want to frame Patrick for murdering Lucy? I turned my attention back to Agnes, who remained white as the proverbial bed linen.

"You really know nothing about it?"

"Nothing."

I yanked open the door in time to see Mrs Fairbanks hurrying down the corridor; she was as displeased to see me as everyone else.

"Is this about your lighter, sir?" she asked.

"It's about murder."

She gasped, Agnes dropped a spoon and the butler pursed his lips.

"Mrs Fairbanks, on the night of Lady Duker's murder I heard you talking with Agnes about the cloakroom key going missing."

"Precisely because I was trying to locate it," she responded tartly.

"And you still don't know why it vanished?"

She shook her head.

"Pinks, can you shed any light on the matter?"

"No."

I noticed he did not address me as *sir*. I was overstaying my welcome and I'd barely arrived.

"You're quite sure?"

"I wasn't aware it had gone missing."

"Even Sir Lionel and Patrick can't shed any light on the matter," I said.

"I think you'll find," added Pinks, "that no one in this house knows why that key went temporarily missing."

"No one alive!"

On that, I left the servants' quarters for the hall whereupon I entered the cloakroom. Getting down on hands and knees, I inspected the spot on the floor where I'd found the fallen letter. Then to the keyhole, decidedly empty, then through the dining room and into the drawing room. I strode to the fireplace and stared into the empty grate. If only I could gather all the suspects together and ask them the relevant questions one by one until I had the solution. Alas, I was not a police officer nor Hercule Poirot, I was just a humble bank clerk with an audience of three bemused household staff ready to have me sent to an asylum.

If this were an Oscar Trolloppe novel, the ghost of Lucy

would appear to me and reveal the final, case-solving clue. Instead a memory of that evening came to mind – I saw a hand reaching up into the darkness. Four fingers and one thumb were held aloft and placed against the cool glass. Beyond was the darkness of the night and from it had emerged another hand. It looked simply as if the hand had touched its own reflection.

"Of course!"

The curtains were all closed, but I went to the ones that covered the French windows and pulled them back. Pinks and Agnes looked on in discomfort. The garden beyond was dark but I surveyed the panes of glass until I found what I wanted, five small, circular smudges. I withdrew a handkerchief from my pocket and wiped at the glass. Nothing. I wiped again and still the smudges remained. How fiendish!

"Mrs Fairbanks," I said, turning to face the trio. "You say you saw a man?"

"I beg your pardon?"

"You said you saw a man hanging around by the gate in the garden wall."

"One of those nasty journalists," she said, more to the drinks cabinet than to me.

"What makes you think it was a journalist?"

"He was lurking, sir. That's what all the journalists have been doing, lurking."

"At the front of the house, surely?"

"I suppose, but what's to stop them going around the back?"

"Could you make out his face?"

"Not in detail, sir. The gate is a fair distance from the house."

"But you say he had a beard."

"Yes, that I do remember. It was terribly scruffy, I'm sure."

I went out through the other door this time and back down the corridor of doom. I stopped between the doors to the billiard room and the one into the water closet. I chose the latter and locked myself inside. There was a small cupboard in one corner, which I opened, only to find cobwebs and a roll of toilet paper. I looked around again, even trying the tiles on the floor with my feet, but they all held fast. There was nowhere else to look apart from the toilet.

"By Jove!" I exclaimed.

"What are you doing in there?" asked Pinks.

"Something of the utmost importance."

I could still picture the drops of blood from Lucy's hand. They'd been cleaned away by now, but there had been some on the sink and the floor. There had even been blood on the toilet seat. I'd thought nothing of it at the time. I climbed gingerly onto the seat and reached for the lid of the cistern. It was a porcelain thing and I readied myself for a struggle. But it rose with surprising ease. I gasped. Something had been attached to the underside of the cistern lid with what looked like a great deal of sticking plaster. It was made of leather and designed to hold a revolver.

"The holster!"

I returned the cistern lid to its rightful place and climbed down from the toilet. Unlocking the door, I made my way past the shocked servants and carried on down the corridor back into the hall. The events of that night were easy to recall as Patrick, Lucy and I made for the stairs, only to be interrupted by Morrow's quiet knocking.

"*Nothing too loud*," I whispered, quoting the letter and beginning to marvel at the ingenuity of it all.

Except this time a loud sound did ring throughout the hall. The doorbell. Pinks rushed past me to open the door.

"Thank you, Pinks," said Sir Lionel, stepping into the house. Then he saw me. "You! What are *you* doing here?"

"Selby Bigge is my name, Sir Lionel, and I was rather hoping we might have a word."

CHAPTER 24

"I would like to tell you a story, Sir Lionel, if I may."

We had retired to the drawing room. He was sitting in his usual armchair and I had taken the one opposite. The staff had been ordered not to follow us and no drinks had been poured. The fireplace remained empty, the mouth of the fish-shaped spill jar remained open and I remained one frayed nerve from the edge.

"You may not."

"A short one," I said. "Its ending will shed new light on the murder of your wife."

"That tragedy has ended. There is nothing more to say on the matter." He did not look at me, instead he stared at the place where warming flames might have been. There were dark circles around his eyes and once again I was reminded of the Parthenon – he looked to be a man on the verge of collapse. I tentatively offered a little more.

"You are right to call it a tragedy, Sir Lionel, but it started out as something quite different. It started as a love story." Truth be told, I did on occasion rather like the sound of my own voice. "Two people deeply in love. One a knight of the realm, the other a beautiful young woman. It was the stuff of Greek myth – you the Orpheus to her Eurydice, willing to go to the very depths of Hades. From the moment I met you at the Ritz, I never doubted your devotion to Lucinda. She was your second chance at love, but..." Here I paused to heighten the drama. "There was someone else in love with her."

With the slightest shift of his head, his gaze came to rest upon me. I felt myself at the opening of the labyrinth on Knossos about to take my first step inside, possibly never to return.

"That someone was Morrow Davenport."

"Rubbish, that man was a pervert."

"A pervert, really?"

"Of the worst kind."

"How did you know?"

"It was obvious."

"As many would seem to think. Pervert, prancing pansy and painted cockatoo are all terms that have been used to describe the late gossip columnist."

"All thoroughly accurate."

"I beg to differ. The self-respecting Englishman is taught to despise any man of difference and prejudiced to think he can be identified from his high voice, limp wrist and artistic temperament." I paused for breath, wishing for a cup of tea to sip, even a tumbler of whisky. "Many accused Davenport of possessing these things and were quick to label him a stereotype, but I never saw it."

"What difference does it make? Queers take all forms these days."

"Indeed they do, but I would like us to entertain the notion that Davenport did not take that form."

"Poppycock, he was worse than Oscar Wilde."

"I think he was as normal as you and... I."

Sir Lionel laughed, a bitter, mirthless laugh, and I blushed. Was it emblazoned upon my forehead?

"I visited him shortly after the affair at the Ritz and he spun me a yarn about his first love, heavily implying it was a man called Rupert Pethybridge. Then along came the villainess Lucinda who stole him away for marriage." The more I described it, the more like a pantomime it sounded. "Davenport spoke of love with conviction, as if he knew it well, and I believed him. But his love was never for Pethybridge, it was for her."

"This story is utterly ridiculous," said Sir Lionel coldly, but he did not stop me from continuing.

"Then I found a letter. A love letter from one lover to another, positively singed from the heat of passion." I silently congratulated myself on a metaphor worthy of Octavia Stubbs. "I always suspected Davenport was its author, with a brief detour via your friend Colonel Price and even Mrs Stubbs, but to whom was Davenport writing? I thought he might be deceiving poor Agnes, I even wondered if he was in some mad affair with Pinks, but it wasn't until I reconsidered his persuasions that the piece fell into place. It was the letter of a couple I thought never could have existed."

"Don't be absurd! I know of no such letter," said Sir Lionel. His eyes were firmly fixed on me but he seemed a little excited. The Minotaur was getting hungrier and I, the hapless peasant, was getting deeper into the maze. But here was when a repressive education at an English boarding school came in handy. I'd be damned if I was going to let him see how truly terrified I was.

"Let us say, for the sake of my story, that you did know of the letter. You will have found it shortly after the dinner at the Ritz. Lucy must have hidden it somewhere she thought you'd never look when really she should have burnt it. But I know how hard it is to part with such a thing.

"I can only conjecture at your feelings on finding it but, given the strength of your love, I can't imagine you were best pleased. However, the letter was signed with an X and, now your suspicions were aroused, you decided to follow her. She said she'd had a shadow on her the day she went to the National Gallery and she thought it might have been Patrick. But it was you. You followed her out the gallery all the way to Davenport's apartment and must have been quite surprised to learn he was the object of her affection. You hid outside, listening through those thin walls, presumably expecting to overhear them making love."

"Your story beggars belief," he said dismissively. "Those two hated each other with a passion, everyone knew that."

"Because that is precisely what they wanted everyone to know. It was all part of their plan."

"What plan?"

"The one you heard them discussing through those thin walls. A plan worthy of Machiavelli."

If I'd been Sherlock Holmes, I would have sucked

dramatically on my pipe at this moment or clapped my hands together to applaud my own genius. Instead, I had to remind myself to breathe and ignore the fact the man sitting opposite was on speaking terms with the Prime Minister.

"It began at the Ritz. The so-called pansy turns up and hurls all sorts of abuse at you and your wife. In shock, she breaks her glass and cuts her hand. They played their parts perfectly; he the villain and she the damsel in distress, and not one of us could deny their animosity. The scene was now set for the real event, your birthday.

"This part of the plan required patience. First, numerous courses had to be eaten and much alcohol imbibed, although I do remember Lucinda doing her best to avoid drinking too much. She needed her wits about her. As the evening wore on, so the guests departed. First to go were Octavia Stubbs and Theodora Smythe, then Colonel Price was escorted upstairs and you took yourself to bed. Once the staff had been dismissed, Lucinda and I were alone in this very room. I remember she did something so seemingly simple; she pulled back a curtain so she could place her hand on a windowpane. I thought I saw her reflection in the dark glass, but I realise now it was his hand, reaching out on the other side and leaving behind his fingerprints. That was the signal – they were both ready.

"Then she manoeuvred Patrick and I into position, reminding us to keep our voices down. Davenport arrived right on cue, knocking but not ringing, which was an oddly considerate thing for such a drunk, angry man to do. *Nothing too loud*, he had written in the letter because they couldn't risk waking anyone. Even the ensuing argument was had in muted tones, *No cries or screams*, and she did neither of those things when he grabbed her hand to aggravate the wound. I remember the look of pain on her face, impossible to fake. So she sent Patrick to the telephone and ordered me outside, as she clutched her bloody hand and made for the WC. I imagine the second I was out the door, she turned back and locked Patrick in the turret with the key she'd stolen earlier that day. Then she went to the WC to wrap her hand in a bandage and enact the next stage of the plan."

"We all know what happened next," snapped Lionel. "Davenport snuck back into the house and killed her."

Even broken men are capable of lashing out but on I went – the truth demanded it.

"That's what the newspapers say, yes, but it's not so simple."

"It never is."

"There was another angle to their plan, you see. As well as Davenport being seen to hate Lucy it was crucial that he hate you as well – you were the one threatening to sue him for libel and put him in prison. He had a very good motive to bump you off."

"But he didn't. He killed my wife instead."

"Almost," I replied. "Enter stage left one rather unfortunate, distant acquaintance of your son – namely me. I met Lucinda at the Ritz and rather haplessly played the part of the would-be hero as I tended to her wound, which was when she realised how I could be drawn into their scheme. I was to be Davenport's alibi for the night of the murder. That's why she sent me outside to chase him, to ensure he'd never be out of sight and, therefore, incapable of having killed you."

"Have you quite failed to realise I am still alive?"

"Trouble was," I said, ignoring his question, "I proved an awful alibi. As soon as I was out the door, I went the wrong way. In the end it was Davenport who had to find me, which explains his odd choice of words when he did: *there you are*. Even though I was supposed to be the one looking for him! Quite unwittingly, I had scuppered their plan because in that scenario he might well have had just enough time to re-enter the house and shoot you."

"No one shot me, you damn fool!"

Under normal circumstances I would not advise antagonising a knight of the realm but these were desperate times. "But the funny thing was," I said, "that, in failing to follow Davenport, I inadvertently created the possibility that he'd gone back into the house to kill Lucinda."

"Which is precisely what he did."

"Not if we are to believe my story, which has them working in cahoots."

"Then who did kill my wife?"

"You did, Sir Lionel."

"And why would I do such a thing?"

"Because she had been planning to kill you."

So I arrived at the centre of the maze, standing face to face with the Minotaur, unsure as to whether I fancied my chances.

"Why on earth would Lucy want to kill me?"

"Two reasons. Firstly, you threatened the man she loved."

"But *I* was the man she loved."

"I thought so too. From the moment I met her, it was clear she was in love. It's impossible to act something like that, but it is possible to lie about who it is one loves. All she had to do was substitute your name for Davenport's and she could talk of love to her heart's content."

"Secondly?"

"You are very rich."

He had nothing to say to that.

"I told you my story began as a love story and it began when Lucinda met Davenport; she the middle-class daughter of a doctor, he the struggling poet. It must have been very romantic at first, but for those of us who don't own gold mines, money quickly becomes an issue. So they hatched a plan and Rupert Pethybridge was their first target. A man of wealth with an uncomfortable secret, a veritable sitting duck. I imagine Davenport verified the nature of his secret while Lucinda offered herself as the perfect bride-to-be. Once married, it can't have been long before Davenport threatened him with exposure. Hell hath no fury like a gossip columnist scorned. Lucinda played the victim and Pethybridge, terrified of exposure, offered her a quiet divorce and a nice, tidy sum. Off he went to Berlin, leaving the lovers to spend their money. Which they did, meaning it wouldn't be long before they needed a second target. You."

He hadn't called the police yet, or punched me in the jaw for that matter, so onwards it was. "An older, widowed man of incredible wealth, rumoured to have a penchant for loose women."

"A pack of lies," he retorted.

"Indeed. Patrick told me about your near brush with a prostitute and how you'd dismissed her before anything happened. But rumours must have spread, leading Lucy to your front door. She seduced you and it wasn't long until wedding bells.

Meanwhile, Davenport donned his disguise once more and took to the gossip columns to insinuate your dalliance with a woman of the night. Doubtlessly they expected you to avoid a scandal at all costs and let Lucinda off with a golden handshake. But putting it into print was their biggest mistake. You had no intention of backing down and accused Davenport of libel. A gossipmonger versus a knight, he didn't stand a chance, prison was inevitable. The couple had never expected this. Lucinda must have tried to persuade you to retreat but to no avail. The lovers found themselves backed against the ropes with no hope of victory. So they resorted to more desperate measures.

"I assume that when you followed Lucinda from the National Gallery, you had expected to learn of her infidelity, which you did, but I doubt you expected to learn of a plot to kill you. You had given her everything, loved her beyond devotion, and this was the ultimate betrayal. So, as you listened through those walls, you formulated a plan of your own."

This might have been the moment for him to pounce and throttle me, except he didn't. He inclined his head ever so slightly as if he wanted me to go on, further into his trap perhaps, but further I went.

"You let them do all the hard work on the night of your birthday. All you had to do was not drink too much and feign fatigue. You took yourself to bed, or so we believed, playing the part of the happy husband. You waited at your door, listening for Davenport's arrival, and then tiptoed to the stairs. You saw me leave and then watched as Lucinda locked Patrick in the turret. Then you slipped downstairs and followed her to the WC."

"Then I strangled the woman I loved, did I?"

"You did. And if I had passed the billiard room moments later that evening, I might have seen you doing it. She had betrayed you. Her infidelity, her murderous scheme, this Orpheus would drown his Eurydice in the River Styx. And it was because you knew their scheme that you got your hands on Davenport's revolver. It always niggled at me that he'd threatened to shoot you and Lucinda, but now I see that it was part of their plan because you *were* to be shot that night. When you surprised Lucinda, she must have already retrieved the weapon. Perhaps you pulled it from her hand or she dropped it as you dragged her body into the billiard room, not forgetting to unlock the French windows to cast suspicion elsewhere.

"It must have come as a huge shock to Davenport to discover that the body found in your house was hers and not yours. There was also the matter of his revolver, which he assumed was still hidden in the house. If that were ever found and traced back to him, it might point to an entirely different plan. He had to get it back. Mrs Fairbanks said she saw someone at the garden gate, she assumed a journalist, and how you'd gone to shoo him away. But it was him, spying on the house, and you'd gone to confront him. I don't think it took him too long to put the pieces together and work out what you'd done. Now you both had secrets to keep, call it a stalemate. Perhaps you offered to return his revolver in exchange for his silence. Whatever lie you told him, he believed it, and he returned that night. *Bang*, you disposed of him and a very convenient suicide was reported in the papers."

My thoughts went back to that night on the Heath when my priorities had been Patrick's lips. Not a stone's throw away, his father had been lying in wait, ready to kill Morrow with the revolver that was meant to have killed him.

"I much prefer the story of the murderous pansy who strangles my wife and ends up shooting himself," he said, as calmly as if he were asking for a cup of tea.

"I can imagine. But what I realise now is that there must have been parts of their plan you didn't overhear, which explains a few inconsistencies concerning the holster and the key."

"What holster?"

"The one I found hidden in the cistern. If you'd heard that part of the plan you most certainly would have removed it, given it points to Lucinda and Davenport's masterplan."

"And the key?"

"I overheard Mrs Fairbanks say that the key to the turret had gone missing the afternoon of your birthday. Yet, when I questioned you and Patrick and the staff, no one knew who'd taken it. Someone could have been lying, of course, but the key's disappearance implied premeditation, it hinted at a plan. It only occurred to me much later that the person who might have taken it was no longer alive – Lucinda. She had easy access to the larder and locking Patrick in the cloakroom was crucial. As was making the scratch marks."

"Why?"

"Because it hinted that Patrick might have locked himself in the tower using a pair of pliers."

"Whatever for?"

"He was their prime suspect for your murder – the bitter son fearful of losing his inheritance. They would have let him hang for your murder. The question now is, will you?"

"What?"

"If the police can make sense of the key and the holster, they might come to realise that Patrick is also the prime suspect for Lucinda's murder. What's to say he didn't plan it all himself? He may even have been in cahoots with Davenport." If I had a moustache I might have twirled it. "So, I ask myself, would you let your son be hanged for your crime?"

A brief flash of fury crossed his face. I do not recommend poking at a Minotaur with a stick. But then he calmed himself.

"What evidence do you have to support this little story of yours?" he asked.

"Well, th... there's the holster in the cistern, for starters."

"I can assure you it won't be there for much longer."

Oh bugger.

"The scratches on the key!"

"Just scratches on the key."

I felt the blood drain from my face.

"But I have the letter from Davenport to Lucinda. It adds a whole new angle to the case. All I have to do is encourage the police to consider such an angle."

"How will you encourage them to do that?"

"I... well... I'll have them analyse the handwriting," I said, thinking on my feet.

"You will hand this letter to the police?"

"If I have to, yes."

"Where did you happen to find such a convenient clue?"

"I... in your cloakroom."

"And what evidence do you have that you found it in my cloakroom?"

His tone was cold and unattached. There was none of the gloating so often associated with criminal masterminds but nor was he going to concede any ground.

"I... er... well..." Something told me that the walls of the labyrinth were closing in.

"Do you know, I think there's another story to be told," he said. "One in which Davenport wrote that letter to you because *you* were his accomplice."

"That's ridiculous!" I said, my turn to protest.

"From the first moment I met you, I knew what sort of a man you were – finagling your way into my house and trying to corrupt Patrick. But all along you were scheming with that hideous man to murder my wife and frame my son."

"The police will never believe that."

"You're forgetting that the Commissioner's wife sends me a card at Christmas. They'll believe a knight of the realm long before they believe some nobody from Horsham. So will the newspapers. They'll enjoy having a second villain. Except this one won't slip the noose."

"B... but you have no proof."

"Haven't you been seen sniffing around the Bullion Club a number of times, doubtlessly stalking my son?"

"Only because that's where you told me he'd be."

"And maybe you were even on the Heath the night Davenport got shot."

"You'd only know that if you were there too."

"And what if Chief Inspector Lisle were encouraged to search your place of residence – might he find there a love letter written to you from the murderer? You just told me you still have it and it'll be easy enough to verify the handwriting. It's most likely also covered in your fingerprints."

And then it clicked, just as the maze fell in on top of me.

"You put the letter in the cloakroom because you wanted me to find it!" I said. "You saw me snooping around the gardens and were worried that I was getting closer to the truth – that Davenport didn't kill Lucy. Of course, you never thought I'd arrive at the actual truth, but what if I were ever to suspect Patrick, well known for hating his stepmother? And if I could suspect him of murder, then anyone could, so you had to prepare a scapegoat. Me!"

"To think, Mr Bigge, that all your snooping has achieved is to incriminate you in the crimes you were attempting to solve."

"You... you won't really have me hanged?"

The silence that followed was truly excruciating. If this man could strangle his wife and shoot her lover, then having a relative stranger executed would be nothing. Of all punishments, the hangman's noose was the worst.

"It is rather an irony," he said, "that if you were to repeat what you've said to anyone else, then it could kill you."

"But... but it is the truth," I said feebly.

"The truth," he echoed quietly.

"You said to me once that you wanted justice done."

"And it will be."

"Having me killed is not justice. Your confession is."

Here I was appealing to the better angels of a murderer. Even Inspector Glover would have arrived with evidence and at least one witness, but I'd walked into this trap alone, and willingly!

"Do you know your Bible?"

"A little," I replied, baffled as to the turn in conversation.

"In the book of Amos it says justice shall roll like the waters and righteousness an everlasting stream. It's an image I think apt. Yet you, Mr Bigge, are nothing like a stream. You are a puddle."

I thought it best to nod.

"I'll admit your words have rather dampened my evening, but they are far from a flood."

"But they are not far from the truth."

He shook his head, smiling, knowing much better than to give me an eleventh-hour verbal confession.

"Do you know where I was earlier?" he asked.

"No."

"I was dining alone at the Ritz; steak and champagne in honour of the woman I loved above all. The woman who, as you put it, gave me a second chance at love. And now that chance has been extinguished."

By your own hand, I ought to have added.

"It was to be my last supper. I had not anticipated your interruption, nor that you would provide me with the rope with which to hang you."

"You... you wouldn't?"

"I will do what I must to protect my family and, if you value your life, you will do the same."

"But..."

"I have listened to your story, Mr Bigge, and now all I want is to put an end to this."

"By having me killed?"

He shook his head wearily. "After everything you claim to

have deduced this evening, it surprises me you cannot see the final piece."

Suddenly the door burst open and in rushed Patrick, Theodora close behind.

"Father, you mustn't talk with this man," he shouted. "He cannot be trusted."

"I'm already well aware of that."

"He's insane!"

I couldn't believe my ears!

"Patrick," I pleaded. "What do you mean?"

"Stay away from my father."

"But he's just confessed to double murder."

"I did no such thing," said Sir Lionel, much too calmly for my liking.

"You're the dangerous one, Selby."

"Patrick, you can't really believe me capable of murder? I've been trying to help."

"I invited you to the Ritz as a friend, not so you could drag my family's name into the dirt."

"But Lucinda and Davenport are dead."

"No one will mourn them and I won't have you making wild accusations at my father."

"They're not wild."

"You need to get out of this house at once."

"Patrick, what I'm saying is true."

He rushed towards me and, before I could do anything, he had me by the collar.

"Get out," he screamed, pulling me to my feet. "Get out!"

"Pat, let go of him," pleaded Theodora.

"I've had enough!"

He dragged me out the room, down that awful corridor and back to the hall. I tried to resist, but he was strong, he had a rower's musculature after all. Pinks, Mrs Fairbanks and Agnes stood on the far side of the room, watching the events unfold in complete shock. Even Mrs Stonehouse the cook was there.

"Back to your quarters," yelled Patrick, pulling open the front door and shoving me to the top of the steps.

"You mustn't hurt him," implored Theodora.

"He'll ruin me, given half the chance."

"Patrick, please," I begged. "I'd never do anything to hurt you. It's Sir Lionel who's the criminal."

"He's no criminal, he's my father."

Patrick lunged forward, his right hand balled into a fist aimed for my face. I'd dodged enough punches at boarding school to avoid this one and off he went tripping down the steps and falling onto the gravel below. He shouted in pain and I ran down to offer him my hand.

"It doesn't have to end like this," I said. "The truth can save us."

"The truth be damned," he roared, crawling away from my outstretched arm.

"What are you doing?" demanded Theodora as she rushed out to join us. I readied myself to answer but realised she wasn't talking to me.

"I'm protecting this family from a madman," he said.

"You really think him mad?"

"I do."

He scrambled to his feet, Theodora at his side. I backed

slowly away down the drive. He was stronger than me, much stronger, but if I had a head start I might be able to outrun him. He watched as I sidled away.

"I'll have you locked up," he hissed.

"You won't," I said, finding an inner resolve that surprised me as much as it did him. "I'll make them believe me and I'll start with the letter."

"Where is it?" he demanded and then he looked down to my pocket, he already knew. He tensed but, just as he leapt forward, I saw Theodora, ever so subtly, put her foot in his way. He tripped and fell again, his palms scraping against the gravel.

"Oh Patrick," she cried. "My poor Patrick."

I saw Sir Lionel framed in the doorway, watching the drama unfold. But where I expected to see fury or menace, all I saw was grief. Slowly Patrick rose to his knees and that's when I decided to run as fast as I could.

CHAPTER 25

Autumn on the Heath is typically associated with beauty before buggery, but for men such as myself we risk to touch despite the falling leaves. What else are we to do? Most of us rent rooms in houses with nosy landladies, always listening at walls with upturned glasses and biblical judgements, or we have the misfortune of still living with our families. Only a few of us are lucky enough to own houses near Fitzroy Square Garden, but even they aren't as safe as the proverbial Englishman's castle. We are criminals wherever we are and our homes are often more dangerous than the Heath. So we take to the streets, the alleyways, cinemas, woods, toilets and any place that might provide a moment of cover for a moment of connection.

I was on my favourite bench at the top of Parliament Hill, wrapped up in coat, hat, scarf and gloves, and puffing on a cigarette. It was the third Sunday in October and the weather was much colder. The russets, ambers and oranges of the trees were magnificent, as they bared their trunks to the world. There were fewer afternoon walkers; they'd be busy at home reading newspapers in front of fires or criticising the maid's efforts at the dusting. I could have been doing such a thing at Miss Wickler's, but I couldn't face her endless torrent of banal observations and prying comments, even if lemon drizzle cake was the reward for my endurance. Arthur was nowhere in sight – presumably still across the pond, enjoying his French fruitcake – and I didn't fancy the warmth of a stranger. How nice it would be for a man to put his arm around my shoulders and pull me in close. I closed one eye and eradicated Big Ben with the smouldering tip of the cigarette.

"Got a light?"

The voice was very close to my left ear, it quite startled me. I turned, only to be startled again.

"Theodora!"

"The very same," she said, sitting down on the bench. "Are you obliterating the city?"

"I beg your pardon?"

"With your cigarette."

"I'm trying to keep it in perspective."

She held up the index finger of her left hand.

"There goes Big Ben and the Houses of Parliament," she said. "It can get overwhelming, can't it?"

"Yes," I replied gloomily. "How are you?"

"That is a tricky question to answer at the moment."

"It is rather, isn't it."

So we sat awhile in silence observing the view as our breath left our mouths in great misty plumes.

"Have you heard the news?" she asked.

"It's impossible to miss."

"Too many pills before bed."

Just as the newspapers had been full of Lucinda's death, now it was Sir Lionel's turn to have his face on the front covers. The headlines were far more sympathetic.

"That evening I confronted him," I said, "he told me he had just eaten his last supper. I didn't understand what he meant, but now I do."

"He was planning suicide?"

I nodded, "He quoted the Bible, something about justice and rivers from the book of Anus."

"Amos, Selby. The book of Amos."

"But no justice has been done. He got away with murder."

"Although the end was the same."

"The means quite different. I'm not one for the noose but with certain individuals I could be persuaded."

"It lessens the scandal. *Would-be murderers murdered by intended victim*! The headlines would be incessant."

"Instead the vengeful pansy takes the blame."

"Yes, that is unfortunate."

At least he was dead, wrote some of the journalists, *killing himself was the best thing he'd ever done*. The list of Morrow's perversions was long and included a predilection for sodomy and homicidal mania, as well as being part Scots. Little did they know he was guilty of only one of those sins.

"How did you know?" she asked. "That he was faking it?"

"Because every time I catch a man's eye, I have less than a second to intuit whether he's the sort to reciprocate my passions, punch me in the face for them, arrest me or pass me by none the wiser. So on the night I went to visit Morrow, I had to get the measure of him. I used a little Polari, but he didn't understand a word. And, after all his flirting, I thought I'd give him a kiss."

"You didn't?"

"But he recoiled."

"Highly suspicious!"

"Now, now," I said with a smirk. "Still, men hate being kissed by men for all sorts of reasons. Take Patrick, he hates it not because he doesn't want it but precisely because he does." I took another drag on my cigarette and let Theodora wait a moment. "He also proved suspiciously absent from the bars and clubs. My chum asked at various preferred haunts and it was as though he didn't exist."

"He might have been lying low."

"Indeed. But what really aroused my suspicions was everyone else."

"How so?"

"Whoever I spoke to – be it Sir Lionel, your aunt, even my colleagues at the bank – all had Morrow down as a flamboyant, mincing quean. To them he was the quintessence of the effeminate monster. But apart from longer hair than most, he was as square as any brick. He gave them a whisper and they echoed it back with a shout. They turned him into the villain they needed him to be."

"How they hate our kind."

"How they do and how that forces us to be stronger than all of them combined. The courage it takes to search for love in uncommon places, to have a limp wrist and painted eye, to strive simply to mince. And after all was said and done, Morrow just didn't strike me as the sort." On that remark I vanished St Paul's with the tip of my index finger. "And while that still wasn't enough to know he was faking, it gave me pause for thought, which let me entertain the notion that he and Lucy were first-rate liars."

"They were a fiendish pair," she said. "Their plan was dastardly but quite ingenious."

"She was acting from the moment I met her. How she'd gushed at the Ritz, calling me her hero. And all those lies she spun me the evening of the birthday party. I even mentioned the missing key and misbehaving toilet, which must have rattled her because that's when she cast poor Agnes as a would-be poisoner. She played her part so convincingly. I was just a fly in their web, as was Patrick."

"Do you think the scratches on the key would have been enough to implicate him?"

"If I were them I would have taken a leaf out of your aunt's book and hidden the holster under Patrick's bed." I shivered. "She was a siren all along, luring men to their demise."

"Although I don't think she married Sir Lionel with the intent to kill him."

"Nor I."

"With Rupert Pethybridge it had just been about money."

"Extorting vulnerable men," I said. "How charming."

"A tried-and-tested method."

"I hope you aren't making excuses for her."

"Absolutely not," she said. "But we aren't all born the third child of a baronet. I can't blame her for wanting finer things. You of all people must be able to understand that."

"I beg your pardon?" I replied defensively, my cheeks blushing despite the chill.

"Selby, why did you do a favour for Patrick in the first place?"

"Well... I... because..." I stuttered. What an embarrassingly direct question, from an Englishwoman no less. "I admired him, it was as simple as that."

"And you hoped he would come to admire you too?"

"I thought it worth a shot. I can be good company."

"That I know to be true but, still, you aren't like Patrick and I."

"What, because I'm from Horsham!"

"Exactly!"

She laughed, not a mean-spirited sort of laugh, a tinkling one, as if I'd just told a rather good joke. I, on the other hand, found nothing funny.

"I am simply saying, Selby, that there are quite a few people who wish to live the high life and I can hardly blame them."

"No, no, no," I repeated emphatically. "I'm no gold-digger. I cared for Patrick."

"You cared for his handsome face and firm physique."

"That may well be true, but we'd shared a connection so long ago and I thought I could rekindle it. Two men are perfectly capable of loving one another. I deserve a great romance just as any other."

"That you do."

"Why can't my love be considered normal, like that between Sir Lionel and Lucy?"

"What? The love between the wife plotting to murder her husband who ends up getting murdered by him instead?"

"Good point, not them, how about..." I racked my brains. "Morrow and Lucy?"

"The two extortionists quite willing to turn their hands to murder when their backs were up against the wall. Not sure I'd say that's a normal love, either."

"Fine," I huffed. "But I want to make it very clear I am not a gold-digger, a blackmailer or a murderer."

"I should hope not. But you do know what it is to want more than you have *and* to want someone. Can you imagine those things put together? The obsessive love Lucinda and Morrow had for one another combined with their love of getting more. It pushed them to extremes. But they hadn't reckoned on Lionel. Like them, his love was born of the desire to possess but, unlike them, he already possessed the things he desired, be it a diamond or a woman."

"You're right," I said, thinking back to the Ritz. "Lucy was his possession, just like his precious stones."

"Except a diamond isn't capable of betrayal. He too was pushed to extremes."

"You sound most sympathetic towards them all."

"Don't be daft. Murdering for love; have you ever heard of anything so absurd? They're stark raving mad, the lot of them. Lionel could easily have told the chief inspector of their plan, but instead he chose to wrap his hands around his wife's neck and squeeze."

"And let us not forget that Eurydice was bitten by a snake, not strangled by Orpheus," I said. "Honestly, if that's what passes for a normal love, count me out."

"Quite right," agreed Theodora. "It hardly seems like love at all."

"Three parts obsession to two parts lunacy, I'd say."

"With a generous dose of insecurity."

"To think they call us the deviants! All that time spent quaffing champagne and eating canapés with murderers, it makes me shudder. I wish I'd never bumped into Patrick at all." I pictured his furious face the night he attacked me. "How did you both know to find me at the house that final evening?"

"You said you were off to get the evidence and it was hardly to be found at Miss Wickler's. I think Patrick was worried you'd confront his father."

"Which I did."

"Yes, but not about him murdering his wife, but about his son's persuasions."

"Gosh, Patrick must really have feared the man. To think there is something worse than having a bank manager for a father."

"The engagement is off, by the way."

"You don't wish to inherit the Duker kingdom?"

"Patrick is not the man or the friend I thought he was. He refuses to believe the truth about his father and I do not like the way he treated you one bit. Quite abysmal." She looked scathingly across the city, ready to burn it with a withering glance. "Besides, why should I strive for a kingdom when I have a queendom all of my own."

"That you do."

"Better than that, I have a dominion."

"Patrick must hate me."

"Naturally, but he hates Lucinda the most."

"I want you to give him this for me."

Out of my pocket, I produced the letter. It was only a handful of words, yet provided the crux of the mystery.

"*My love,*" read Theodora out loud, "*My forbidden love. How I yearn to be yours again. But, for now, we must be quiet, nothing too loud, no cries or screams. Until we are away and can make all the noise in the world. Forever yours. X.*"

She folded it back up and placed it discreetly into her handbag.

"I did think about taking it to the police, you know…"

"I should hope so," she replied.

"… Encourage a posthumous charge of murder for the late, great Sir Lionel Duker."

"It wouldn't have worked. If there's one thing you need to know about the rich, Selby, it's that we know how to endure. Until very recently, Sir Lionel's name was a byword for the very strength of our economy. He was made a knight for his gold and now he's a martyr. The police are about as interested in your version of events as Patrick is."

"I could write the truth in a gossip column."

"And be done for libel?"

"Chief Inspector Lisle and his tiresome constable are just waiting for an excuse to throw me in jail. I've already stolen from a crime scene."

"That's the spirit, a good dose of self-preservation."

Somewhere a dog yapped on the Heath.

"Lionel, Lucy and Morrow, that lot deserved each other."

"And now they're all dead," she said.

"Where do you think Lucy and Morrow were planning to escape to?"

"America, perhaps, like Crippen and Neave. They didn't get away with it either."

"What hideous plans these people concoct," I declared, thinking of that other infamous couple who'd hacked a woman to death and hidden her corpse under the floor. "To think of the risks they take."

"Lovers take the biggest of risks."

"Murder?"

"They were madly in love, emphasis on the *madly*."

I managed a chuckle; it was hard to dislike Theodora Smythe.

"I've been meaning to ask you, Selby, about what you said when you rushed from the suite at the Ritz. Something about your going to Corpus College, Oxford."

"No!" I said, not bothering to hide the exasperation from my voice. "I was at Fitzalan. And Lucy was the only one who remembered. She mentioned it not long before she was murdered. She said it was Patrick who'd told her, but he adamantly denied ever talking to her about it. So, if not him, then who? No one else bothered to enquire into my past achievements, yourself included. It was only after we'd found Patrick in the suite that I remembered there *was* someone else I'd told – Morrow, the evening I visited him at his flat. He must have told Lucy afterwards. It was only at that moment did I think to ask myself the impossible – what if Lucy and Morrow had been lovers?"

"How clever, Selby! You're rather good at this detecting."

"I never meant to be," I said modestly. "If Patrick hadn't asked me to dig the dirt on Lucy I never would have got caught up in their plan."

"Are you telling me that the only reason you're involved in all this is because you wished to get your hands on Patrick's…"

"Heart!" I said quickly. "The things I do for love!"

"Honestly, you men are all the same! I make a far more tactful man."

"I bet you do."

We couldn't help but laugh; it was nice to ease the tension.

"So what next for you, Selby?"

"Yet more tedious conversations with my colleagues at the bank, avoiding my family as much as is socially acceptable, maybe the odd trip to the countryside."

I saw the life I had described playing out before me and it filled me with dread – yet more weeks of tedium and loneliness. And there was I thinking that a life with Patrick might have been possible. Unsurprisingly, he'd chosen loyalty to his father and now lived alone in a big house on the Heath. He hadn't cared for me one jot. All he'd wanted was for me to confirm his suspicions of Lucy. Not altogether baseless ones, mind!

"I've heard news that Wall Street is quaking."

"That's just the markets for you, Theodora. They go up and down, it's what they do."

"Said like a true schoolmaster. You're welcome to pop by fourteen Wilkington Mews for a cup of tea or something stronger."

I turned to her and she was looking at me, her large brown eyes moist from blinking back the cold.

"Do you mean it?" I asked, sounding as pathetic as I felt.

"I do like you, Selby, even if you are from Horsham." I opened my mouth to protest but she raised her hands in entreaty. "I'm teasing you. It's not such an awful thing to come from Horsham. Percy Bysshe Shelley grew up there *and* he went to Oxford. He was at University College, just like you."

I rolled my eyes. "You can be most trying, Theodora Smythe."

"You're much too easy a target," she said with a wicked grin. "The Watson to my Holmes."

"I think you'll find I was the one who put the final pieces together."

"With much help from myself."

I harrumphed into the distance and obliterated most of London with my right hand.

"But do pop back every once in a while," she said.

"I will."

"Because I think we make quite the trio."

"Trio?"

"Theodora, Selby and Theo."

"You contain multitudes," I said, smiling.

"As do you."

ACKNOWLEDGEMENTS

Many books helped me create Selby's world, including *Queer London* by Matt Houlbrook, *The Morbid Age* by Richard Overy and *The Naked Civil Servant* by Quentin Crisp. Unlike Octavia Stubbs, I will always be a superfan of Agatha Christie and her canon.

I would like to thank Antony Harwood, my agent, and all those at Titan Books for bringing this book to the shelves. Special thanks to editor Rufus Purdy, publicists Bahar Kutluk and Katharine Carroll, and designer Julia Lloyd – the cover is beautiful.

I have many friends and colleagues to thank for reading the manuscript at various stages of its development: Anna Machin and Sally May of the Mystery Gang; Eleanor Wasserberg of memorable Garsdale trips; Jo Cunningham, Catherine Jarvie and Sean Lusk of my Curtis Brown Creative group – thanks also to the rest of the group for your support throughout the years; and special thanks to Heather Jackson.

I am deeply grateful to my friend and fellow novelist Stephanie Scott, whose support remains invaluable. Thank you also to Julia Oertli, for the long walks and wisdom, and to Jeffrey Marsh, for Selby unbound.

Finally, I would like to thank my parents – Elizabeth and Bruce. You have always loved and supported me, which is why this book is for you.

ABOUT THE AUTHOR

ROBERT HOLTOM is an award-winning playwright and storytelling coach, based in London. Their play 'Dumbledore Is So Gay' won a VAULT Festival Origins Award for new work and an Offies Commendation. It has since played at the Pleasance and the Southwark Playhouse, receiving five stars from the *Daily Express*, *Broadway World* and *Theatre Weekly*. Robert also runs workshops in writing and communication skills. You can find Robert on Twitter/X at @Robert_Holtom; on Instagram at @robertholtomwriter and at their website robertholtom.com.

For more fantastic fiction, author events,
exclusive excerpts, competitions, limited editions and more

VISIT OUR WEBSITE
titanbooks.com

LIKE US ON FACEBOOK
facebook.com/titanbooks

FOLLOW US ON TWITTER AND INSTAGRAM
@TitanBooks

EMAIL US
readerfeedback@titanemail.com